MAFIA PRINCESS

S.J. Smith

*To Matt for inspiring me to do what's right for me.
To my parents for always supporting me and
encouraging me to make my dreams come true.
To Adam. Not because you asked for it but because
you have so much blind faith in me I feel like the new
goddess on the block.*

PROLOGUE

Since Alexis Angelo was dropped off on the first day of high school, she'd been the subject of many whispered conversations and nervous glances. Every time her father made headlines or was the subject of some second-rate blogger, she heard her classmates and teachers alike wondering if she'd turn out to be just like him. Some of them wondered if her mum knew what she was in for when she married Anthony Angelo. Others believed that she had married him because of the danger and excitement of it all. A real-life mafia movie.

There were the few who were either very brave or very stupid who actually asked Alexis what it was her father did for a living. At first, she would give them ridiculous answers: lion tamer, pet psychologist, conquistador. She enjoyed watching them scramble to google the name for a Spanish explorer.

Now, two years on, she just glared at them until they left, which they now did very quickly. The same people who had once been her friends all through primary school suddenly treated her like the kid who ate his own snot.

One of them had been brave enough to tell Alexis that their parents told them to stop being her friend. They didn't want their precious god-fearing children associated with a mobster's daughter.

There were others of course who actually believed all the stuff written about her family and they stayed away from her without any prompting from their parents. Those were the people that warned all the new kids about her, told them to stay away in case they got sucked into her family's criminal ways.

After her uncle got arrested the summer before she started high school, Alexis had only a few friends outside of her Family that didn't care what other people said. They'd stuck by her through everything, all the snide remarks and invasive questions. They didn't care who her father was or what her uncle had been accused of, they just liked her for who she was. When you're surrounded by overly privileged, silver spoon fed brats, finding a few that weren't looking to work some kind of angle of their own was pretty rare.

What her classmates and teachers weren't aware of during all of their whisperings about her family, was that Tony Angelo, her dad, had one strict rule about his daughter and the family business; they were to stay very, very far away from each other. He'd actually added a few more 'verys' when he originally made the rule, but for the sake of time, it was shortened to two in recent recollections of that fateful day. How-ever, her father didn't realise that Alexis had every intention of one day being a part of the family business.

Some psychologists might think that the whole lifestyle had been romanticised by TV shows and movies, but that wasn't it. There was something about having the power to protect the people you love; she wanted that power. She knew everything that her parents did, it didn't scare her like it probably should, but then again, being a criminal was in her blood, it was as natural to her as breathing.

After all, she was a mafia princess.

CHAPTER 1

There was something to be said for a man who could take a relatively boring topic and make it absolutely coma inducing. Alexis struggled to keep her eyes open as the vice principal reminded everyone of the school's uniform code. Dress hems must touch the knee. Shirts tucked in. Hats worn whenever not undercover during the summer terms. Welcome to the snooze fest.

Alexis found her gaze drifting away from the front. She scanned the crowd in front of her, not looking for anyone or anything in particular. She remembered how she'd done the same thing four years ago and been met with countless pairs of eyes. The memory sent a spark of sadness through her. Alexis tried not to think of the events that had led to her becoming a social pariah at twelve, but sometimes it couldn't be helped.

◆◆◆

Alexis had known from a young age that being an Angelo meant certain things. It meant that sometimes her dad went away for days at a time, and then came home with bruised knuckles and a weary look in his eyes. Sometimes he came home and she heard him hissing in pain whenever he moved too fast in a certain way. It also meant that once a week they swept the house for bugs.

The first time her dad explained it to her, she'd been so confused which wasn't surprising since she was six at the time. How does one explain to their six-year-old that the magnet she found attached to her Disney princess statue was actually a listening device planted by the authorities to get information on a suspected mob boss?

Once it had been explained to her how dangerous these little devices were, she would search the house for them every day for months, even after her parents assured her that they'd gotten them all. They believed that she thought it was just a game, find all the listening devices and get a prize!

What Tony and Carmen Angelo didn't realise was that their only child had picked up on a lot more than they'd ever dreamed. She had overheard their conversations about police raids and not keeping anything incriminating at the house. She'd overheard the weird conversations Tony had with his brothers, whom she later found out were actually his capos. She also knew about the hidden floor safe that was in her dad's office with all their passports and getaway money.

So six years later when her Zia Claire pulled into the driveway, her headlights off, Alexis knew that it wasn't going to be a normal visit. She knelt on the couch watching from the living room window as her dad opened up the front passenger side door and pulled her Zio Marco out. Zia Claire reached into the back seat and pulled a sleeping Damian into her arms. Alexis marvelled at how her aunt was able to pick up her ten-year-old cousin with such ease. She'd tried herself once, it wasn't easy. She'd once commented that instead of being all skin and bone he was made up of skin and rocks shaped like bone.

Alexis rushed to the front door pulling it open just in time for her encumbered aunt to reach the front steps. Her aunt spared her little more than a glance as she carried her son across the threshold. Alexis tried not to take it personally.

Her mum came next placing two bags at the top of the stairs before running back to the car to grab what was left. Her uncle Marco was limping so badly that her mum was able to return from the car and bring all the bags inside before they even got to the steps. Once they stepped into the light of the house, having not dared turn on the porch light in case the neighbours looked out their window, Alexis could see why.

A belt was tightened around Marco's upper thigh, his entire left pant leg was soaked in drying blood. His face was pale and a sweat had broken out across his forehead.

"Hey slugger," Marco breathlessly greeted his oldest niece.

"Hi Zio Marco," Alexis said, staring up at him wide eyed, panic rising in her chest. Her dad had come home with his fair share of injuries, but never had he looked this bad. The only people she'd seen look this bad before were actors in TV shows, and generally once they were made to look this bad, it meant they were dying.

"Carmen, can you get an ETA on the Doc?" her dad asked as he helped his brother past the living room and down the hall to the guest bathroom.

"I already did, he's three minutes out. He said to try and keep Marco from slipping into shock before he gets here."

"Yeah, right," Tony muttered almost dismissively. He could feel the cold sweat soaking through his baby brother's clothes, and he was starting to feel more and more like dead weight.

"Alexis, go with your mum and get some blankets for your uncle, preferably ones she doesn't mind getting bloody or I'll be hearing about it for weeks," he called behind him.

The rustling of her clothes as she ran after her

mother was all the acknowledgement he needed of his request. As he settled his brother into the bathtub a soft but firm knocking on the front door had Tony letting out a breath he hadn't realized he'd been holding.

Alexis made her way down the hallway, her sock covered feet slipping on the wooden floor. Catching herself against the wall she set off for the linen closet as quickly as she dared. Her mum was already there, a pile of folded blankets at the ready. They were the scratchy ones that every household seemed to have, the ones no one really remembered where they had come from or why they were kept due to how uncomfortable they were. Before she could take the blankets away, her mum plopped a spare pillow on top of the pile as well.

Alexis considered making a joke about her uncle being forced to sleep in the bathtub but thought better of it. Hearing her uncle's voice as she approached the bathroom door, Alexis slowed down to a full stop.

"Boss, I'm so sorr-"

"Shut up you *mamaluke*! He's trying to concentrate." Alexis listened outside the ajar bathroom door as fabric ripped. There was an odd sound, almost like when her mum cutting raw chicken and then the tinkling of metal against porcelain. All the while Zio Marco kept hissing and let out a low groan.

"Alexis, stop hovering outside the door would

you?" Alexis almost jumped out of her skin. Why was she even hiding, her uncle needed the blankets. Not wasting anymore time she pushed the door open just enough for her small body to slip through, a sheepish smile on her face.

"Sorry, daddy. Sorry Zio Marco."

Doctor Lee, at least that was what Alexis had called him since she was small and couldn't pronounce his last name, was kneeling outside the bathtub. It reminded Alexis of when her dad used to give her baths as a toddler.

Her uncle was laying inside the bath, his left leg elevated so his foot rested on the end, his hands gripping the edges so hard his knuckles were turning white. She tried not to look at her uncle's exposed and bloody leg.

"We're almost done here, the doc does quick work. Why don't you help me get your uncle comfortable, he might be in here for a while," her dad instructed.

"I think mum figured the same thing," Alexis smiled weakly as she placed the pillow gently behind her uncle's head. Once it was firmly in place he leaned his head back against it, sighing in relief.

"Thanks for that sweethear-" he sucked air through clenched teeth as Dr Lee made sure the wound was well and truly disinfected. "My neck was killing me," Marco finally breathed out.

"Oh so long as it's just your neck that hurts," Alexis smirked down at her uncle trying to appear calmer than she felt. Zio Marco wasn't just her dad's favourite.

"Zio, how'd you get shot?" The question slipped from her lips before she could stop herself. Slapping a hand over her mouth Alexis stared at her father wide eyed. He just looked back at her, his own face not giving away any clues as to his thoughts.

"Well *bambina*," Marco drew her attention back to him, "I was working and got into a bit of a disagreement with some guys and one of them shot me." As simple as that.

"Are they going to come after you again?" Alexis knew exactly what her uncle meant by 'working', and she knew that whatever had caused this particular disagreement wasn't just some construction timeline issue.

"That's a good question Lex. Are they going to come after you Marc?" her dad asked from his place beside the tub. Dr Lee remained focused on stitching up the leg in front of him, but that didn't stop him from being interested in the answer himself.

"We're all good boss. We eventually came to an agreement and decided to... amicably part ways. I've sent a few guys to clean up the mess at the workshop so that we're ready for business as usual tomorrow."

Sometimes Alexis wondered why their 'codes' were so easy to interpret. Even if she hadn't been listening in on most of her dad's work conversations since she was five, Alexis still would've been able to figure out what her uncle had meant.

"Well good, everyone knows that loose ends are bad for business. Baby girl why don't you go ask your mum to put together a plate of food for your Zio Marco?" And with that, she was dismissed. Whatever was about to be discussed wasn't for her ears... unfortunately.

Dropping a kiss onto her uncle's cheek with a wish for him to feel better, Alexis slipped from the bathroom.

Alexis started her search for her mother. She didn't want to call out for her in case she woke her cousin Damian. How he'd managed to sleep through everything she had no idea, but it wouldn't help anything to wake him up now. So she went from room to room, her socked feet making next to no noise on the tiled hallways. As she neared the kitchen she heard her mum and Zia Claire talking quietly.

"What happened Claire, really?" her mum asked, concern thick in her voice.

"I married an idiot, that's what happened. I should've listened to my father, God rest his soul. He said that marrying a made man would only bring me heartache, and he was right." Claire started to get louder and more hysterical.

"Claire, for God's sake pull it together and quiet down or you'll wake Damian."

Alexis heard a cupboard opening and the sound of glass being set down on the stone benchtop. Then the fridge door opening and shutting before a top was unscrewed. She didn't need to be in the room to know that her mum was pouring her aunt a very generous glass of wine.

"Don't worry about Damian. He'll be out for at least another six hours," Claire stated.

"What did you do? Drug him?" There was no humour in her mum's voice.

"Oh, it was only a sleeping pill. I crushed it up and put it in some milk. He was freaking out about his father being shot, and I couldn't deal with him and Marco at the same time," Claire said, no hint of remorse in her voice.

Alexis suddenly felt a wave of anger towards her Zia Claire. She knew that it was wrong and she should respect her aunt, but wasn't it also wrong to drug your children? Damian was only ten after all. Why didn't she try talking to him? How was she going to deal with it when Damian woke up? Explain the truth to him or play it all off as a bad dream?

Not wanting to stand there any longer and possibly be caught eavesdropping again, Alexis pushed open the kitchen door and called out to her mum.

"Hey mum, dad asked if you could put together some food for Zio Marco. Hi Claire," Alexis said, barely sparing her aunt a glance. She would hear it for that one later. In their family respect was key and referring to one's aunts and uncles as anything but Zia or Zio was seen to be disrespectful. To not even call Claire 'auntie' was as much of a slap in the face as Alexis could get away with.

For now.

Damian was the closest thing that Alexis had to a little brother and she didn't like anyone messing with him. Including his mother.

From the way her mum's right eyebrow arched and her lips pursed, Alexis knew that her mum knew she'd been eavesdropping and that there would be a conversation about it later. Not that it would be the first time she'd gotten in trouble for that exact crime.

"I take it then that Dr Lee is wrapping things up?" Alexis' nickname for the Family doctor had caught on. Alexis nodded the affirmative and went to the cupboard to grab a dinner plate for her uncle.

Setting down her still empty wine glass Carmen went to the fridge and fetched the leftovers from dinner. Taking the dinner plate from her daughter, Carmen started dishing out a generous serving of chicken and roasted potatoes. When the plate was full she covered it with cling wrap and put it in the microwave to heat up before dishing out tossed salad into a separate bowl.

"Claire what kind of dressing does Marc like on his salad?"

Claire scoffed into her wine glass. Swallowing her mouthful, she smacked her lips together. "Marco hasn't eaten a salad in years, the man's diet is atrocious."

"Aren't you meant to be the one making sure he eats healthy?" Alexis muttered under her breath. She'd never really liked Claire. Apparently when she was a baby, whenever Claire came near her Alexis would start screaming. Over the years it became obvious that Claire had the same aversion to her, though if what Alexis overheard was anything to go by, then Claire's aversion was to their entire family.

Claire was too involved in her wine to be paying attention but Carmen was all ears. While she agreed with her daughter's snide remark, she still sent Alexis a warning look. "Lex can you get a plate for the doctor. We can't send him home on an empty stomach, now can we?"

The rest of that first night passed without incident. Marco and Dr Lee ate. They got Marco set up in one of the spare bedrooms where Claire eventually passed out as well. The next morning Alexis thought about how it was a good thing Marco didn't need anything during the night since Claire was too drunk to have been any help to him.

Damian woke up the next morning, a few hours later than Claire had predicted. At Alexis' insistence they had moved him into her room. He didn't say a word when he opened his eyes, just took in his surroundings, saw his cousin sitting at her desk and remembered the night before.

He remembered his dad bleeding and his mum swearing. He remembered hovering in the doorway wanting to know what was going on. Then he remembered his mum giving him some chocolate milk, but it tasted weird, and then he remembered nothing.

Alexis got up from her desk chair and made her way to Damian in the same way she would approach a scared animal. Not wanting to break the silence until he did, she just reached out to him, her arms wide. He didn't wait for her to close the distance, instead getting up from the bed and closing it himself. The cousins wrapped their arms around each other. Maybe if they held each other tight enough, for long enough, all the bad stuff that had happened in the last twelve hours, all the risks that came with their family name, maybe, just maybe, it would all go away.

They might've been there for minutes or hours. Alexis wasn't letting go until Damian did, but when he did, she knew that it was time to take him to his dad. Gently taking his hand in hers, Alexis led Damian from her room and downstairs to the living room where his dad was resting watching morning talk shows.

The look on Damian's face when he saw his dad, alive and more or less well, almost broke Alexis' heart. She knew exactly how that look felt because she'd felt it a dozen times before. His hand slipped from hers, and in a split second he was across the room and flying into his father's arms. Marco didn't even flinch. From where Alexis stood she could see Damian's shoulders start to shake.

It was time for her to leave them alone.

From what she'd gathered the night before, this was the first time that Marco had ever been injured like that. There had been a few minor scrapes and close calls, but nothing that he hadn't been able to hide. She sometimes thought that it was because her dad never sent his baby brother on any jobs that he thought were too dangerous.

Over the next week Alexis continued to share her room with Damian while his parents slept down-stairs. Zio Marco was moving around on his own now but with a considerable limp. Damian spent his waking hours waiting on his father hand and foot. Zia Claire on the other hand spent her waking hours sipping on mimosas before noon and glasses of white wine from lunch until... well whenever she ended up passing out. On more than one occasion she'd heard her dad muttering under his breath about Zia Claire being a lush.

All in all it was a pretty nice visit.

Unfortunately, it wasn't meant to last.

Damian had been having nightmares every night, it was only one and always the same. He wouldn't tell

Alexis what it was about and she didn't mention that he talked in his sleep. Neither of them mentioned it to their parents.

Alexis had started staying up until the nightmare ran its course. She would calm Damian down when he woke up, reassure him that everything was okay and then rub circles on his back until he fell asleep again. Only then would she lay down on the other side of the bed and let herself sleep.

That night though, it was different. They'd gone to bed later than normal and had spent a few more hours talking through the early hours. Damian had just started to toss and turn and make panicked noises in his sleep. Any moment now he would start calling out for his dad.

Out of nowhere there was a loud banging. It didn't wake Damian, but Alexis was suddenly on high alert. Shouts from outside had her flying from the bed to the window. Throwing open the curtains she instantly noticed the flashing lights. Looking down she saw they were coming from police cars on the street. They were everywhere.

More shouting.

More banging.

"Zio Marco," Alexis breathed. That first night she had asked if those men were going to come after him, she'd never thought to ask if the police would be.

Racing to the bed she shook Damian awake. He was instantly alert, his eyes wide with fear.

"Stay quiet and stay behind me," Alexis instructed Damian who gave her a single nod of confirmation. With that she moved to the bedroom door and eased it open. The shouting was clearer now.

"Police! Anthony Angelo we have a warrant! Open up!"

Her heart felt like it was trying to beat its way out of her chest. She didn't dare look back at Damian now.

"Carmen, get the kids." Her dad came rushing from her parent's bedroom, her mum hot on his heels. "I'm coming, I'm coming! Hold your horses!" He made quick work of the locks, only hesitating on the last one to look over his shoulder and up at the landing. Alexis stared back at him, barely registering that her mum had made it to her and Damian, pulling them both against her.

Then he undid the last lock.

The door burst open nearly knocking him over. Men in uniforms and vests rushed through the open doorway. Guns drawn. Alexis hoped they had the safety on.

"Where's Marco Angelo?" a man with a moustache wearing dress pants and a button up shirt under his vest asked her dad.

"Where's your warrant?" he asked in return.

As if anticipating the question, the man was already pulling out a folded piece of paper from his back pocket.

While her dad and the man had their standoff, the other police officers spread through the house. At least a dozen of them had come through the front door, most of them dispersed through the rooms on the ground floor but three started climbing the stairs. Her mum immediately pulled herself and Damian behind her, backing them all into the corner of the landing. Did she really think the officers were going to hurt them?

One of them broke off from the other two who kept going up the hall, checking each bedroom as they went. The one who stayed back gestured down the stairs.

"Ma'am, please take the children downstairs." Until the officer spoke Alexis hadn't been able to tell if they were men or women due to their bulky equipment and the masks and fabric covering their faces. They didn't need to be told twice and followed the female officer's request.

"Where's my dad?" Damian whispered to her as they made their way down the stairs. Alexis merely shrugged, not wanting to give any information to the police before they discovered it themselves. If she had to guess though, Zio Marco was still passed out in bed. He'd had to take some strong painkillers the night before.

Tony watched as his wife herded Alexis and Damian to the couch. She didn't let go of the children, and she never stopped watching the officers as they searched the house. They both knew it wouldn't take them long to find Marco. If they had been honest with themselves from the beginning, this moment was coming as soon as he showed up at their front door. Tony loved his baby brother, but he wasn't meant for this life.

The problem with Marco was that he always tried so hard to keep up with his older brothers. All of them followed in their father's footsteps, and as the eldest, it fell to Tony to take up the mantle of Mafioso when their father died. The girls were never expected to stay in the Family business. The boys though, it was expected of them. It was a path that Marco should never have been forced to walk.

"What is it exactly that you suspect my brother of doing, Detective Smith?"

"I think the shorter answer is what we don't suspect him of being involved in Mr Angelo. Now please, take a seat with your family."

He resisted the urge to spit at the detective's feet. It wasn't the first time this house had been subject to a police raid. It was however the first time that Alexis had been home when it happened, and for that he was angry. His *bambina* shouldn't have to witness this.

On the other hand, maybe it was good that she was seeing this, the bad side of the Family business. He'd noticed how interested she was becoming in his work and everything that went along with it. He'd tried his best to shield her over the years from the worst of it, but perhaps it was time that she saw it. It might squash whatever desires she was having to follow in his footsteps.

Not that he'd ever allow that to happen to begin with.

"Detective! We've found him!" Five minutes. It had taken them five minutes to find his baby brother, still in bed and dead to the world. They probably searched every nook and cranny on the way. There were only so many rooms down that hallway.

Alexis could do nothing but listen as Zio Marco woke from his drug induced slumber and started swearing. It sounded like Zia Claire managed to wake up quickly, and her subsequent screaming probably hurt the neighbour's dog's ears.

Damian tried to leap from the couch at his parents yells but was held back by Alexis and her mum. It broke her heart to do it. Alexis knew that if she were in his position, all she would want to do was run to her parents, to do everything she could to protect them. She also knew that there was nothing that could be done now.

She heard the detective reading Zio Marco his rights, only interrupted by Zia Claire's abuse once. One of the other officers must have restrained her after that.

Zio Marco was then frogmarched down the hall and into the living room. His face was grim and his shoulders pushed back. It looked like he was trying his best not to limp. He truly had the Angelo pride.

Alexis' eyes started to sting and she realised that they were filling with tears. She didn't notice when she reached up to wipe away the tears running down her cheek, that she had also let go of Damian.

Taking his chance, Damian burst from between his cousin and aunt and ran for his dad. Ducking around the officers in front, Damian wrapped his arms around his dad's waist, burying his tear stained face into his belly. It was then that Alexis saw her uncle truly break. His arms strained behind his back against the cuffs, his entire body yearning to embrace his son.

One officer stepped forward as if to pull Damian away, but a look from Detective Smith stopped him in his tracks. The detective stepped forward himself and whispered in Marco's ear, who gave a sharp nod in response.

Marco did his best to move smoothly towards the closest armchair, which was made even more difficult by the ten-year-old attached to his abdomen. Eventually, Damian realised what was happening and helped his dad sit down and stood in front of him.

"Damo, I need you to listen to me very carefully, okay? I love you, son. More than anything, I love you.

Your mum likes to think she's tough, but she's going to need you, alright? Be strong for me bambino, be strong for her."

Damian just wrapped his arms around his dad's neck, "I love you too, daddy."

Alexis could feel her heart shattering just watching the exchange. Imagining herself and her dad in their places was just too easy.

"Alexis." She locked eyes with her uncle, not expecting him to address her at all.

"Look after my boy okay?"

She could only nod and wonder at the cruel twist the morning had taken. Damian had no sooner woken up from one nightmare to be faced with another, one that was all too real.

CHAPTER 2

A vibration against her thigh pulled Alexis from her memories. Two weeks after her uncle had been arrested a number of things started. His trial for one. Damian started year five, for two. And thirdly, she started high school.

Damian only stayed at school for a total of three hours before his mum was called to pick him up.

Alexis had lasted even less time than that. The first kid who mentioned her uncle in some derogatory way got a bloody nose for his trouble. She didn't wait to hear whatever smartass thing his friend had to say, she just kept swinging. She was suspended for a week. The kid who taunted her got no punishment, but she had sent a clear message. It didn't matter that her parents banned her from fighting at school for those kinds of reasons.

Very few were brave or stupid enough to try the same thing again.

Damian had ended up going back to school after a few days. The principle had stepped in and called an assembly for the whole year group, informing them that whatever happened with a student's parents was not to be used as fodder for schoolyard rumours and bullying.

Alexis had known even then that Zio Marco had done something illegal and gotten caught. That was his fault. No one loved him any more or less because of it, except maybe Zia Claire. Damian shouldn't be paying for his crimes though.

Looking around subtly, she made sure that none of the teachers scattered throughout the gymnasium were looking at or near her before pulling out her phone.

8.42 - *Try and checkout the guy in front of me to the left, so hot!!! Jessica.*

Jessica was Alexis' most fashion orientated friend. She also knew a hot guy when she saw one. Truth be told, their year group was severely lacking in the hot guy department. Looking around the gymnasium where her friends sat scattered, separated into their different houses and years, Alexis finally found Jessica's dirty blonde, perfectly curled hair. Barely.

She was on the aisle, two houses over. Alexis

leaned forward to try and get a look at the people around Jess. In front, to the left.

He was tall. Maybe. It was hard to tell for two reasons. The first being that he was sitting down and the second, just because she could tell that he was taller than Jess didn't actually mean anything. Jess stood at a tiny five feet two inches. Alexis had ten-year-old cousins taller than Jess. Then again, Alexis herself was only five foot eight so there was a good chance he was taller than her. She liked tall guys.

Leaning forward bit by bit, Alexis tried to get a glimpse at the possibly tall, brunette's face. Now if the guy blocking her view of the new guy could also lean forward, she'd have a clear-ish view of the right side of his face. A cough off to her right caught Alexis' attention. Glancing to the side, she sat up straight and gave the tired looking teacher one of her classic guilty smiles.

Finally, the assembly came to an end and they were dismissed. Picking up her chair, Alexis tried lingering in the foyer but Mrs Rauser, the Head of the Math Department, old and royal pain in the ass, narrowed her steely gaze on Alexis.

Talking to Jessica could wait.

Dropping the chair off inside her homeroom, Alexis grabbed the books she'd left in there for her second period class and started across the school. There were plenty of faces that she hadn't seen since the end of the previous year, most of which she couldn't say she had actually missed. The majority of her classmates were nice enough, but they'd never stay friends once they graduated. The only thing holding most of these friendships together was this academic hell which they were all stuck in.

Someone much taller than Alexis, dropped their arm around her shoulders. Looking up at one of the only people who would willingly invade her personal space, Alexis smiled at Seth. He was six feet tall, blond and still carried some baby fat. He was cute.

"Meet me in our spot at lunch?" He made it sound like a question, but she knew better. It was a demand and Alexis just rolled her eyes.

"Lex, it's good to see you. You too Seth, it's been like three whole days since you've annoyed me. How you been?" she mocked.

"You know, all that sarcasm of yours is going to get you in trouble one day," his brown eyes narrowing playfully at her.

"Haven't you heard? I live for trouble." It was the joking boast of someone who'd watched too much television over the summer holidays.

Alexis hadn't been paying attention to their surroundings and didn't realise when Seth turned them down a walkway behind the demountable class-rooms. Before she had a chance to question why they were back here, Seth leaned down and captured her mouth with his, his hands gripping her waist. Her right hand still held her books and pencil case, but her left hand moved up to grab the back of Seth's neck.

She really needed to stop getting into these compromising situations with him.

Hearing the voices of students getting closer, Alexis pushed away the boy that would only bring her trouble.

Moving back around the building she asked him, "What's gotten into you?" She'd tried to sound incredulous but really, she found this side of him hot. It made her feel wanted when he kissed her out of the blue like that. *That*, however, was where the good feelings ended. They both knew the repercussions if they were caught. Getting caught by a teacher meant detention. Getting caught by another student, particularly one from their year, meant that their friends would find out. That was something neither of them wanted.

Well... Alexis had wished they could come out as a couple, but that was before the summer holidays.

She'd had a crush on Seth for so long that when he finally expressed an interest in her she couldn't believe it. He was her ex-boyfriend's friend. The two of them having an interest in each other wouldn't have gone over well with their group of friends, so they decided to keep it a secret.

Then Seth told her that Brennan, one of their best friends, had admitted to liking her - a lot. They'd decided to end it, so no one would get hurt. That lasted for all of two days before Seth was calling her, asking to meet up. They'd spent months stealing kisses and hiding their feelings for each other.

Alexis had thought that the rules they had set down were clear:

1) Their friends don't find out.

2) If they want to hook up with someone else, things end between them first.

3) Don't be weird with each other around other people.

Rule number two had proven to be particularly difficult for Seth to follow. Alexis held no delusions that they were in a monogamous relationship, or a real relationship at all for that matter. She did however think that Seth would be a decent enough person to tell her that he hooked up with someone else. So they ended things officially a few weeks after the Christmas break started and went back to how things were before.

Well, Alexis was trying to. It was safe to say she still had a massive crush on him. She hated herself for it every day.

◆ ◆ ◆

Brushing off the encounter with Seth, Alexis joined the group heading into class. Once she got inside she found a seat next to her oldest friend. "Well fancy seeing you here."

Had it been anyone else, they would've thought Alexis was flirting with the way she propped her chin in her hand and batted her forest green eyes.

"You're so weird." Emilia however was very used to Alexis' flair for the dramatic entrance. And exit. And general existence. Alexis had always felt that with a small camera crew, and a hair and makeup artist, her life would make a great TV show. If it weren't for a few small issues, for example - the law, they might be able to pull it off.

"You love me." Blowing a kiss to her less than impressed best friend, Alexis turned to look at what was written on the white board at the front of the classroom and Emilia got a look at the back of Alexis' dress.

"Why is your back covered in dust and..." There was a pause as she reached out to take off what looked like hair. "Cobwebs." It wasn't hair.

Ridding her hands of the sticky substance, Emilia brushed her hand over her friend's back until it was more or less clean. When she looked to Alexis for an answer she found her brunette friend steadfastly avoiding her gaze.

"Lex-" Before Emilia could continue the teacher, one they'd never had before, started the lesson. She introduced herself as Miss Peters and she was the new Modern History teacher. Maybe this one would stick around for more than a term.

A piece of paper slid across the desk towards

Emilia, and she glanced down as though to make a note about the syllabus they were going through.

Seth -.-

Emilia looked over at Alexis, rolling her eyes.

Honestly, she wasn't even surprised - Seth had issues letting go. He was a manipulative little shit and she didn't know why Alexis still hung out with him, even if it was just as friends.

A few days after New Year's, Alexis came to her ready to burst into tears. She was ranting about Seth and an agreement they had, and how she found out he was hooking up with other girls and not telling her. Then he went and hooked up with one right in front of her. It took some time, chocolate and water before Alexis calmed down enough to get the whole story out, about how they'd started, ended, started again and then ultimately, this.

That night, Emilia helped her write the message ending things, and then helped her write the responses. Normally, Alexis was better at expressing herself with the written word. However, what Alexis wasn't great at, was staying strong when it came to her own personal devil on her shoulder. To Emilia's knowledge, she was the only one that Alexis had told about all of this. She'd also been informed of the rules they'd set down and knew why they wouldn't want something like this getting out to the student body. Alexis already went through enough shit for what people thought her father did for a living.

◆◆◆

Thanks to the morning assembly, they only had to suffer through one proper class before recess. As they walked from class to their respective homerooms, Alexis filled Emilia in on everything that had been said and done.

"Are you going to meet him?"

"God no Em, what do you think I am? A masochist?"

"Well sometimes, you make me wonder, I'm not gonna lie." Emilia wondered if maybe she was being too harsh.

"Your lack of faith in me hurts a little." The smirk that spread across the pretty brunette's face told Emilia that she took no offence.

After grabbing their recess snacks the pair went to their usual spot where the rest of their friends had already gathered and were unsurprisingly, having a heated discussion about something.

"Did you see the size of him?" Marty asked, a tinge of jealousy could be heard in his voice.

"He's taller than Seth," Jessica pointed out.

"Pfft, no he's not," Seth argued.

"Fine, I dare you to go stand next to him," she taunted back.

The girls slid in on the ends of the metal bench, Alexis mentally noting that the only one who hadn't said anything was Brennan, who was too busy moping into his jelly fruit cup, his long black hair flopping into his eyes.

"Okay so, what are you lot on about, or I guess, who are you on about?" Alexis asked.

Jessica was practically vibrating in her seat. It must've been killing her waiting this long to talk. "Lexi, did you get a look at him? Was I right? Is he hot?"

"Jess, sweetie relax. And only sort of. The guy next to him wouldn't move his head."

Jessica deflated only slightly, disappointed that she had no one to discuss the new guy's attractiveness with. Seth on the other hand looked relieved, which made her heart float just a little bit. She was going to need to nail that thing to the floor of her chest cavity soon.

"So, moving on, how's everyone doing?" Alexis asked, effectively changing the topic.

When the bell rang again, they started dispersing, but Alexis lagged behind to walk next to Brennan. They hadn't had a chance to talk this morning and she knew he must be feeling anxious today. His anxiety flared up whenever there was a major change. This year the school was opening up their new trade centre, a TAFE within the high school, and Brennan was one of the first ones to be in it. Once he got settled and made some friends he'd be fine, but now he needed someone to lean on, and she was his designated someone. She'd asked him once before why he preferred having her around when he was feeling anxious – apparently he found her to be a calming presence.

"Hey, I haven't heard from you for a couple days, what's been going on?" she asked, bumping his shoulder with hers. Instead of answering, Brennan gathered her up in a spine cracking hug. Which wasn't actually too bad since her back needed a good crack. When he put her feet back on the ground they started heading to their bags.

"Well my mum came down for a few days so that was good. Then it was just working and stuff. Sorry, I didn't get back to you."

"Don't worry about it, I was just curious. It's good that your mum could come down though. I'd better head into class, but we'll talk more later?"

Finding her seat next to Jessica, Alexis thought about how weird her friendship with Brennan had become over the past year. She'd thought of him as a best friend and had believed that he felt the same way about her. Turned out that wasn't the case at all, and while she had been careful to not let on that she knew, it felt like he knew that she knew.

Things had gotten weird. It also occurred to her that this was the second time she'd sat down today thinking about how her relationships with people had changed. That was something that needed to stop.

One of the great things about having classes with Jessica was that Alexis didn't even need to finish her thoughts half the time. Jessica just knew what she was thinking. The other great thing was that they were both good at texting without looking, a skill that freaked their friends out for some unknown reason.

For now though, their teacher, Mr Kyle, was busy sorting out his papers and passing out the semester syllabus. "Right, so do you know anything about this guy other than he's apparently a giant?"

Jessica's green eyes lit up with excitement. "Imagine if... Jensen Ackles and Cody Christian had a love child." Alexis had to admit that what she was imagining was insanely hot and hoped that the real thing at least came close. There was also the consideration that maybe she had enough boy drama to deal with without adding more into the mix.

"Is he actually in our year?" Alexis asked, not sure what she wanted to answer to be.

"Yep. Brennan had second period with him. Didn't really say much about him though."

"Yeah, he seems a little off today, for the past few days actually. Has he said anything to you?" Alexis didn't fail to notice how Jess' face expression became more closed off and she suddenly became extremely interested in the paper in front of her.

"Not really, he seemed fine when we caught up on the weekend."

Alexis couldn't help but feel hurt. She had messaged Brennan asking if he wanted to hang out on the weekend, and he'd told her he had family stuff. Family stuff he'd been telling her about just before class. So why had he lied to her and hung out with Jess instead?

Jess obviously knew something. For someone who tried to be all mysterious and 'interesting', she was a terrible liar. If you asked the right questions and paid attention, you could find out everything you needed to know without her actually saying anything.

"So, what'd you two do?"

"We met up with Seth and just hung out really, rode our bikes around. They ended up staying for dinner. My mum is not a fan of Seth at all, thinks he's creepy."

And sometimes, she just spilled the beans.

Jessica went on about what her parent's thought of the two boys, but Alexis' own thoughts were centred around how Brennan had lied to her. She went through all the different reasons she could think of as to why he avoided her and then lie about it.

Last time he ignored her, it had been because she bailed on their plans last minute. In her defence, it had been a code red situation on the Family business front, and no one was allowed to leave the house without an army of bodyguards, but she couldn't exactly explain that to him. Instead she'd told him she got a massive headache. He didn't buy it. A part of her wondered if maybe she should ignore him for so obviously lying to her about why he couldn't hang out, but decided it was far too childish.

For the rest of the period Alexis half listened to what Mr Kyle was telling them. Jessica kept whispering to her about what had happened when the guys were over her house, acting as though the constant attention was something she hated, but in reality, she thrived off it. Alexis didn't understand why it wasn't enough that Jessica had the undivided attention of her actual boyfriend. The few times that Alexis had floated the idea of her and Seth becoming a thing, Jessica had gotten all jealous and territorial, while trying to act like she was indifferent, in pure passive aggressive teenage girl fashion.

Alexis had learnt to hide how she felt about Seth and not talk to Jess about it, which was hard because they used to be able to talk about everything.

When her fourth period Maths class was let out for lunch, Alexis looked at her messages, seeing the same text from Seth that she had been ignoring all period. He was reminding her about how they were going to meet up in their spot at lunch.

For a second, she even considered it, until she happened to glance across the room and saw Anna, the girl that Seth had hooked up with over the break. Just seeing her was more than enough to steel Alexis' resolve to not meet Seth.

She'd already let him hurt her and she wasn't going to be a sitting duck again. As Alexis walked, she saw the recreation building come into view. A mental image of Anna and Seth making out flashed behind her eyes, and Alexis took a sudden right turn towards her homeroom.

Before she knew it, she was sitting on the lawn at the front of the school. She'd been in such a rush to be as far from that gym hallway where Seth was waiting for her that she had practically run here.

"Lex! What the hell? Are you deaf? I've been calling your name since you nearly bowled me over outside your homeroom."

Brennan.

"Um, shit, sorry. I wasn't ignoring you, just got a lot on my mind is all." *Like how you lied to me and I don't understand why.* She waited until he'd taken his usual spot on her left and turned to look at him.

"So, Jess was telling me about her weekend, pretty interesting stuff." She saw how his shoulders stiffened ever so slightly, and he paused unwrapping his sandwich, not looking at her. Something that she and Jess had in common was their passive aggressive streaks. Alexis didn't like it when her friends lied to her. Ironic since she was carrying around her own huge, guilt and shame inducing, secret.

Brennan was now looking at her like a wounded puppy.

"Why didn't you just tell me that you didn't want to hang out with me on the weekend?" The look deepened and he moved closer to her, reaching for her hand. She let him take it, pushing down the uncomfortable feeling she got.

"You know I love hanging out with you. It's just Jess asked us first and Seth thought that maybe we shouldn't tell you in case you got jealous or something. He's an idiot and I never should've listened to him."

It was obvious that he was genuinely sorry, but what he said about Seth pissed her off. She tried to brush it off though, Brennan had just listened to the wrong friend.

"Yeah, you're right, he is an idiot and no one should listen to him, ever." He squeezed her hand. "Why would I be jealous that you've already made plans? Yeah, I'd be a bit bummed that we can't hang out, but I would get over it. You don't need to feel bad about making plans with other people."

He awkwardly leant over their food to give her a hug, muttering his apology into her hair, "I'm really, really sorry."

She pulled away the best she could without making it obvious that she was getting uncomfortable, especially with so many people now making their way to their lunch spots established from the year before.

With Brennan, his issue was boundaries. He didn't seem to understand that other people had them. He was one of her best friends, and she always felt like she could tell him anything, unless it was about guys she liked, then he got really uncomfortable. Before she had a chance to assure him that they were good, their other friends started to arrive and put an end to their private conversation.

Looking up to greet the new arrivals Alexis was glad that they were forced to wear hats outside during the first and fourth terms. She remembered being blinded quite a few times last year whenever the sun had hit Marty's orange hair at just the right angle. She also wondered why it was that they didn't find a shadier spot to eat lunch since out of all of them, only she and Emilia had olive skin. She was surprised the rest weren't already turning pink.

It wasn't until halfway through their lunch break that Marty questioned where Seth was. Alexis had been, up until that moment, successfully ignoring the vibrating phone in her dress pocket. She had a feeling that if she were to check those missed messages, they'd all be from Seth, and they would all be shitty.

Alexis slowly ate her sandwich, listening to the group throwing around ideas on where Seth was, nodding along whenever someone looked in her direction. She figured if her mouth was full then she didn't have to lie.

Ten minutes and two topic changes later, Em looked over Alexis' shoulder and pursed her lips in annoyance.

"Well, speak of the devil and he shall appear, he'll be late, but he will appear."

This prompted the rest of them to look up from their conversations and food.

"Dude, where have you been? Lunch is almost over," Brennan questioned their tall friend as he dropped down on the grass next to him.

Seth shot a glare at Alexis as he answered, "Sorry, got held up."

Alexis hoped that he had a better excuse than that. They were friends with some of the nosiest people on the planet, all of whom could pick apart a story like nobody's business. Except Em and Marty. Em just respected people's privacy. She might know you're lying, but she understood sometimes people needed to have secrets, and she knew it better than anyone that Alexis knew. Marty was just too self-absorbed to care unless the lie directly affected him.

Just as Seth was gearing up to tell them all some obvious lie, or maybe all his lies were just obvious to her because she always knew the truth he was hiding, the bell rang, saving his ass.

"And back into the depths of hell we go kids." Alexis got up, brushing away any dirt or grass that might be caught on the ass of her dress. Two more periods, and then she could run away from this place, until tomorrow.

◆ ◆ ◆

Alexis' phone vibrated in her pocket sporadically for the rest of the school day. She knew that she would have to talk to Seth eventually. They were still friends... sort of. Sometimes when she thought about their history, she couldn't remember a time that he hadn't been obviously interested in her. Most people thought he was just a very friendly guy. When she had been going out with Marty, he had made it very clear that Seth had a habit of falling for the girls his friends dated. Marty had then proceeded to make things awkward anytime they all hung out, accusing Seth of flirting with her when they were just talking as friends.

In hindsight, Alexis couldn't help but admit that in this one instance, Marty had actually been right about something. She would, however, deny it to anyone who asked.

Alexis avoided opening the messages from Seth for the rest of the day. She didn't know why she was feeling so guilty about not showing up. She had no reason to feel guilty. Right? They had set rules for their arrangement for a reason. And he broke a rule. He hooked up with someone else, didn't tell her, and then tried hooking up with her like normal. She understood why he didn't tell her he wanted to hook up with Anna. If he had, then their thing would have stopped for good. Why risk losing what he already had on the off chance he'd be able to hook up with someone else.

Just because she understood why he did it, didn't mean that she would ever agree with it. She'd made it clear to him back then that what they had was over and yet, here he was once again trying to manipulate her into doing what he wanted. And he was making her feel guilty in the process. It wasn't right.

At the end of the day, her not showing up only wasted half of Seth's lunch break, which could've been avoided if he wasn't always assuming that she would do whatever he wanted. What he did to her... breaking their rules and lying about it... that broke her heart. She had felt so stupid, holding out hope that he would realise he wanted a relationship with her, no matter who knew or what their friends thought. When she ended things with him, she thought that she was free of his manipulation, but obviously she'd been wrong about a lot of things.

Walking to the pickup zone where her mum would be waiting for her, Alexis gave in and looked at all the messages Seth had sent her through the second half of the day. There was a combination of instant messages and texts, which explained the constant vibrating of her phone.

12.47 - *I'm here*

12.50 - *Waiting for you*

12.55 - *Where are you?*

12.57 - *Did you get detention or something?*

13.05 - *It's starting to look weird, me just standing here*

13.10 - *I'm gonna head to the lunch spot.*

13.45 - *Dude what the fuck!?*

13.50 - *You just went to lunch and didn't even bother to tell me you weren't coming anymore?*

14.15 - *So you're just going to ignore me? Fine. Be a bitch.*

By the time Alexis made it to her mum's waiting car, she was full of renewed anger. She had told him that she was done with whatever it was they were, and she meant it. When she had gotten upset about him hooking up with Anna, he acted like it was no big deal and she shouldn't have been upset about it because they weren't together, so it wasn't like he cheated.

"Um, hello? Earth to Lex?" Alexis looked to her right at her mum, Carmen.

"What's wrong?" There was a look of concern so genuine and protective in Carmen's eyes, that it could only come from a loving mother. It was that look that made Alexis want to spill her guts about everything that had been going on.

She knew that her parents hadn't wanted her dating yet, but it couldn't really be classified as dating, so she kept everything a secret.

"Just a long day and I have a headache." She would continue to keep it a secret. There was no way her perfect mum could understand what she was going through right now. Nodding sympathetically, Carmen turned down the music and turned up the aircon, directing the vents towards Alexis, then they started the slow crawl through afterschool pickup traffic. While her mum was focusing on the other impatient mums and dads trying to escape the school parking lot, Alexis turned her attention back to her phone. There was no way she was letting Seth win this.

15.30 - *Did you maybe consider that I was in class and trying to not get detention. And since you've forgotten, I never actually agreed to meet you at lunch, so you wasted your own time there. You also made it very clear that we weren't together, and I made it*

very clear that what we had was done. So you have no reason to assume that I would meet you just because you told me too.

15.32 - *What are you talking about? You said you'd meet me.*

15.35 - *No. I didn't. You walked up to me, told me to meet you, I mocked you for not even saying hello and then it was end of discussion.*

15.38 - *So? You never said you wouldn't meet me.*

15.45 - *Really?! That's what you're taking away from that? That even though I didn't agree just because I didn't disagree then I still should've met up with you? What is wrong with you?*

Alexis tossed her mobile into her bag, too frustrated with Seth's attitude to even wait for his response. While she'd been lying about having a headache fifteen minutes ago, she had one now. When she looked up she realised they were in the drive through at McDonalds.

"Mum, not that I'm arguing with your choice of afternoon snack, but what's the occasion?"

"Well you look like you've had a rough day, and I

thought you might like a thick shake to help with that headache."

Alexis leaned over the centre console to rest her head on her mum's shoulder.

"Also, I'm craving something salty."

"Oop, there we go, the truth comes out. You're just using me as an excuse to satisfy your own desires."

"Mm, well what good is having kids if as a parent you can't use them as an excuse every now and again?"

"I'm starting to wonder what else you've used me to get out of."

"Shh, what those overly involved mums at your school don't know, doesn't hurt me."

"Pft, whatever. You could destroy those women with your savage wit alone." Alexis sat back properly in her seat when they got to the speaker box to order and located her mum's debit card.

"So you think I'm savage do you?" Carmen smirked at her daughter after she finished putting through their order and moved the car forward a few more feet.

"Yes, mum. You are the most savage parent I've ever met. Seriously though, I don't buy it for a second that those women could force you to be involved in something you didn't want to be."

As they left the payment window Carmen pulled up the arm rest in the centre console and pulled out a packet of painkillers, tossing them into her daughter's lap.

"Thanks mummy." Alexis put on her best toddler voice, or worst toddler voice depending on your feelings about imitating toddlers. She couldn't help it though. It was one of those things that came out whenever she was feeling particularly pathetic or talking to someone or something that was insanely adorable. In this instance she was definitely feeling pathetic.

Once they'd gotten their drinks, Alexis popped two pills out of their foil and took them with her thick shake. She didn't know why, but painkillers always went down better when taken with a liquid that wasn't water, at least it did for her.

"So, you want to tell me about school now?"

"It was fine. Same old same old."

"Lex." The tone in her mum's voice was all the warning Alexis needed. It was always easier to at least tell half the truth, it was normally enough to satisfy her mum's curiosity.

"It's just, the guys. They've been really weird lately, Like, last week, I asked Brennan if he wanted to hang out on the weekend, and he said he couldn't because he had family stuff, which you know, fine, whatever, family is family. I'm Italian, who am I to stand in the way of family stuff. But then, today I was talking to Jess, and she said that on the day I wanted to hang out with him, he and Seth were over at her place and they stayed for dinner. Like what the actual hell?

Then, when I asked Brennan about it at lunch, he said that it was all Seth's idea to lie to me. I mean, come on. Firstly, why did they feel like they needed to lie to me about having plans to hang out with Jess? We're all friends. We're allowed to hang out all together or only some of us. What's the big deal?"

"Do you think that maybe they were worried that you'd be jealous?"

"Brennan actually said that Seth thought that I would get jealous, and that's why they shouldn't tell me. Why would they think that in the first place though? I don't get it."

"Well, you normally all hang out together. Have they hung out without you before? Or you and the guys with Jess? I know you and Jess hang out on your own more than enough." Carmen was always trying to make sure her daughter looked at situations from both sides before she reacted.

"Yeah, of course, it's nothing new. If someone can't make it then we still go ahead with the plans even if they can't come. We just try and make new plans for when that person is free."

"Mm, but what I'm suggesting is, hasn't there been a time when you've organised something with Brennan and Seth, without Jess ever being a part of the plan, whether she could come or not?"

Alexis took a moment to think about it. She was always making one on one plans with Jess or Brennan. And she knew that Brennan and Jess hung out just the two of them sometimes, and of course Brennan and Seth did the same because they're best friends. She couldn't remember the last time she'd made plans specifically just with Seth and Brennan though. Normally Brennan was the one messaging her to see if she was free, and whenever Jess wasn't there already, the guys had said that she was busy.

"I'm going to guess by your two-minute silence that the answer is that you haven't made plans that didn't include Jess, not to exclude her, but because you wanted to hang out with just the guys."

"What I don't get though is why-" Alexis cut herself off, making her unfinished sentence sound like a question. Leaving her mum hanging, Alexis dug around her bag for her phone. She ignored the message from Seth and composed a hurried text to Brennan. She didn't know what it was that had made her realise why Seth had decided that she needed to be lied to. It was as though all the clues that had been right in front of her face had just leapt at her all at once and formed a bigger picture.

Now she just had to wait to see if Brennan confirmed her suspicions correct.

For the remainder of the drive home, Alexis vented to her mum about her classes and the teachers she didn't like, as well as how useless assemblies were to have every Monday morning. As if Monday's weren't torturous enough, why did the school feel like they needed to add to it?

By the time they walked through the front door, Alexis felt so much lighter. In all her ranting she managed to forget about how shitty Seth had made her feel and the hurt she was still feeling over his betrayals.

She was able to give her dad a watered-down version of her day, which she knew he appreciated after he had been conducting interviews all day. It was as Alexis was getting dressed in her lounging clothes after her shower that she got a reply from Brennan.

It was a short message, but it was enough to make her heart drop into her stomach as all the new realisations sank in.

16.25 - *Yeah he does, who told you?*

CHAPTER 3

16.25 - *Yeah he does, who told you?*

Seth liked Jess. All this time. Seth had liked Jess. But he couldn't get Jess. So he settled for her. She had felt genuine feelings for him, and she'd just been a consolation prize. No wonder he never wanted an actual relationship with her, and why he insisted that they couldn't tell anyone about what they were doing. He thought that if it got back to Jess then he'd lose any chance he might've had with her. He didn't actually care about hurting his friendship with Brennan. He only cared about how Jess saw him.

Fuck him.

There was so much hurt bubbling up inside Alexis that she didn't know what to do with it.

If she started crying now and her mum or dad

came in, they would demand to know what she was so upset about, and she didn't think she had it in her to come up with a convincing lie right then. If she went down to the basement training room to the punching bags, then it would have the same outcome. She never exercised unless she was angry, and she'd have to explain to her parents why she was riled up enough to do any kind of physical activity.

Her phone vibrated with another message.

16.46 - *Lexi?*

Brennan again. She shot back a quick message, something along the lines of having guessed and that she'd message him later. When she was about to shove her phone under her bed pillows she remembered the new message from Seth and decided to see what he had to say.

16.10 - *I'm sorry for being an ass, I've missed you the past few weeks. Still friends?*

Prick. Absolute prick.

God, she felt so used and dirty. She was done... for good. She didn't care who figured out that there was something wrong between her and Seth, she just didn't want to be anywhere near him.

For the rest of night Alexis hid out in her room. She didn't message Brennan or Seth back, just lay in bed and watched old movies on her laptop until she fell asleep.

The next morning when she got to school she managed to strategically avoid both the boys, with Em's help of course. As soon as Em saw her friend's face, the black-haired mother hen whisked Alexis off to a quiet part of the library, hidden from the prying eyes of others, where they were frequently able to discuss the current events of their lives.

Rain pattered against the library windows. Considering it was the middle of summer it was strange for there to be rain. Then again, Australian weather was always a bit unpredictable. Normally the sound of the rain would make Alexis feel better, but with the summer heat it just created a humid mess that made an unbearable day worse.

"I'm such an idiot, God, I should've seen it." Alexis's eyes were still a bit puffy, and there were shadows under her eyes from the lack of sleep. She also forgot to put concealer on before leaving the house and left her backup tube in her other dress. Thankfully, part of her autopilot mode included putting deodorant on, otherwise she'd never be able to live down the day.

"Lex, come on, I've seen him around you. Anyone would've thought he had a thing for you. As a matter of fact, a lot of people do. They also reckon he's got a thing for Jess, so there's a bet going on who he'll end up with. My money is firmly on neither of you. You deserve so much better."

When Alexis let out a half-hearted chuckle, followed up by smile, Em took it as a good sign. Even though the chuckle sounded more like a dramatic exhale and the sad eyes made the smile look more resigned than amused, it was progress. "Do you have any classes with him today?"

Alexis was suddenly grateful that they'd all shared their class timetables to the group chat after school yesterday. Well except herself. She had shoved her phone under her mountain of pillows and forgotten about it as much as she could until this morning. Then she remembered she hadn't charged it the night before, which resulted in a frantic charge while she stumbled through half of her morning routine.

"Nope, not until Friday. We have the same study period."

"Which is tomorrow. Alright... Well between now and then, let's see just how much you can avoid him."

Before they had a chance to go into any depth of how they would achieve this feat, the first bell rang, forcing them to head off to their separate homeroom classes.

While the other kids in the room scrambled to finish homework or even grab another twenty minutes of sleep, Alexis was focused on her phone, flicking between her schedule and Seth's. She figured, if she could remember where he would be heading each period, she'd be able to avoid him. At least she knew that today Brennan was in the trade centre all day. While the tradies spent most of their class time in the large building at the back of the school, they did come out and mingle with the rest of the school population for certain classes and breaks.

It wasn't that she didn't want to see Brennan, he was one of her best friends. She just knew that he'd figure out something was wrong. Avoiding him and Seth would also lead to this realisation, but at least if she was far away from them, then he couldn't question her about it and possibly figure out the truth. As adamant as she had been the previous night about not caring who found out the truth, she knew deep down that it was just easier that the secret didn't get out.

By the time Alexis was heading for first period she had a decent mental map of where the two boys were heading right now, where they'd be going for the rest of the day, and what were the best routes to take to get to her classes in relation to that. How she was keeping this all straight without a drop of caffeine in her system was a miracle in and of itself.

On the way to second period, Jess suddenly pulled up next to Alexis, looped their arms together and wordlessly redirected them to the nearest toilet.

"If you wanted someone to go with you to bathroom

all you had to do was ask," Alexis pointed out confused, but not unused to Jess sometimes forgetting to speak certain thoughts out loud. Jess didn't speak or stop pulling her along until they'd barged through the doors to the toilets and stood in front of the sinks.

"Girl, what is going on with you today? You look like crap."

Alexis felt her face scrunch up in confusion at Jess' words and turned to look in the mirror hanging over the closest sink. During first period she'd actually managed to forget that she looked worse than she felt. "Oh, yeah."

Rolling her eyes at her friend's uncharacteristic air headedness, Jess dumped her books on the countertop and pulled a handful of cosmetics from her pencil case. The other girls in the room spared them passing glances, but since they were from different years, none of them stopped to question what was wrong.

"Fix yourself up, and while you're at it, maybe spill about what's got you looking like you haven't slept for three weeks," Jess said, passing Alexis the various beauty products and started fixing her own hair in the mirror.

When Alexis didn't immediately start, Jess glared at her through the mirror. "Tick tock, we've got about five more minutes before Miss Hileman gets to class, and it would be a good idea if we were there in four."

Not wasting another second, Alexis uncapped the concealer and dapped it around her face, particularly under her eyes. A few swipes of mascara and a re-adjustment of her hair from the askew ponytail into a messy bun had Alexis looking worlds better. It was so like Jess to not let a friend wander around all day looking like something the cat dragged in. All of that *Seth stuff* aside, Jess truly was a good friend.

Yes, it was obvious that part of the reason she didn't want Seth and Alexis together was her own craving for Seth's attention, but from their numerous conversations about it, Jess also only wanted what was good for her friend, and she knew that Seth wasn't it.

Regardless, Alexis hated keeping such a big secret from Jess. They'd been friends for most of their school lives, and it just didn't feel right.

"Okay, I know that there's something to tell, but right now we have to get to class. Don't think you're off the hook though." Jess returned the cosmetics Alexis had used to the pencil case. They took one final look at the countertop to make sure they'd grabbed all their things and hurried from the room. Their class was just around the corner so it took them all of ten seconds to leave the toilets and blend in with the group of students streaming into the classroom. All the while Alexis marvelled to herself how she managed to get through that whole interaction without actually saying more than a few words.

◆ ◆ ◆

During class Alexis made it clear to Jess that while there was something to tell, and that she would definitely be telling soon, today was not the day.

When they parted ways at the end of class, Jess reassured her that everything would work out. For years they had always told each other everything, even being sworn to secrecy by others didn't stop them. For Alexis to not immediately spill the beans, it had to be bigger than anything they'd ever dealt with before.

Alexis was still trying to figure out what the right thing to do was. Jess was one of her oldest and best friends. It was her duty to tell her friend when a guy had a thing for her. But she and Seth had promised they wouldn't tell anyone about what they were doing. But who did she have more loyalty towards? Jess obviously.

She supposed that she could just tell Jess about Seth's feelings for her and not divulge anything about their secret *friends with benefits* relationship. She knew that Seth wouldn't tell anyone. He'd said it before, people finding out would ruin friendships, and while he hadn't mentioned his greatest fear, she knew that Jess would never consider dating him after she found out about their past. She tried to ignore how that thought gave her some small relief.

For the rest of the day Alexis tried to forget about

the secrets she was carrying around and focused solely on avoiding Seth and Brennan. She did so well at avoiding them that halfway through lunch she got a text from Brennan asking if she was actually at school. Seth hadn't messaged her again, so either he'd seen her, or he didn't care that she supposedly hadn't shown up that day. She told Brennan that she was spending her breaks working on a group assignment with some classmates, claiming she didn't want to fall behind. Meanwhile she and Em had snuck their food into a study room at the back of the library and were talking about everything but Seth.

One topic of particular significance was who Alexis' father was going to hire as his new head of security. Their previous one had disappeared a few weeks ago and Anthony Angelo was not one to take risks. A crew had been sent out to find him, but when their search had been fruitless, Tony had begun his own search for a new guy. Since Emilia's father was her father's consigliere, Tony's most trusted advisor, it wasn't unusual for Em to know things. Her dad did a lot of research and always had his ear to the ground. He prided himself on how thorough he was.

Emilia took after her dad like that. She was an amazing listener and she strived to give good sound advice to her friends, after sympathising and joking about the many ways they could inflict pain on who- ever it was that was causing trouble. Whenever the two friends talked about Alexis taking over the Family business from her father, Emilia was always there as well, taking over from her father as Alexis' consigliere.

As it was, Em was sharing about how her dad had set up 'interviews' with three guys over the coming weeks. One of the 'interviews' was simply a courtesy, the son of one of the capos wanting to step up. Em didn't think that this one stood much of a chance. He was a competent enough guy, but they were looking for someone more experienced, someone who had proved their unwavering loyalty to the Family. The second candidate sounded far more promising.

"So, apparently this guy has two kids. They recently moved up here from down south, and he's been working in the private security and tech fields since he was eighteen so he knows the ins and outs of the old and the new. He's been an associate of the family since he was twenty-three. Um, what else, what else... oh um, one of his kids is meant to be about our age. I didn't get an exact date of birth, but from what I overheard, they're in their final years of high school. Not yet sure of where they go. I don't think it came up in the part of the conversation that I overheard."

"Well that's all very interesting, but at the same time insanely unhelpful. Okay so we've covered nepotism and the working dad, who's the third one?"

"The third one our dads are interviewing for a laugh."

"A laugh?"

"Yeah, so they reckon that this third guy is actually a cop. It has not yet been confirmed, but there are very strong suspicions."

"Wait, so if he's a cop then why are they even bothering with the interview?"

"I forget that you aren't as in the loop as people would think you are."

"Yeah well, dad likes to keep me in the dark. Thinks it'll keep me from joining the family business. Whatever keeps him happy and in denial." Alexis chuckled to herself, remembering how annoyed her dad would get whenever she mentioned her desire to join the Family when she was older.

He was always so concerned with keeping her separate from that life. She remembered one argument they had where she questioned why he even bothered having kids if he didn't plan on having an heir. It was a very dramatic stand for her to take at the time, but she'd been watching a lot of period shows.

"Honestly, I don't think anything would make my dad happier than me following in his footsteps. Though to be fair, being the consigliere is considered to be a lot less dangerous than being the head honcho mafioso."

Alexis rolled her eyes at her friend, a smile on her face. Her dad could live his life swimming in a sea of denial if he wanted to, but she knew where she was headed. There would come a point when she would reach a crossroad, she would have the choice of washing her hands of everything that came with the last name Angelo, or she could embrace it. All of it.

Before Em had a chance to continue the discussion, the bell rang, signalling the end of the lunch break. The two girls gathered up their empty food wrappers and the books they'd used to hide their food with and left the library.

Only two more periods and then Alexis was home free. Or so she thought. Coming out of her sixth period English Lit class, she didn't see Seth until it was too late. He was leaning against a wooden pole across from the classroom door. Time to face the music.

Putting on her most convincing fake smile, Alexis approached the boy she'd been trying and failing to get over. "Hey Seth, long time no see, how's your day been?"

Instead of replying, Seth corralled her away from the bustle of students and behind the building. Alexis wondered how many déjà vu moments she would have before the year was over.

"Stop avoiding me."

"Excuse you?" she urged herself to keep eye contact without it being obvious that she was forcing it. "What are you talking about? I haven't been avoiding you."

"Okay, then what do you call not being around all

day?"

She knew that he would notice her absence eventually. Even if he didn't actually care about whether or not she was mad at him, he cared about keeping up the appearance of them being friends.

If people caught on that there was something wrong between them, they'd start to wonder why, and then they might figure out that they were more than just friends. "Well, I call that being in class, and I was working on some group assignments at lunch. I thought Brennan would've told you."

"Alexis, knock it off. You can lie to Brennan all you want, but I know that you're still mad at me and you need to get over it. I'm sorry about yesterday, I crossed the line. I wasn't lying when I said I missed you. We had fun together."

Alexis couldn't stop the unamused expression that came over her face.

"No! Not like that. Well yeah, that was pretty fun, but I mean when we weren't doing that. When we were just hanging out, the talking and the joking around, it was fun."

She wished that she could tell him how wrong he was, but she would've just been lying. What he was talking about, the talking and joking around, that was her favourite part of when they were together. Sometimes that was when he was at his sweetest, they'd be sitting in his car and he'd wrap his arm around her, her head would rest on his shoulder and he'd drop a kiss on the top of her hair. They'd just sit there and talk about everything from their friends to shows and movies, until it was time to go home.

Seth looked down at the girl he'd developed such a complicated relationship with. Once upon a time he had considered a relationship with her. He'd even started flirting with the her, hoping that maybe she liked him back and all their joking and flirting wasn't just her being friendly.

Then Brennan had confessed how he felt about her, and Seth knew that he could never publicly pursue a relationship, not unless he wanted to risk losing his best friend.

So instead, he'd risked his friendship with Alexis and proposed the *friends with benefits* relationship that they now have. Had. They had a relationship until he fucked it up.

And now he was paying the price - their friendship. "Please Lex, I miss you."

He was breaking her walls down, brick by brick. He could see it in her eyes. He'd seen the hurt and apprehension that flashed in her eyes when she first saw him as she walked out of class. She'd put up the mask pretty quickly, but he'd spent a lot of time watching her when she didn't think anyone was. Now, he could see the hesitation fading away, but the hurt was still there. Reaching out, Seth ran his hand down her arm, trying to give her some comfort. She squeezed her eyes shut and took a deep breath. When her eyes opened up again they were void of all emotion, but she smiled brightly at him.

"You're right, we did have fun."

Seth took her books from her and put their stuff on top of a locker. Then he stepped toward her, wrapping his arms around her shoulders. When Alexis had secured hers around his waist, he tightened his grip on her.

She was so confused, so conflicted, and so very angry with herself, but she couldn't stay mad at him, no matter how set in stone she was about her decision.

For now, she enjoyed being in his embrace and the comfort it brought.

CHAPTER 4

When Alexis got home that afternoon she'd contemplated calling Em and telling her what had happened with Seth, but she knew that the reaction she'd get wouldn't be a good one and for good reason. So she decided to keep it to herself. This lasted until sixth period Friday afternoon. Seth for some reason decided to walk Alexis to her human biology class despite the fact that his next class was in the other direction. As soon as they got near the classroom, Em zeroed in on them, and the look on her face spoke volumes about how unimpressed she was. Once Seth had left, Em approached her friend.

"Really? How long did you actually manage to stay mad at him for this time? Three hours? Four?"

"I know, I suck at holding a grudge. He caught me after last period yesterday. Wouldn't let me leave until I heard him out."

"Mmhm, that's fine. I've already told you my feelings on the matter. So long as you know what you're doing."

There was something in Emilia's tone that suggested she knew Alexis had no idea what she was doing. There was no point getting upset at the insinuation, Em was right.

Yesterday she'd been certain about ignoring Seth's messages and avoiding him at least until next Monday. Then he came and apologised and looked all sincere and she changed her mind. For the sake of self-preservation she needed to massacre her feelings for Seth.

"I swear, we're just friends now. Nothing else. I'm not going there again."

"I'm not the one you have to convince."

"What are you talking about?"

"Well, Seth. You told him that you were done and he tried to get you to *meet* him at school."

"You say that like there were going to be virgin sacrifices involved."

"Would there have been virgins around to sacrifice?"

While Emilia hadn't intended for her words to come across as snarky, they came out that way and Alexis' eyes narrowed ever so slightly. The teacher opened the classroom door and ushered everyone inside, saving Emilia from putting her other foot in her mouth. She'd never judged her friend for doing what she wanted and she wasn't going to start now. It was just this whole *friends with benefits* thing worried Em. Alexis wasn't the kind of girl who could have a no strings attached kind of relationship.

Alexis sidled up next to Em once they were inside the classroom. "We didn't- I mean I haven't-"

"Come on in everyone. Look at the whiteboard, find your seat, sit in it. Thanks to the term starting in the middle of the week, this class is already a lesson behind." Miss Leschenelle was a good teacher, if not a little intense at times. She was also quite strict and wouldn't allow them all to stand around forever. Em gave Alexis' forearm a squeeze, letting her oldest friend know that she'd heard her and she was sorry. Alexis gave her a small smile and they shuffled closer to the whiteboard to find their assigned seats.

When Alexis had read her timetable that morning she'd thought that there could be nothing worse on a Friday than having a content heavy class for the last period of the day. Then she read the board and realised that something could actually make this worse. April Hale.

Themis College was a Catholic school, so it made sense that there would be a lot of deeply religious people here. Most of them were really nice people who held strong to their beliefs without enforcing them on others. April Hale however was not one of those people. She used to be one of their closest friends. That was until Em confided in her that she was a lesbian. April had laughed in her face, thinking the whole thing was a joke. Then she had started telling Em that it was just a phase, she was wrong about being a lesbian. She said that a woman could find another woman pretty without being gay.

When Em finally convinced April that she wasn't confused, but that she was actually attracted to women, that was when April cracked. Alexis hadn't needed to be there to know the look that Em had described on April's face. She'd seen that look of disgust before, but she'd never thought it would be directed at someone April had claimed to love like a sister.

That day Emilia was left sitting in the empty dance classroom as one of her only friends walked away without another word. The next day it was almost as if they had never been friends, like they didn't even know each other. Alexis gave April a day to process, not happy with how unsupportive she'd been, but understanding that what April was raised to believe in was in direct conflict with her own forming beliefs.

When nothing changed the day after that, Alexis stepped in. She confronted April about Emilia's confession. Rather than acknowledging that she'd handled things badly, April started on her diatribe about how being a homosexual was wrong and Emilia was going to hell. Then she told Alexis that she felt uncomfortable around Emilia, sure that the girl had a crush on her and was going to make a move now that she'd come out of the closet.

Alexis hadn't been able to believe it. What shocked her more was that April thought she would agree with her. After a number of choice words detailing where exactly April could shove her homophobic opinions, Alexis walked away. It had been almost a year since that happened. Since then, Emilia hadn't spoken a word to April, and all the ones that Alexis spoke were dripping in sarcasm and disdain.

Normally having April Hale in the same class wouldn't have been an issue. They would just sit on opposite sides of the classroom and ignore each other for the four hours a week that they would be breathing the same air.

Unfortunately, the powers that be had decided that not only would they be inhabiting the same half of the classroom, but April was sitting between them. Em was in the front row, April had the seat directly behind her and Alexis sat behind her.

The girls looked at each other, the apprehension was clear on Emilia's face.

"So, this is going to be fun," Alexis said, knowing there were better times for her sarcasm than this, but it was how she dealt with most situations.

As the girls walked to their seats, Alexis was scanning the room, looking for the demon spawn and Em was suddenly extremely interested in the floor. Once everyone present had taken their seat Mrs

Leschenelle started the lesson. The seat between the two friends remained empty, prompting Alexis to risk sending a text to Em.

14.10 - *Maybe she finally burst into flames or got struck by lightning*

She watched as Em kept watching the teacher, as though she hadn't noticed her phone vibrating in her pocket. A few seconds later Em's hand reached into her pocket slowly and moved her phone between the books in front of her. When she was sure that she wasn't going to get caught, she looked down at her phone.

Twisting in her seat as though stretching her back, Em gave Alexis a small but grateful smile. The mental image that had accompanied the text had cheered her up a bit.

However the good times were not meant to roll that day. At that moment, almost ten minutes after class had started, April walked through the classroom door, put a late slip on the teacher's desk, and walked straight to her seat.

Alexis had a burst of irrational anger at how April didn't even bother to look at the whiteboard to find her assigned seat. It was irrational because every other seat in the room was taken, so her place was obvious. She smirked at Alexis as she took her seat, which of course resulted in Alexis sneering back at her. The rest of the class took an eternity to pass by, and that was saying something for a Friday afternoon.

By the time class let out, April had flipped her hair twelve times, 'accidentally' kicked Emilia's chair three times and smirked at Alexis four times, not including her initial smirk when she sat down. When Alexis relayed this list to Emilia as they walked to the pickup zone, she felt the need to question it. "So why did you include the hair flipping?"

"Because... it annoyed me. Her breathing annoys me. Arrogant homophobic bitch. How do you think her parents would react if they found out about all the guys she hooked up with? Bet they wouldn't think she was a perfect pure little angel then, would they?"

Em found Alexis' anger towards April heart-warming. Ever since she'd found out about how April reacted that day, she'd been unbendingly protective and loyal. Not that she hadn't been before, but it was different this time. It wasn't directed towards someone they didn't have any relationship with. This righteous anger that Alexis had, it was for someone that they had been best friends with for years.

For as long as Emilia and Alexis had known each other, Alexis had always defended her friends to a fault. Even if she knew they were wrong, she wouldn't let other people attack them. She made sure they understood they were wrong, but no one else was allowed to. She was like the big sister they all needed.

So for her to turn her back on someone she'd been friends with since they were nine, that was a big deal. Emilia also knew that Alexis' anger could land her in a lot of trouble one day, especially if she lashed out at the wrong person at the wrong time.

"Lex, please promise me that no matter what April does, you'll let me handle her."

"What's wrong with the way I'd handle her?"

Em hesitated in responding for a moment, wanting to put it as delicately as possible, "Well, you don't exactly think before you act, you let your anger get the best of you. Just promise me that unless she comes at you directly, you'll stay out of it."

"Yeah. See, I don't think that's going to work for me."

"Alexis. Please." There was a seriousness in Emilia's eyes that Alexis rarely saw. For some odd reason that she didn't understand, it was important to her friend that she not get involved. It wasn't for her to question though, so Alexis agreed.

"Ugh fine, if you're going to give me that face then I don't have much of a choice, do I?"

The pair walked down the line of waiting cars till they found Emilia's driver and hopped in the back seat.

"Home, Jeeves," Alexis grinned at Kyle, the driver, through the rear-view mirror.

"Never gets old for you, does it miss?"

"Nope, I like my traditions." Alexis liked Kyle, he

wasn't like some of the drivers her dad had gotten for her over the years. He was a lot more chilled out and let them play whatever music they wanted, plus he always took them through the drive through after school.

CHAPTER 5

Now while it was fair to say that Emilia avoided all forms of communication between herself and April, the same could not be said for April herself. No, April was a taunter. It was her life's work to try and taunt people into punching her in the face. At least that was how Alexis had described it one day when Em had vented to her about her interactions with the she-demon.

Today, it seemed, would be no exception. It was a Tuesday, week three of the semester. Miss Lesch, as she had insisted on being called rather than listening to another student stumble over her name, had been forced to go back to her office to reprint the assignment sheets. April was taking this teacherless opportunity to once again, torment the shy lesbian she knew wouldn't fight back. Her latest brain fart was to sing under her breath, "Dykes going to hell, dykes going to hell, all the ugly dykes going to hell."

"Shut the actual fuck up." Alexis emphasised her curse by slouching down and kicking the back of April's chair. The students around them slid their chairs away ever so slightly. All of them too timid or too smart to get in the middle of this. Every class had been like this for the past week. A pot ready to boil over, but always settling to a simmer before anything could happen.

The energy in the room was different today. April had been going out of her way to be more of a bitch then she normally was, and Alexis had become far less tolerant of people being pricks to her friends. Especially those who didn't fight back.

April turned in her chair and gave Alexis a sinister smile. "Oh, don't you worry Lex, you'll be joining her. I'm sure there's a special section for lesbos and mob sluts to get together."

Mob slut, that one was actually new. She'd been called a lot of things referring to the mob, and a slut, but never had the two been put together, or at least if they had, then no one had said it to her face until now.

"So long as it's far away from the ring of hell they've got waiting for you," Alexis replied with her own sweet smile.

April's smile died away and she turned back to face the front. She was the kind of person who had to prepare her insults in advance and once she ran out of smart comebacks, she resorted to general name calling and senseless cursing.

The class had been instructed to do their worksheets on nerve cells, but as it was, Miss Lesch had been gone for more than five minutes and seventy five percent of the class had the attention span of a goldfish. There was a lot of whispering and the rustling sound of notes being passed between friends, but the sound Alexis was trying to focus on was April's voice. It pained her to do it, but she needed to pay attention, especially since April had rocked her chair onto its front legs so she could lean further over the work bench and was now telling Emilia how no one would ever love her, whether she stayed as a dyke or went back to being straight.

Alexis could feel herself becoming more and more angry, but she'd made a promise to not interfere, to let Em to deal with it her way. They had argued about what the best way was. Em believing that if she just ignored April, eventually she'd go away and bug someone else. Sure, maybe she would move on to someone new, but she shouldn't be able to.

It was closing in on the ten-minute mark when it happened. April was leaning over the work bench again, this time it wasn't so she could say something else cruel, no, this time it was so she could reach for Em's hair. As her fingers made contact, they curled and pulled, dragging Em's head backwards. The moment she let go of the other girl's hair, April fell forward. Her chair had tipped out from under her, causing her to fall in such a way that she clipped her chin on the edge of the wooden work bench.

Before anyone else had a chance to react Alexis was out of her seat and by April's side, 'checking if she was okay.' She seized the opportunity to whisper some words of her own. "You lay a hand on my friend again, you even speak to her again and this mob slut is going to do a lot more than just make you bleed."

As if on cue, Miss Lesch was running back into the classroom. It took her a moment to absorb the scene in front of her before she took charge.

Another science teacher was called in to supervise the rest of the class while Miss Lesch took a now sobbing April to the nurse. The poor guy tried to keep them focused on nerve cells, but no one was paying any attention to what they were supposed to be doing. They were all trying to figure out what happened.

Everyone nearby had seen April rocking on her chair and leaning over the work bench. They'd seen her touch Emilia, they'd heard the things she had said but what they hadn't seen was Alexis' foot coming up to give April's chair that extra little push it needed to tip, and what they hadn't heard was Alexis threatening April. To the rest of the class it looked like divine intervention.

CHAPTER 6

The day after the incident in the science room was surprisingly devoid of drama. Only a few people were talking about April splitting her chin open, and most of them were laughing about how she'd deserved it.

She knew she shouldn't have, but Alexis swelled with pride. For so long April Hale had been the torment of their year group. Now, maybe, they could all get through year eleven without the sound of her voice throwing judgement at anyone she deemed to be a sinner.

For the rest of the day, there was a spring in Alexis' step that she wouldn't explain to people. It was one thing to secretly cause an injury to another person, but another stupid thing entirely to brag about it. No, if there was one thing that Alexis had learned from her father, it was to never brag about the bad things you do, even if doing them helps someone else.

Brennan was instantly suspicious of her good mood. Though when Jess suggested it was because she'd met a boy, he suddenly became very uninterested. Even after Alexis assured everyone that her good mood wasn't because of a boy, Brennan avoided her.

Every time she was with Emilia, Alexis could feel her friend watching her every move, almost like she was studying her, contemplating her existence. Alexis hadn't told Em what she'd done either... better her friend stay in the dark.

Thursday morning however, was a very different day. Alexis was running late for school. So long as she made it to first period on time no one would really care, but for some reason, when she walked into her homeroom class that morning all eyes were on her.

She didn't even have a chance to sit down before her homeroom teacher, Mrs Allsop, was calling her up to the front of the room.

"Alexis, you're needed up at the office. Katie will walk you up there. Take your bag with you."

"I know where the office is."

"Katie will take you." There was a finality in the woman's voice that dared Alexis to argue, and she hadn't even looked up from her computer screen. Alexis was starting to feel like a criminal.

Her mind raced as she went back outside and grabbed her bag from the rack while Katie trailed hesitantly behind.

"So, what'd you do?" the other girl asked when she caught up.

Alexis had a feeling that she knew exactly what she'd done. Other than *April* she hadn't done much in the past few days that would warrant a visit to the office. However she wasn't going to go and admit that to anyone, especially not the biggest goody two shoes in their entire year group.

"Your guess would be as good as mine. Did anyone say anything before I got there?" Alexis deflected.

"No, if anything Mrs Allsop went all quiet and serious. Then she called me over and asked me to walk you to the office when you got in." Katie's curiosity was obvious on her face, and Alexis wasn't going to be the one to satisfy it.

Even dragging her feet as much as she was physically able without going backwards, they reached the office within a few minutes. When they got to the doors of the office Alexis stopped and turned to Katie. "Yep, okay, I think I've got it from here." Whatever was to come next, she didn't need an audience.

Katie shifted awkwardly. "I think I'm meant to walk you in."

Alexis lost the fake smile and her eyes hardened. "Go. Away."

It worked. Which wasn't a surprise. Her dad called it her Mob Boss Face, the one that threatened to spill blood.

Katie tried to save face, but Alexis could see the fear dancing in her eyes.

Good.

Once she was sure that the girl wasn't going to reappear and snoop, Alexis went into the office. There were two receptionists behind the desk; one was on the phone, probably dealing with a parent calling in to say their child was sick, the other, an older woman that Alexis had never been able to learn the name of, but every time they'd interacted, she'd always been nice. The nice lady looked up from her computer screen with a smile. When she saw who it was that had come in, her smile faltered for a split second. Anyone else might've missed it.

"Apparently I'm needed?"

Before the lady had a chance to say a word, a door opened down the hall and heavy footsteps could be heard. A few moments later the principal appeared behind the receptionists.

"Alexis, why don't you step this way."

"Do I really have a choice?" Alexis asked with a cheeky smile.

"Not today, Alexis." He didn't smile back. Today he had his serious face on.

She'd always liked Mr McNeil. As an Angelo she was well known to all the teaching staff. She was just one in a long line of Angelo cousins that had attended Themis College. McNeil had pulled her into his office when the rumours about her family had hit an all-time high after her uncle Marco went to prison. He'd wanted to make sure that she was okay. It had seemed like he was insinuating that he was a *friend of the family*, or maybe he was just concerned about one of his students being singled out.

When they reached his office, she took a seat in one of the visitor's chairs on the other side of his desk, dumping her school bag at her feet. McNeil took his seat, unbuttoning the single button on his jacket.

Alexis had always wondered why it was that men wearing suits would do up that single button on their jacket when they stood up, only to then unbutton it the second they sat down again. Especially when those two things were barely minutes apart. Her wonderings were interrupted when he finally spoke.

"Do you know why I've called you in today?"

"As part of a new regime to discourage students from being late to homeroom?"

"You're very funny, but no. Alexis, this is very serious, so I'm going to need you to pay attention." And just like that, all the humour left her. Maybe it wasn't what she'd thought it was. Maybe it was something else that she hadn't actually been a part of. "Now, I think we should wait until your parents get here before we get into it, but there's been some trouble getting a hold of them."

Nodding slowly Alexis pulled out her phone. There was a text from her mum.

"Don't worry, my mum's already here." Looking up

and seeing the look of confusion on the man's face, Alexis explained. "I texted her when I first got told to come to the office. She'd only just left from dropping me off."

"Okay, well that certainly makes things easier."

As if on cue, they heard the outer office door open and Carmen Angelo's voice floated down the hall.

"Hi, I'm Alexis Angelo's mother, she's meant to be here."

McNeil stood from his chair, did up that one single button on his jacket and left the room. A few moments later he followed her mother into the room.

"Lex, are you okay?" Carmen didn't take her eyes off her daughter, scanning over every inch that she could, looking for some kind of injury or sign that she wasn't okay.

"Actually, Mrs Angelo, that's somewhat why we're here this morning. If you'd like to take a seat I'll explain." But she didn't. Carmen ignored the man. She knew that he had been a friend to their family, always looking out for each Angelo that came through over the years. He was a smart man. He didn't know if the rumours were true, but on the off chance they were, he wanted to be seen as an ally. Even so, her first concern would always be her daughter.

"Mum, I promise, I'm fine." This seemed to calm Carmen enough that she took the seat next to Alexis.

"Now, I'm sorry to have to disrupt your day Mrs Angelo, but this is quite a serious matter we have on our hands. Alexis, what can you tell us about your human bio class on Tuesday, in particular, what happened with April Hale?"

Alexis didn't look away from the principal, instead she adopted a look of confusion. "What do you mean? She fell."

"Yes, she fell, but she is claiming she didn't fall on her own."

Maybe it is what I thought it was, Alexis thought to herself.

Before she had a chance to reply or he had a chance to continue, Carmen interrupted. "Um, excuse me, can someone catch me up on what happened to April?"

"During class on Tuesday, there was an incident in which April fell and hit her chin on the edge of the work bench. She's had to have stitches." While that answered Carmen's question, it also raised another.

"Well that's unfortunate, but what does it have to do with Alexis?" Never one to beat around the bush, Carmen was slowly growing frustrated. She hated small talk and distractions, actually hated anything that hindered someone from getting to the point of the matter at hand.

"Well, April is claiming that Alexis caused the accident, and Mr and Mrs Hale are prepared to press charges."

"They're what? I didn't do anything. That's insane!" Alexis felt her mum's hand over hers and realised that she'd been gripping the arm rests of the chair. Taking a deep breath and releasing her grip, she went to speak again, with a much calmer tone, but her mum beat her to it.

"Wait, how did April fall? Did she trip? Slip? Fall from the sky?"

"Well, they're saying that as April was sitting down, Alexis pulled her chair out from under her."

The hand on hers tightened. Alexis knew she had to keep her cool and couldn't start shouting about how bullshit that story was. Instead she waited for Mr McNeil to look to her for a response.

"Does that sound like what happened?"

"Not even close. Sir." She added the 'sir' as an afterthought. "I'd be happy to tell you what actually happened, if you'd like."

"Please, by all means."

So Alexis launched into a retelling of the events of two days ago.

"Well for starters, no one was standing up. The teacher had gone to her office because the assignment sheets hadn't printed properly and we were all working through the tasks for that lesson. I sit behind April who sits behind Emilia, and at one point when I looked up I saw April leaning forwards to say something to Em, but it wasn't anything nice. This kept going so I told April to shut up. She turned around and said something to me and went back to harassing Em. Then she rocked her chair forward so she could lean over her desk to grab Em's hair. She must have over balanced because the next thing we all knew she was on the floor next to her chair. Everyone around us saw it."

"So, April was bullying Emilia?" Her mother's tone said it all. She was angry. Alexis couldn't tell if it was at her for supposedly doing nothing to stop it, or if it was purely directed at April for being such a bitch.

"I promised Em that I would stay out of it, she wanted to deal with April her own way. I didn't like it, but I promised."

Carmen's eyes softened, realising that her anger was being misinterpreted.

"You did what she asked you to do." Then she turned to Mr McNeil. "So April is trying to cover up the fact that she was bullying another student by saying that Alexis caused her to fall?"

Mr McNeil started to nod in agreement but shook his head at the last moment. "There's more. She's also saying that you threatened her."

So the little bitch thinks she can throw me under the bus but come away unscathed. Oh honey...

"And when is she claiming that I did this?"

"After she fell. She said you were the first one to get to her and that you threatened to do something worse to her if she told anyone."

"So did I threaten her before or after I asked if she was okay? Do I like April. No. Am I sad that she got hurt after being a bitch to my best friend? Also no.

But when someone hurts themselves, I'm going to check if they're okay, whether I like them or not. If I'd known she was going to try and pin the whole thing on me I wouldn't have bothered."

Before Mr McNeil had a chance to respond Carmen raised a very valid question. "Does she have any proof to back up her absurd allegations against Alexis?"

"I... don't know, they never said. April and her parents are actually waiting in the conference room. If you'd like we can continue this conversation with them. Perhaps we'll be able to get to the bottom of this."

"Yes, let's."

And with that the three of them rose from their seats. Alexis grabbed her bag from the floor and the trio made their way to the conference room with Mr McNeil leading the way. When they got to the closed door, he held it open for them as they stepped through.

Alexis hadn't seen April since she got taken to the office, trying to staunch the blood flow with a bunch of tissues. Back when they had been friends, Alexis had considered April to be a pretty girl. Now though, any attractive physical qualities she had were over-shadowed by what a terrible person she was. Her parents sat on either side of her, and Mr Hale had his left arm over the back of her chair. Her parents had always been nice enough to her back in the past. You could tell that they were a family. April had the same dark brown hair as her mother, and they shared the same large build which in itself was a sign of what was to come if April didn't take care of herself. Mr Hale had darker hair, closer to black than brown, but he shared his eyes and mouth with his daughter. All of the Hale children were like that. They were all a mix of their parents and you could tell they all belonged together. Alexis had always felt out of place when looking at pictures of herself with her parents. Sure, they looked like they were related, but not like she was actually their daughter. A cousin, maybe.

Alexis took the seat to the right of her mother, who sat across from Mr Hale. Mr McNeil took a seat at the head of the oval table closest to them.

"I've asked Alexis and Mrs Angelo to join us so that we can get to the bottom of what happened."

Drew Hale didn't waste any time voicing his opinion, "What happened is that delinquent assaulted my daughter."

"As far as I'm concerned the only delinquent here is your kid," Carmen said as calmly as she could.

"April doesn't go around assaulting other students!" Mr Hale all but leapt from his seat.

"Bullshit," Alexis scoffed. She hadn't realised she'd said it loud enough for everyone to hear until she looked up to see everyone looking at her. She looked to her left at her mum who just nodded at her encouragingly. Mr and Mrs Hale just sat there as though her curse had frozen them in place and April glared daggers at her. Mr McNeil didn't look as though he was going to interrupt either, so she went on.

"April is a bully. That day, she was harassing Emilia, calling her names, saying horrible stuff about her going to hell. I told her to shut up, so she spat some crap at me before she went back to being a horrible person to someone who was once her best friend. Then she leaned forward in her chair, grabbed Em's hair and pulled it. Em didn't do anything to provoke this, and she didn't retaliate. April must've leant too far forward and since she was trying to balance the chair on two legs it didn't end well for her. When she fell, I went to see if she was okay, and that's when the teacher came back. Everyone around us saw what happened."

"You're just making that up to try and get out of trouble," Sue Hale finally spoke, her words were laced with disgust.

"I don't have to lie. There's at least six other people who saw April being a bitch if you don't believe me. I didn't make her fall, she just fell all on her own. Instant karma."

"You did make me fall! I was balancing just fine, and then you pushed my chair or something, and now my face is scarred forever!"

Alexis couldn't see the extent of the injury due to the bandage covering the girl's chin.

"Honey, it wasn't such a treat to look at before either," Carmen muttered quietly enough that only Alexis could hear. It took all her self-control to not laugh. She waited another few moments for someone else at the table to click on to what April had said. And she wasn't disappointed.

Mr McNeil was the first to speak. "April, you said originally that Alexis pulled your chair out from under you as you went to sit down. But just now you've admitted to not only already being seated, but also rocking on your chair which is quite dangerous."

"I... she... you..."

"I think it's time that we investigated this matter further. Carmen, Alexis, if you wouldn't mind, I'll have Mrs Poole escort you to our new cafe so you'll be a bit more comfortable while I'm speaking to the other students."

"What about us?" Mr Hale didn't look as high and mighty as he had when they had walked into the room.

"I'll have some coffee and tea brought in for you. Excuse us." Without another word, the principal rose from his seat and held the door open for Alexis and her mum. They went back to his office briefly so she could write down the names of the other kids who sat nearby. She didn't include Emilia's name, but chances were, he'd call her in anyway.

Mrs Poole, the nice older receptionist, dropped the mother and daughter at the cafe, with instructions for the cooking teacher to make sure they were taken care of. It was a weird experience for Alexis. She knew that all of this was because of McNeil's assumption that her family was involved in the Mafia and he wanted to keep her mum happy. While she always had to endure the scrutiny of being a part of a suspected crime family, she had yet to experience the perks that came with it. Her parents made a lot of money, that was true, but she didn't get to run around spending it like a lot of her rich classmates did. And she'd never had someone suck up to her because of her last name. It was unsettling, but not the worst feeling in the world.

While they waited for their coffee and whatever dessert the culinary students were preparing for them, Alexis texted Emilia to let her know that the shit was hitting the fan but she'd tried to keep her friend out of it as much as possible, and while there was a list of students McNeil was going to be questioning, her name wasn't on it. Em messaged back almost straight away, the call had already come for her to go to the office.

"So why didn't you tell me what happened the other day? Something like April splitting her chin open would normally be the biggest news you had."

"Tuesday was just a really long day I guess. I had a lot of homework, it must've slipped my mind."

"Mmmhmm." The look on her mum's face said it all. She wasn't buying what her daughter was selling.

Alexis decided to shift the topic of conversation away from anything that could circle back to April's *unfortunate accident.*

For the next half hour she managed to distract her mum with tales of Jessica's drama with her boyfriend and the new gossip surrounding the new guy that she was still yet to actually see, let alone meet. The entire time Carmen just sat there, letting her daughter stall. There was more to this whole thing than Alexis was letting on, that much she knew. What she was more concerned about though, was why Emilia was being targeted.

Bullies were bullies. Simple as that. Sure, they *had their reasons.* She'd seen all those daytime talk shows about how bullies had been bullied themselves. That didn't give them an excuse to be assholes. She'd met plenty of people who had been through hell and were the most caring people she knew. She'd also met people who had had the perfect lives, most loving parents and family and yet, they still turned out to be pricks. Sometimes people were just born evil.

Carmen looked up to the doorway just as Mrs Poole was walking through it.

"Mr McNeil is ready for you again, ladies."

"Thank you, Helen." Alexis looked at her mum in surprise. "We'll just be a minute, I have to finish this coffee, it's wonderful." Carmen was not lying, it was wonderful.

"Well, if you'd like, I can have them make you

fresh coffees to go?" Helen offered with a genuine smile.

"Oh, I would hate to be an inconvenience."

"Of course not, it's no trouble at all. Alexis, would you like one as well?"

"Yes please, that would be great."

The moment the kind woman was out of earshot, Alexis looked at her mother, a single eyebrow quirking up.

"Helen?"

"What? That is her name."

"Yes, I know that's her name... well now I do, but my question is, how do you know her name?"

"You should always make it a point of knowing who it is you're dealing with." It was only for a second, but her mum's face changed and her words seemed to have a serious edge to them. This wasn't just some piece of useless advice that parents gave their kids to try and guide them to becoming good adults. No, this was something that her mum had figured out the hard way. Before she could say anything back, Mrs Poole came back from the kitchen with two brand new reusable travel coffee cups.

Back in the conference room, sitting in the same chairs as they had the first time, everyone was quiet, waiting for Mr McNeil to reveal what he'd learnt from his interviews with the students. From the look of the papers on the desk in front of him, he'd typed up each student's statement and then had them sign it.

"Alright, I had some remarkably interesting conversations with a number of the students from your human bio class, girls. To say that I am disappointed by what I've learned is an understatement. I would like to state that these students who were called in were unaware of the accusations made and were simply asked to provide their point of view for the events of Tuesday afternoon. Now, I'm going to read some excerpts from the statements that were made."

The Hales all sat in rapt silence on the other side of the table. April actually looked worried about what the principal was about to say, and her parents didn't look quite so certain that their daughter was the perfect, harmless angel they thought she was.

"I sit a few seats away and I could hear every-thing she was saying. She wasn't trying to be quiet about it, she was just being mean.

"Onto the next page. *She was rocking on her chair and she fell.* I then asked this student for clarification on one of April's statements about how she fell. *No, once we sat down at the start of class she didn't get out of her seat until she was on the floor.*

"The next page. *We all try and ignore her, but it's almost like she's mean just because she can be. Emilia was just sitting there trying to do her work and April was behind her, saying all this horrible stuff and pulling her hair."*

With each new excerpt Mr McNeil read out, the glaring contest between Alexis and April intensified. Drew and Sue Hale were sharing looks that were a mix between embarrassment and angry. They definitely weren't jumping to their daughter's defence anymore.

"So, April, I think this is quite substantial evidence that contradicts everything you said happened that day."

April didn't answer. She didn't even bother breaking eye contact with Alexis to acknowledge that he'd spoken. April's rudeness didn't faze McNeil, he was used to moody teenagers getting caught in a lie.

"Mr and Mrs Hale, in light of this new evidence I don't believe that I have a choice but to suspend April for three days. This will be an in-school sus-"

"What about her? She threatened me!"

Mr McNeil took a deep breath through his nose, his eyes narrowing in barely contained frustration.

"Miss Hale. As per the interviews I conducted with your classmates, not a single one of them can corroborate your claims that Alexis threatened you, and seeing as every aspect of your story has been pulled into question, I find myself inclined to believe that you are once again making up stories so as to get yourself out of trouble. Now, I think it's time I show Mrs Angelo and Alexis out. Please remain here. We have more to discuss."

The Hales were beyond the point of caring what their daughter had to say, as Carmen and Alexis grabbed their things Alexis could hear April being berated by her parents for lying about everything. She almost felt sorry for the hell spawn.

Almost.

Mr McNeil opened the door for the mother and daughter and followed them out into the hall, closing the door behind him. That didn't stop April from glaring at Alexis through the wall of windows. Alexis had won both this round and the last, but the look in April's eyes promised that there would be a round three.

"I'm so sorry that your day has been interrupted by this nonsense, and I apologise for the abrupt exit, but I wanted to save you both from what I'm sure is going to be a very tedious conversation."

"That's quite alright Rob, and please call me Carmen. I'm just glad that you went to so much effort to find the truth rather than just punishing Alexis on that child's word alone."

Alexis smirked through the window at April before turning her back on the conference room.

"Yes, I really appreciate it Mr McNeil." Something Alexis had learned from watching her parents interact with people over the years, when they do something to help you, no matter how small or insignificant, you show your gratitude for that act. The more gratitude you show, the more willing they are to help you in the future. It was something amazingly simple to grasp, but it made the world of difference in the long run.

"Alexis, you have been a model student and I have been given absolutely no reason to suspect that what April said was true. Now, I must let you both go. Alexis, I hope to not see you in my office anytime soon." He gave her a smile to show he was joking and she gave him a small nod in return. Mr McNeil walked them the short distance back to the main reception area, and after speaking softly with Mrs Poole, bid them goodbye again and went back to the conference room to deal with the Hales.

Ten minutes later Carmen and Alexis were driving away from the school. As they had passed through the reception, Mrs Poole informed them that Mr McNeil had excused Alexis from the rest of the school day, his way of apologising for the 'inconvenience'. He was also probably trying to minimise the chances of the entire eleventh grade knowing about what went down in the office conference room before lunch.

"Well hun, I've gotta say, you getting called in to the principal's office gave me an amazing reason to cancel my coffee plans with your aunt. Love the woman, I really do..." Carmen trailed off.

"But she drives you insane when you have to inter-act with her on your own?"

"Mmhmm, exactly. Now, it's almost eleven, so why don't we get some brunch before we go home?"

"Mum, I did it." Alexis didn't know why she said it, she wasn't planning on telling anyone the truth about her involvement in April's disfiguring. She hadn't even started feeling guilty about it until now, and even then, she didn't feel guilty about actually doing it. She just felt guilty about her mum thinking she hadn't.

"And what pray tell, is it that you did?" There was an amused smile on her mum's face, and Alexis wondered how long she could keep her mum looking happy. "Lexis, you've got stalling face, what did you do?"

"It. April's face. I caused it." Alexis watched her mum like a hawk, waiting for the anger to show.

When her mum started talking again, there was no sign of anger or disappointment, just more amusement. "Well I don't think you can be blamed for that. I'm quite certain her parents had more to do with that than you did."

Alexis was confused for a second, unsure what her mum was on about, she was too focused on confessing her physical violence against another person.

"What? Mum, no, that's not what I meant."

"Yes honey, I know what you meant, and I know."

"You know what? I'm so confused." Carmen held back her laugh. She loved driving her daughter crazy.

It was one of the few joys she was able to get on a regular basis.

"I know that the further disfiguring of that girl's face was something that you played a part in."

Alexis couldn't hide the shock she was feeling. "But if you knew then why..." she trailed off, not quite sure how to ask the question without throwing herself into the fire.

"I didn't know what was going on until Mr McNeil explained it this morning. At first I thought that maybe you were telling the truth about having nothing to do with it. Then I heard what that demon child was saying about Emilia and I knew that you wouldn't just stand by and let someone hurt a friend like that, and definitely not your best friend."

"I tried to stay out of it, mum. I swear. Em made me promise not to get involved and I tried. It was one thing when all she was doing was running her mouth, but then she actually put her hands on Em, and I wanted to kill her." It felt good for Alexis to finally get it out and to tell someone. There were still no signs of anger on her mum's face, no disappointment either. She stayed quiet for another minute, not wanting to say anything else that might provoke a negative reaction.

"Do you feel bad that you did it?"

"No." There was no need to think about it. The words were out of Alexis' mouth before she could even pretend to give it some thought.

"So you don't feel guilty about sending that girl to the hospital where she had to get stitches in her face because you somehow caused her to fall and split her chin open?"

"No, I don't. It was one thing to be saying all that crap to Em, but then she went and actually started physically harassing her. That was it, I was done. I only felt guilty that you didn't know and that you thought I was completely innocent. I don't care what those assholes at that school say or do to me, but they don't get to attack my friends and get away with it."

They stopped at a red light just before hitting the main shopping complex, which gave Carmen a chance to look at her daughter. Alexis was looking back at her, a look in her eye that Carmen had never seen in her daughter before but recognised all too well. She didn't condone violence for the sake of violence, and she certainly didn't want her daughter going around knocking in the head of every bully at that school. But she was proud of Alexis all the same. She stood up for someone who couldn't or wouldn't stand up for themselves.

"Good. Now, you never answered me about brunch."

CHAPTER 7

For most of Friday Alexis was able to avoid the speculative looks and whispered conversations. After all she'd been dealing with it for most of her life, what was another day? It wasn't until after lunch when Alexis was in the library for study period that she had the misfortune of overhearing a conversation between three girls about April.

"Talk about a double whammy, splitting your own face open *and* getting in-school suspension," the first girl said.

"Bitch had it coming." The voice of the second girl sounded more familiar, but Alexis couldn't quite place it.

"Well yeah, she's awful but come on."

"No, she's not just awful, she's actually the devil. You just haven't been on the receiving end of her crap."

"She's right. God, I actually wish that April's story about Alexis being the one to make her fall had been true. Totally wouldn't have blamed her," the third girl piped in.

"Look, I'm not saying that she didn't deserve to be punished in some way, but I just don't think that physical violence is the way to go."

"Hun, we're not talking about physical violence, though April did start it when she put her hands on Emilia. But April fell all on her own. It was like God himself decided he'd had enough of her bullshit."

The three girls laughed softly.

"Yeah, I guess you're right. If anyone hurt you girls I'd be furious. I wouldn't stop at chin splitting."

"Ahh... No! You wouldn't hurt a fly and you know it."

Before the trio of girls could continue their argument over who was the most protective amongst them, a short bell sounded signally the end of the period. Alexis gathered up her books and brushed past the girls.

"Oh shit-"

"Was she-"

"Did you kn-"

Their guilty whispers were swallowed up by the sound of the two dozen students in the library heading to their next class.

Unfortunately, Alexis couldn't get their conversation out of her head. She spent the next fifty-five minutes in a daze, absentmindedly making notes that she would later find out was unintelligible scribble.

Alexis' absentmindedness didn't go unnoticed by Emilia. When Mrs Lesch told them to pair up and quiz each other for the test next week, Emilia had expected Alexis to slide into the seat next to her, but when she looked behind her, her friend just sat there staring down at her textbook. It wasn't even open.

Emilia moved over to her, trying to initiate a conversation, but she might as well have not been there at all.

In Alexis' defence, she was completely unaware of her surroundings. There was something about what those girls had said in the library. How they'd been so ready to accept that April deserved to be disfigured. That for everything she'd done and said to people, the ways that she'd hurt them, she deserved to bleed for that. The way they spoke, Alexis knew that if she had admitted to being the cause of April's injury, they would've looked up to her. Did she want that? People to look up to her because she inflicted pain on someone else?

What if that someone else was a bad person? What if they deserved the pain?

And when did that become her decision to make? Who said she got to decide?

Alexis couldn't help but think about her dad and the line of business he was in. She knew that he had guys in his crew that hurt people. People that betrayed the Family. Bad people.

Once when she was eleven, she'd snuck into the boot of her dad's car before he went to a 'business meeting'. She had no idea what she was getting herself into. At the time she still had this image in her head of who her dad was when he went to work. However, the idea in her head was shattered that day. When she opened the boot and peeked out, she was surprised to see that the car was parked in a back alley. Then when she climbed out she could see that they were next to a warehouse. She went through the only door she could find.

Looking back, she was surprised that the door was even unlocked. Alexis could hear noises and she followed them, not sure what she was expecting to find but she wasn't scared because her dad was there somewhere.

When she finally made her way through the maze of pallets and wooden crates, she saw something that to this day, she couldn't forget. A man, duct taped to a metal chair, surrounded by men. One of his eyes was swollen shut while blood dribbled down from a gash on his forehead into his other eye. All the fingers on his right hand and two on his left hand looked broken.

"Tell us what we want to know Petey and we'll let you go."

She knew that voice, it was her dad's bodyguard

Ty. Whenever he came over he would bring her ice cream. She loved his hugs, he'd always pick her up when he hugged her, no matter how tall she got. It made her feel precious every time.

"Pfft, do I look like an idiot to you dumb-fucked wogs? I know that the second I tell you anything you'll kill me." Petey spat at Ty but his blood-filled saliva didn't go far. In fact it didn't do more than dribble down his own chin. He was weak. They could've left him there in the warehouse and he'd probably be dead in a few days.

Out of nowhere there was a bang and Petey was screaming.

Alexis didn't realise that she had screamed out too. It was just a short scream of surprise, but it was enough to alert everyone in the warehouse to her presence. Scrambling backwards, Alexis knocked into a stack of crates and froze. Ty had just shot Petey in the knee. She hadn't even seen the gun, but she saw the way his knee jerked to the side and the blood spraying out.

"Boss! You're gonna wanna come here!" Ty stood in front of the little girl he'd known since the night she was born and was at a loss. Her eyes were wide open and she was there against the boxes, still as a statue. There was a look in her eyes that he couldn't decipher. He then became very conscious of the fact that he was still holding the gun.

"Boss!" Ty didn't know why he sounded so

panicked. It wasn't the first time that someone had walked into something they weren't meant to. It was easy enough to deal with. However, this was the first time that someone had been the boss' daughter. Tony's whole crew knew Alexis, and they all loved her like family. She was precious to them. She was a miracle.

"Lexis, *bambina*, can you hear me?" Tony went to his knees in front of his little girl. There were so many questions running through his head. *How did she get here? How did she get in? How much did she see? What does she think of me now?* Alexis just crouched there staring blankly ahead, her breathing was fast and shallow.

"Ty, she's in shock. I've gotta get her home, you finish up here."

His second in command nodded and straightened up. Taking a deep breath, he schooled his expression and walked back to the open space in the middle of the warehouse.

Alexis didn't remember going home with her dad. She didn't remember being carried up to bed or how Ty had stood in her doorway for what must have been hours.

The next day she pretended that she didn't remember anything from the day before. She acted like it had been any other boring school holiday day. Her parents looked relieved, but Ty was still nervous around her for weeks after. He still brought ice cream whenever he came to the house, but he hesitated to hug her. It took her a few weeks to realise why. She'd thought that he was upset with her for being at the warehouse that day, but finally she overheard a conversation between Ty and her dad. She realised then that he was scared of what she might think of him after what she'd seen.

From then on, every time she saw him, she showed how happy she was that he was around. Between that and her dad's reassurances that she remembered nothing from that day in the warehouse, he finally went back to normal.

When he finally picked her up in a bear hug for the first time in almost two months, she actually let out a happy *"Finally"*. He pretended he didn't hear it, but his hold on her tightened.

When Alexis was eleven, she hadn't understood the reasons behind the torture that Ty was inflicting on Petey. She still didn't know what it was that he had done to deserve being kneecapped and having his fingers broken, but it hadn't changed how she felt about Ty. He wasn't a blood relative but he was like an uncle to her, even more so than some of her blood related uncles. She could've seen him kill Petey with his bare hands and it wouldn't have changed anything. She didn't feel unsafe when he was around. If anything she felt safer. To this day no one knew that she remembered that day.

◆ ◆ ◆

Alexis barely noticed when Emilia shook her at the end of class. She did notice when Emilia dug her nails into her arm.

"Ah, stop that."

"Yeah well you were like a zombie. Except zombies tend to make more noise. I had to do something to bring you out of it. Class is over... let's go."

The two girls gathered up their books and made their way for the door. Alexis started to get lost in her thoughts again, trying to figure out if what Ty did to Petey was any different than what she'd done to April. Because of this she didn't notice that she was walking straight towards someone who also wasn't looking where they were going.

She did however, quickly learn that he was a solid wall. Most teenage boys their age were all gangly with no real muscle to them. This one however... he worked out. At least that was the observation she made as she sat on the concrete pathway, staring up at the human obstacle she would later admit, was absolutely gorgeous.

"Shit! Are you okay? I'm sorry, I wasn't looking where I was going."

She saw the hand extend towards her, and for a few moments, she was genuinely confused as to why it was there.

"Lex! What are you doing on the ground, you

loser?"

Emilia. For her, calling her best friend a loser, was the nicest thing you could expect at this time of day and thankfully, it was enough to snap Alexis back to reality and stop checking out the forearm of the handsome stranger. Snapping her eyes up to meet the boy's, she smiled awkwardly and reached her hand out to grab his still out-stretched one. In one swift move he pulled her to her feet and caught her when she over balanced.

"I... um... thanks... mean... sorry for running into you... I guess I didn't see you... don't know how you're huge... I mean... Not huge huge... Tall... You're very tall." *Stammering... I'm stammering. If God had any kindness left he would open the ground and have it swallow me whole right now.*

The boy just smiled sweetly at her before bending down to pick up their books. In the seconds he wasn't looking at her, Alexis turned to Emilia, her eyes wide and panicked. All she saw in return was amusement with a touch of pity. Turning back just in time for the boy not to notice the shared looks, Alexis gratefully took her books back.

"I'm Lucas, by the way."

Those eyes... God they're blue... and that hair - her thoughts were interrupted by a sharp jab in her side, which thankfully she didn't visibly flinch away from... too much.

"Um... yes... thank you... Lucas. Welcome. Bye!"

Then with as much dignity as she could muster, Alexis spun around and started walking away. Emilia quickly caught up to her.

"Hun, you know we're going the wrong way right?"

"Mmhmm." She was too mortified to even form words. They were too close to the scene of the crime. The crime being, any chance of her being perceived as an intelligent and funny person, being murdered. The murderer? Herself. Alexis Angelo. It wasn't until they'd done almost a full lap of the building that Alexis stopped and faced her best friend.

"Em... I froze."

"Yes... I did see that. It's okay. I don't think he noticed."

Now if she'd been able to look as confident as she sounded, Emilia could pass as almost believable.

"Not notice? How could he have not noticed? I was staring at his forearm for the entire time that I was on the ground. How could anyone not notice that? And I was stammering! I don't stammer. When was the last time I was at a loss for words? I'm one of the biggest smart mouth pains in the ass here, all the teachers think so! Yet here I am, lost for words because of some guy. Oh god..."

While Emilia was guiltily enjoying the out of character freak out, the look of horror in her friend's eyes was cause for concern.

"What? What's wrong?"

"I told him he was huge and then called him tall."

"Yeah, sweetie. I think he's aware that he's tall. It's not like you blew his mind with that revelation of yours." *Though I'm sure she'd like to blow something else of his.*

"I know he knows he's tall, that's why what I said was so stupid. I didn't tell him my name either. He introduced himself, and all I had to say in return was, 'welcome' and 'bye'."

"You also said 'thank you', which personally I thought was pretty polite."

Lucas saw the girl visibly freeze again, and although he was behind her, the reflection in the window showed him that her eyes were once again wide and full of embarrassment. It was a really clean window.

"Well, *Alexis*, I think now you've got the chance to introduce yourself."

Giving herself the time to mouth the words 'I hate you' to Emilia before turning around also gave Alexis the chance to school her face into an expression that wasn't one of horror or embarrassment, but instead what she hoped was a cute and confident smile.

"Hi Lucas."

The sound of his name coming from this amusing girl was enough to make him grin again.

"I realised that I had your pencil case in my pile of stuff and thought you might want it back."

Emilia subtly side stepped a few metres away, far enough that she didn't feel like she was intruding on whatever straight flirting ritual was going on, but close enough that if he turned out to be a deranged teenage psycho killer and attacked Alexis suddenly, she could at least jump in a try and save her best friend.

"So, Alexis, was it?" He waited for her nod of acknowledgement before continuing. "It was really nice running into you today. Maybe we could do it again sometime... say this weekend?"

How is he so confident? Teenage boys are never this confident. Answer him before you scare him away.

"Yes! I mean... *fuck*." Though she muttered the curse under her breath to herself, there was no doubt that he heard it. "That would be really nice. Should I give you my number or should we just meet up somewhere?" *And now she sounded desperate, just offering her number up left, right and centre. Asking to meet up.*

"How about this, I give you my number and then, if you want to, call me and we'll do something." A few minutes later his number was in her phone and they were saying their goodbyes.

When Lucas had finally left ear shot, Emilia sidled up next to Alexis again and started peppering her with questions about what had happened. She gushed like a proud mamma when Alexis got to the part where she was able to string an actual sentence together, without swearing and without stumbling her way through it. Then she practically snatched the phone out of Alexis' hand to examine the new contact.

By the time they made it from their lockers to the waiting car and then to Alexis' house, the pair had gone over each interaction with Lucas twice and discussed in length when and how she should contact him. While he had told her to call him, she clearly couldn't be trusted on her own to string a coherent sentence together, so they settled on texting him to make plans. If he ended up calling her after she texted him, well then she was screwed and would have to wing it from there.

A few hours later, after they'd eaten dinner, they rushed back to Alexis' room with enough junk food and drinks to choke a grown man. Alexis pulled out her phone and started to draft a message. It took twenty minutes and five rewrites, but eventually, she was able to send off the text message, *Hey, it's Alexis, I'm free tomorrow, what about you?*

And then they waited.

CHAPTER 8

"Hey mum, um there's something I need to ask you. Well not so much ask you but more just talk about."

Carmen had been waiting all night for her daughter to come to her. When the girls got home from school that day they'd been buzzing. She and Tony could hear them giggling and shushing each other right up until they got called down for dinner. During dinner though, Alexis got quiet and Carmen knew that something else was going on. She just had to wait.

"What's the matter?" Putting down the damp tea towel she'd been using to dry dishes, Carmen moved around the kitchen preparing mugs of hot chocolate for the two of them. Alexis appreciated how her mum gave her time to get up the courage to say what needed to be said. Finally she just opened her mouth and said the first thing that came to mind, and she shocked herself.

"Do you think I'm a good person?"

Carmen spun around, the open can of chocolate powder in one hand and a spoon in the other, her eyes squinting at her only child. She shouldn't have been surprised that she was asking, it was bound to happen after she confessed to being behind April's 'fall'. However with all the girl talk she and Emilia had obviously been having upstairs all night, it wasn't what Carmen had been expecting to be the most pressing topic of conversation.

"Honey, of course you're a good person. What's got you thinking otherwise?"

"Well um, today at school in the library, during study period, there were these girls talking in the cubicle next to me. They were talking about what happened with April, and about me."

"What were they saying?"

"They were saying how they wouldn't have blamed me if I had been the one to make April fall. They were saying that she deserves whatever happens to her. They would've thought I was *awesome* if I'd made April split her chin open. Like, what? Who thinks like that? Is April a horrible person? Yes, a thousand times yes, but they were talking like she deserved to bleed for everything she's ever done to people. They didn't care that she was hurt. They loved that she got stitches and is going to have a scar for the rest of her life." It all just spilled out. When Em had been there, she'd been able to distract herself with talk about Lucas and laughing at how weird she'd been when they met, but the moment Em got picked up it was back to her moral dilemma.

"Lex, do you regret what you did?"

"God no, she put her hands on Em." There was a finality in Alexis' voice that Carmen had heard before, except it was coming from her husband not her daughter.

"I dunno why, but it made me think about Ty and that day in the warehouse when I snuck into the car and walked in on one of dad's 'business meetings'. Afterwards Ty was all worried that I saw him differently, and it took him months to realise that I didn't. But what I was thinking about was how I didn't see him differently. He's my uncle Ty, nothing could change how I see him. But why? I saw him kneecap a man, but I didn't care because he's Ty. I didn't understand everything back then but I get it now, he was doing what he had to do to protect the Family. But listening to those girls today, I felt sick. Two of them were practically singing my praises just on the speculation that I might've been responsible. And I was thinking about the situation with Ty back then and comparing it to now, and I don't understand how in my mind what I saw Ty do is somehow not as bad as what I did. I'm not saying that what I did was good, but it's not as bad a shooting a guy and breaking all his fingers."

Carmen took a deep breath and opened her mouth to speak. And then closed it again. She had two more false starts before she finally got words out.

"So, you do remember that day, I thought you might have."

"That's it? Yeah, I never forgot. I just pretended I did so no one would send me to therapy."

"Oh honey, we wouldn't have sent you to therapy, we would've indoctrinated you right then and there."

"Really? No therapy? After what I saw?" There was a glimmer of humour in Alexis' eyes and Carmen was relieved to see that her daughter was calming down a bit.

"No, they wouldn't have believed you anyway. Would've thought you were dreaming or delusional, but hey sometimes they give you the good drugs for that kind of thing. But seriously, is it the fact that the girls would've been happy if you'd done it, or the fact that you did it to begin with?"

"Mum, I was serious. When I think about what happened, I don't feel remorse for it. Did I intend for her to get seriously hurt? No, but it happened, and yes maybe she deserved to get hurt, but I just wanted her to leave Em alone."

"So you're upset that they were happy about what you did even though they don't actually know you did it, they just wish you'd done it?"

"Yes? But then when I was thinking about the

whole thing with Ty, I felt like a hypocrite because I did the same thing back then that they're doing now."

"But are you?"

"What do you mean?"

"Are you happy that Ty hurt that man?"

"Well... no..."

"So you don't think the man deserved what happened to him?"

"I don't know if he deserved it or not, but I know that for Ty to be torturing him then there must have been a reason."

"There we go. Those girls glorified the violence and are using April's actions as a way to justify how they feel. What you saw that day was significantly worse, but you aren't doing what they did. You know that Ty was doing what he had to do for the Family. He was protecting the Family. You were protecting your family. If you were anything like those girls then you would've been bragging about what you'd done from the get-go. But you didn't. You don't want credit for what you did because that's not why you did it. I hope that you're never in a situation where you need to make hard decisions about what's right and wrong, but I also know the life we live and if you choose to be a part of this life then you will have to make those choices. There are worse things to do to someone than to physically harm them." There was a look in her mum's eyes that Alexis couldn't quite place, but her tone said she knew what she was talking about.

CHAPTER 9

Alexis was going on her first proper date. While she and Marty had dated for a few months, they hadn't actually gone out on a date. But now, in five hours' time, she would be meeting Lucas at the cinema where they would be seeing some movie about a house party that gets out of control.

For the third time in two hours Alexis called Emilia in a panic. As soon as her friend had picked up the call, Alexis let loose, "What do I do if he tries to kiss me? Or puts his arm around me during the movie? What if he wants to hold my hand? What if my hands are all sweaty? What if his are? Oh my god, what if he doesn't try anything at all? What if one of us loves the movie and the other hates it? What if we go to dinner and we have nothing to talk about? Em help me," her final request came out as a desperate plea.

Emilia took a deep, calming breathe and was glad that Alexis couldn't see her rolling her eyes.

"Honey, you need to chill out. Seriously. You're going to give yourself a panic attack and that's not going to do anyone any good. Now do those breathing things you told me about, I'll wait."

Emilia waited until Alexis had opened up the app on her phone and listened to her control her breathing. Alexis had actually downloaded the app for Emilia for when she got an anxiety attack, but there was no harm in using it for herself. After a few minutes Alexis closed the app. "Okay I'm back. Sorry about that."

"It's okay, now that you're not losing your shit anymore. Let's start from the beginning. Do you want him to kiss you? If so then make sure you take some mints with you just in case. There is also the option of getting chocolate at the cinema, make yourself taste extra sweet. As for his arm, same thing, if you want it there then leave it there, if you don't then take it away. Those rules apply for all physical interactions that might occur tonight.

"Sweaty hands just mean you're nervous. Now if he's been listening to any of the rumours they tell new kids in our year about you, then he probably would be nervous to be dating you, but hey, he'll get over it when he realises how amazing you are. As for the movie, whether you love it or hate it then that in itself is a conversation. It can easily take up at least twenty minutes of conversation, more so if you both hate it, then you can rip on it for a good forty-five minutes. This can then lead into talking about other movies and TV shows that you both like. Maybe even hint at seeing a different movie later that you might actually like.

"Ask him where he's from, siblings, what do his parents do. In the event that he asks you these same questions, do not tell him what your parents actually do. Actually, do that, then take a photo of the look on his face when you tell him that your dad is a mafia boss. I think that'd be pretty funny."

Alexis couldn't help but laugh.

This was one of the reasons Alexis defended Emilia so steadfastly. Emilia knew just what to say to get her to calm down.

After another few minutes of talking the pair hung up and Alexis finished getting ready. She was about to go on her first real date.

"That... sucked. I'm sorry, but that was probably the worst movie I've ever seen."

"You do not have to apologise. I totally agree. I'm sorry I ever suggested it to begin with. Seriously the whole movie was a bad home video. If that's what's passing as cinematic genius these days then my parents could make a fortune off my baby videos." Lucas voiced his opinion in such a passionate and dramatic way that Alexis just had to laugh. The pair sat across from each other at the Chinese restaurant across the way from the movie theatre.

"If I'd known you hated it so much I would've suggested that we leave when I wanted to," Alexis grinned.

"God I wish you had, definitely two hours neither of us are getting back." Before Alexis could say anything in reply, their food arrived and they lapsed into silence as they started eating.

"I didn't mean that how it sounded," Lucas said suddenly. Alexis looked up and tried to quickly swallow the mouthful of food so she could speak. Unfortunately, she only succeeded in almost choking herself. After chugging her glass of water, she felt like the blockage had cleared and prayed that Lucas hadn't noticed.

"Are you okay there?" he asked.

"Ahem, hmm? Me? No, I'm fine. So, you were saying something about... something?"

"About the two hours of our lives thing." He looked so nervous about what he was trying to get across and it took a moment before it clicked with Alexis what he'd said. When she opened her mouth to tell him it was okay he rushed to explain himself.

"I just meant that if we'd left we maybe could've seen a movie that we would've enjoyed, not that I didn't want to be in the movie with you... I mean, it wouldn't have mattered what movie we saw so long as we were seeing it together-"

"But that movie sucked ass. Seriously I did not take what you said in a bad way. Maybe later when I decide to over analyse everything you said, but not just then."

The cheeky smile on Alexis' face had Lucas instantly at ease. He felt like an idiot the way he'd stumbled over his words like that. The moment he realised that what he said could've come across as a dig at her, he couldn't stand the thought that he might've hurt her feelings.

"You know it's nice to know that I'm not the only one who turns into a bumbling idiot when I'm nervous," Alexis smiled.

"So, you're saying that you were nervous yesterday?"

"Wouldn't you be nervous if you'd just been knocked over by a giant?"

"I am not that tall."

"Yeah, okay Gigantor." The vibration of her phone stole Alexis' attention, but when she checked the notifications she saw that it was just another text from Brennan.

"You seem pretty popular tonight."

From someone else those words would've sounded snarky, but Lucas seemed genuinely curious and unphased that she hadn't stopped getting texts all night.

"Ugh I know. I'm sorry. I would turn it off, but if my parents try and call me and I don't answer, they'll send an army out for me."

"No, no, it's fine. I was just curious is all. I get how that is, my mum's pretty protective as well."

"It's so fun, right?" Her flat tone and dead eyes contradicted her words and Lucas found himself grinning at her. Before he could try flirting with her again her phone started ringing and he saw Brennan come up on the screen. Alexis didn't decline the call, but instead pressed the lock key on the side of the phone to stop the vibrating and just let the call ring out.

"Your friends seem pretty persistent, maybe it's an emergency?"

"Pft, yeah... I don't think so. I wouldn't tell them what I was doing tonight, and they don't like not being in the know."

Lucas could've been offended that she hadn't told her friends that she was going on a date, but he wasn't sure if these particular friends were ones that she would share that information with.

"Are these the guys you hang out with at school?"

"Yeah, Seth and Brennan. They asked me to hang out with them tonight, and I told them I already had plans, but I wouldn't tell them what those plans were or who they're with, so here we are." As if on cue her phone rang again, this time it was Seth.

Before Alexis could silence the call again, Lucas reached out for her phone but stopped just short.

"Do you trust me?"

Alexis looked into his eyes looking for any reason why she shouldn't. Aside from a glimmer of mischief there was nothing that made her want to say no. Once she'd given him the nod he grabbed her phone off the table and quickly answered it before it rung out.

"Hello."

Alexis couldn't help admiring how his greeting was so laid back but at the same time, so strong. She could've been blind and would've felt safe just from hearing his voice.

"No sorry, there's no Alexis here. Yeah man I'm sure."

Propping the phone holding arm up on the table, Lucas continued to listen, but with his other hand he reached across the table and started stroking the back of her hand.

"Dude I think I would notice if there was an Alexis here."

She held her breathe as his fingers danced softly over her skin. One second he was tripping over his words, and the next he was the most confident guy she'd ever met.

"Okay... well, why don't you describe her?" Alexis covered her mouth with the hand Lucas wasn't occupying to muffle the giggles she could feel bubbling to the surface.

"She sounds gorgeous. I can understand why you want to find her, but yeah no, she's not here. Anyways, gotta go dude. Good luck with that."

The whole time that he'd been on the phone Lucas hadn't taken his eyes off Alexis. He was gauging her reactions to everything he said, not wanting to upset her. Alexis however was the furthest she'd ever been from upset. Lucas had called her gorgeous.

"You know, you probably just sent them into a frenzy. They'll think I've been kidnapped."

His fingers had moved up and now danced over the softer skin of her inner forearm. Her hormones were going insane. All she wanted was for the two of them to leave the restaurant and go somewhere where they could make out in peace for a solid few hours.

"Well if that's what I've got to do to get some time with you. Wait... God, okay that sounded so much smoother in my head, but then I said it and it sounded really creepy." Lucas palmed his face with his unoccupied hand trying to hide his embarrassment. When he looked back up at the girl across from him however, there was no sign that she was creeped out by what he'd said. If anything, the smile on her face was the sweetest thing he'd ever seen.

"So, you'd stage my kidnapping if it meant we could spend more time together. Now if anyone else had said that I'd probably be running for the hills. You however, have me intrigued. So how exactly would we go about pulling it off?"

For the next twenty minutes they discussed the finer details of Lucas' hypothetical kidnapping of Alexis, and by the time they'd finished their dinner, they had a somewhat well thought out plan.

Lucas returned to the table from paying just as Alexis was wrapping up a phone call. He sat back down and waited, trying to think of ways he could draw out their date a while longer.

"Yes Jess, I promise, I'm fine. I can't believe they got you involved in this... I'm sure they were, but they knew I had plans tonight so why were they calling me in the first place?... No I know, I'm not mad at you. I promise I'll message you when I get home. Bye." Turning back to face Lucas, Alexis couldn't hide the frustration on her face and she didn't have the energy to try.

"I'm sorry, I thought it might've actually been something important, but the guys just went straight to Jess to find out where I was."

"It's okay. You have friends that obviously care about you, it's nice."

"I'm sure it would be, except their reasons for caring aren't quite as great. Do you wanna walk around... maybe?"

Without even a second thought Lucas held out his hand, and when Alexis' much smaller hand grasped his, he never wanted to let go.

"So, I know that Brennan likes you, that much is

obvious. Sometimes it looks like Seth likes you too, but then there's also rumours that he likes Jess."

"Yeah, Brennan is my friend, but I just don't like him like that. Seth is a little more complicated, but he does like Jess. I think he's just jealous is all." Alexis couldn't shake the feeling that she was saying more than she should, like any moment now the truth was going to come out about her and Seth, and that really wasn't first date talk. Lucas however, wasn't letting up. He didn't think Alexis knew, but they actually had study period together, and he'd noticed her. Lucas had also noticed Seth noticing her. Anytime he saw Alexis with Seth, Seth had a tendency of positioning himself between her and any guy that was nearby, until Brennan showed up, then he backed off.

"You and Seth were a thing."

Alexis gasped like she'd been burnt. She tried to let go of Lucas' hand, but he just gave hers a comforting squeeze. She could still deny it, lie, and tell him anything else, but she didn't want to. It was insane how she was feeling tonight. It was like she could trust him with anything, but at the same time her head was telling her that he wouldn't understand, that there was no way he could ever accept her history. If he couldn't accept her past with Seth, then how would he be able to accept the truth about her family?

Lucas watched the emotions flash across Alexis' face. She was conflicted, that much was obvious, as obvious as it was that she and Seth had hooked up.

Squeezing her hand again to bring her back from her thoughts, Lucas hoped she told him the truth. He'd never felt so comfortable around a girl he was interested in before, and he didn't want lies to get in the way of that.

Finally, after what felt like an eternity, Alexis finally spoke, looking ahead the whole time not being able to bear seeing the disgust that would come across his face when she told him the truth.

"We were a thing, it started after I broke up with Marty. It wasn't intentional. I mean I did like him, but I never thought he'd actually like me back let alone act on it, and then he did and it's just been a whole lot of secrecy since then."

"But it's over?"

Alexis risked a sideways glance up at him. He didn't look mad, more curious.

"Yes, of course. I ended it around New Years. He didn't seem to understand that, but I made it clear when school started. He does have a hard time letting things go."

"That explains the jealousy then."

"I know, but I swear it's over."

"I believe you."

Alexis cracked her neck with how fast she looked up at Lucas. She didn't dwell on how good it felt to finally get the kink out, she just stared up at him trying to find anything in his expression that said he was lying.

"You believe me?"

"Of course, I believe you. Why would you lie?" Lucas had overheard a lot of conversations in the weeks he'd been attending Themis College. Didn't hurt that he had some help in the eavesdropping department either, but that was a story for another time. Lucas looked around for somewhere they could sit down and spotted a bench a few metres away. Once they were sitting down and facing each other, Lucas put her mind at ease as much as possible.

"Alexis, I like you. Now I could've totally misread the signs tonight, but I think it's safe to say you like me too. If you say that whatever you had with Seth is over and done with, then that's all I care about. I've never been this comfortable with someone before, and I want to see where this goes. How about you?"

Instead of verbally responding, Alexis leaned in and captured his lips with hers. Her left hand moved up to the back of his neck while her right gripped his bicep. While he was initially caught off guard, Lucas got himself together pretty quickly, only making Alexis wait a few seconds before he was kissing her back.

CHAPTER 10

Monday morning came far too quickly and yet not quickly enough. Ever since she'd been picked up from their date on Saturday night, Alexis couldn't wait to see Lucas again. He had messaged her when he got home, confessing that he could've kissed her all night. Just thinking about it brought a smile to her face. After she messaged Jess that she was home and alive, Alexis sent a much more detailed message to Em. It was with her memories of the night that Alexis crawled into bed, happier than she'd felt in ages.

This particular morning Alexis didn't even care that they were about to start their day with yet another fifty-minute assembly. While everyone else in their group that morning was tired and grumpy, Alexis couldn't stop smiling. She was still riding the high of her date, and her friends were noticing.

Jess knew that Alexis wouldn't last the whole day without sharing the details of whatever it was that had her practically floating, so she decided to sit back and let her friend come to her.

Brennan however had a sinking suspicion of what it was that had his best friend in such a good mood. He just didn't know who that 'what' was, and that was giving him anxiety.

Seth had gotten a peak at Alexis' phone over her shoulder before he sat down and had seen the name of who she was messaging.

L.

Seth had scoffed to himself as he sat down. She hadn't even put his full name in her phone, just 'L', like he was some Japanese anime character. He wondered to himself if he should tell Brennan about the mystery guy that Alexis was texting, however one look at his face told Seth that he already knew there was a guy.

The bell rang signally the start of the school day, and the group dispersed to their homeroom classrooms before heading to the school assembly. Alexis chatted happily to a very confused Katie who had grown accustomed to the other girl's bad morning mood. As they took their seats in the gym Alexis scanned the crowd until she saw Lucas halfway across the gym. She gave him a small wave and he nodded his head in acknowledgement, a beautiful smile on his face.

Alexis was crushing hard. The realisation of this led her to question whether or not it still counted as crushing on someone when you know they like you back. Or did liking someone mean you had stronger feelings than you did with a crush? All of these were important questions that she would pose to Jess later.

8.50 - *You look beautiful today x*
        Lucas

Looking up to where she'd last seen Lucas, Alexis found him staring back at her, a sly grin on his face.

He knew what his compliments did to her. Ever since Saturday night when she'd gotten all cute and shy when he called her gorgeous, he'd taken every opportunity he could to see that same reaction. When there got to be too many people in the way, Lucas turned back in his seat to face the stage. As he did so he made eye contact with Seth, who was weirdly enough, staring him down. Not one to back down from a challenge, Lucas held the eye contact. Even if Alexis hadn't come clean about her history with Seth, of which she had also sworn him to secrecy, Lucas would've had to be blind to not see that Seth had a thing for her. And maybe even being blind wouldn't have stopped him from figuring it out.

Neither boy was backing down, though Lucas couldn't understand Seth's possessiveness of Alexis. From what she'd told him, Seth had made it clear that they had to remain a secret, and then he'd hooked up with someone else. But when she'd ended things with him, he refused to let go. He might've wondered why Seth didn't just go after someone who wasn't in a relationship already, and who he could have an open relationship without hurting anyone else, but just from their one date, Lucas already knew that Alexis was amazing. The way she kissed him alone was enough to make him willing to go to the mats for her.

Finally, it was time for them to stand for the national anthem, and Seth was forced to look to the front of the gym. Willing or not, Lucas was counting that as a win.

For the rest of the assembly Lucas thought of the next date he wanted to take Alexis on. For the first time since moving from over east, Lucas was grateful for being held back a year. It had something to do with his mid-year baby status. When they'd moved he had had to repeat year six which he hadn't been enthused about. Now though it meant that he was one of the few Year Elevens' to have their licence.

He considered inviting Alexis with himself and his sister this weekend when they went strawberry picking. His sister had said she wanted to officially meet Alexis, but he'd have to see how Alexis felt about meeting his family so soon. By the time they were picking their chairs up at the end of assembly, Lucas had no less than five well planned date ideas and two rough ideas. Hopefully, Alexis liked the sound of at least a few of them.

◆◆◆

Jessica had been right. No more than ten seconds after the two girls took their seats in their second period English class, Alexis leaned close and whispered the words she had been waiting to hear all morning. *"I went on a date with Lucas."*

And even though Jessica had been waiting for this information all weekend, she still wasn't prepared for the excitement she felt. Her boyfriend Aaron had been speculating for months that there was something going on between Alexis and Seth, and the couple had agreed that if it were true then it wouldn't end well. Besides, Alexis deserved someone better than Seth, and while Brennan was a great guy he was also far too sensitive for someone with Alexis' personality.

"Tell me everything."

Not needing any further prompting, Alexis told Jess everything starting from when they quite literally bumped into each other on Friday afternoon. If their teacher was aware that he didn't have the full attention of the two girls, he didn't let on. They kept up with their notes half-heartedly so they at least couldn't be accused of not paying attention at all.

"So, I kind of just... attacked him, but then he kissed me back, and then afterwards we talked more about our families. He has an older sister who's a teacher and a dog name Zeus. Then before he went to bed he texted me again saying 'sweet dreams', and I got a good morning text when he woke up the next day, and oh my god, he's so perfect."

They were currently meant to be discussing the key points they would be making during their speech next week, but Jess wasn't letting Alexis off the hook until she spilled every last bean. And Alexis was not arguing. While Em was excited for her and wanted to hear how the date went, she didn't get the same thrill from their romantic lives as Jessica did.

"Have you two talked today?"

"Not face to face yet, but we texted good morning and he sent me a message before assembly telling me I looked beautiful, and he put an 'x' at the end."

Jess' eyes widened in excitement. It was like watching a romcom. No, it was like being a part of a real life romcom.

"Do the guys know?"

"I haven't told them anything yet. Can you imagine though? What if this turns out to be nothing, they'd get all shitty for no reason."

"How long do you think you can keep you two a secret from them, let alone everyone else? Someone else is bound to see you two together, and gossip spreads like wildfire."

Alexis had to stop herself from revealing to her friend how she and Seth had kept their *thing* a secret for close to a year. "I know I have to tell them. Just, I like Lucas, and what if they scare him off?"

"Well if that does happen then that just means that he isn't right for you, however I don't think it will. I have a good feeling about this one."

"Jess, let me remind you that you also had a good feeling about Marty, and we all know how that turned out."

"Okay, so I was wrong about Martin, but I am right now. Have a little faith."

Suddenly the sound of classroom doors opening and students streaming out into the fresh air alerted their own teacher to the end of the period. "Alright, go refuel and we'll continue planning for your speeches next period."

"Are you going to go spend recess with Lucas." The way Jess sang his name like a moony preteen did nothing to squash her own lovesick smile.

"No, I don't think so, but he did mention us studying after school."

"Yeah... sure... studying... is that what the kids are calling it these days?"

Alexis laughed at her friend, giving her a soft nudge to the side.

"Oh, heads up. Look who's coming in at two o'clock." Instinctively looking up to her right Alexis saw exactly who it was. He didn't slow down as he neared her, just kept chatting to Tom Barnes. She almost thought that maybe he hadn't seen her there.

That was until he looked down at her as he passed, his hand brushing the inside of her arm from her elbow down to the palm of her hand. A shiver ran up Alexis' spine and goose bumps popped up all up and down the right side of her body.

"What was that? Jesus, did you see the look he gave you?"

"The look who gave you?" Seth... Christ for someone so tall and notoriously lacking in grace, he managed to sneak up on them a lot.

"Don't worry, where's Brennan?"

Don't worry, yeah right. He'd seen that little move of Lucas' and how Alexis had reacted. They thought he didn't know what was going on, but it wasn't hard to figure out.

"Mmhmm, sure. He's already sitting down, I just forgot something." And so the trio walked towards their favourite eating spot.

When they arrived Alexis sat down next to Brennan. She knew that if she and Lucas actually became a couple, then she'd have to come clean to Brennan about it all. And when that happened she'd have to make sure he knew that he was still as important to her as always. The thing was, Brennan had never told her that he like liked her. All of their friends had told her that he did, but he hadn't said a word. She felt like this was more than a valid excuse for not acknowledging his alleged feelings for her, he had not yet claimed to have any. Therefore, if she treated him as though he did have feelings that she didn't return then he'd definitely know something was up. Right?

For the next fifteen minutes the group made small talk and ate, hoping that somehow the bell wouldn't ring and they wouldn't have to go back to class. However, ring it did, and when Alexis stood up she noticed that the familiar weight of her phone in her dress pocket was missing. She hadn't taken it out to text Lucas during the break because she worried that one of the guys would question her about it or somehow see the messages, but she was sure she'd put it back in her pocket before they left class. "Shit, where's my phone?"

Scanning the grass where they'd been sitting Alexis couldn't see it anywhere. Jess dutifully joined in on the fruitless search.

"Did you leave it in class?"

"I don't think so, but maybe I did?" Alexis was sure she had it when she sat down.

"Here I'll ring it," Jess offered.

"Don't worry, I found it." Brennan held out her phone, not quite making eye contact with her, but Alexis took it back with a heartfelt thank you.

"Where was- Why am I locked out?" One look at Brennan's face told her that he was the reason. "Did you try to get into my phone?"

"No! Why would you even ask that? I just found it."

Alexis backed off, but the thing was, Brennan couldn't lie to save his life. She wanted so badly to believe him, to know for a fact that he hadn't had a chance to even try, but she'd been talking to Seth and Jess, both who had sat on her other side. During the whole break she'd only really looked at Brennan when they sat down and he'd rebuffed her attempts at conversation, and then again when they got up to leave.

"Fine, sorry," but she wasn't sorry. As she and Jess headed back to their class, Alexis couldn't shake the nagging feeling in the back of her mind. Brennan had tried to get into her phone, but why? Looking at the time left on the lock down she saw that there was just under fourteen minutes left. He must've been trying to get in for most of the break for it to be so long.

Remembering that she'd turned off her notifications before recess, Alexis breathed a sigh of relief. It wasn't that she didn't trust her friends, just that she knew them too well. When she'd accused Brennan of going through her phone she had of course hoped that he hadn't done it, she knew that the chances of him conveniently finding her phone after someone else had gotten it locked for fifteen minutes... after already being locked out for a cumulative six minutes were slim to none.

When the timer finally ran out and Alexis was able to successfully unlock her phone, the first thing she did was check her messages. Two texts from Lucas sat in her inbox.

10:35 - *How about we have lunch together?*

10:36 - *Also I have some ideas for our next date :)*

Before she replied to either message, Alexis went to her photo gallery. Something that Brennan didn't know was that when she'd gotten her new smartphone, Alexis had installed some decent security. This security included an anti-theft feature which took photos with the front facing camera whenever an incorrect password was entered. Now of course this had led to Alexis having to delete some terrible unintentional selfies, but in this instance, she was glad the feature was active. Sure enough, Brennan's face slowly growing more and more frustrated. Alexis wondered for a second if he'd kept trying the same old password he knew or if he'd actually tried something else. Not that it was really important, but it would definitely say something if he hadn't.

It was time to deal with this. Brennan wouldn't tell her the truth to her face, so she had to message him. It was a short message, straight to the point.

10.55 - Brennan, be honest with me, did you try and get into my phone?

She didn't have to wait long for a reply, almost as

soon as it was sent it came up as having been read.

11.00 - *Yeah sorry, I was just messing around.*

Alexis didn't buy that excuse or that he was sorry for a second. If he was just messing around then he would've owned up to it from the beginning, not lied to her.

11.01 - *Okay, so what were you trying to do?*

It was a simple enough question, it didn't call for any kind of hostility, but that was all she was going to get from Brennan today apparently.

11.04 - *Why are you so paranoid all of a sudden? I didn't think you would get mad about it, jeez.*

11.08 - *I'm not paranoid. It's the fact that you tried to go through my phone behind my back. If you'd done it in front of me then I would've just laughed and taken it away from you, but you were doing it behind my back.*

11.15 - *Alright I get it. I wasn't trying to find any-thing, the worst I would've done was send a snap to someone.*

Alexis rolled her eyes to herself before she passed her phone over into Jess' lap, the chat screen still open. Jess let out a confused sound before understanding set in. Scrolling up to where the conversation had obviously started, Jess quickly figured out what was going on.

"Is he high?" Not being able to exclaim the way she wanted to, a whispered shout was the best Jess could do, and Alexis was quick to follow suit.

"Right! Good God, does he think I came down in the last shower of rain? He knows something, he has to."

"I swear I didn't tell him anything."

"Oh hun, I know you were with me the entire time. I trust you. How does he kn-"

"Saturday night," Jess cut her off. "When he and Seth came over to find out where you were, they mentioned how when they called you, some guy answered the phone. While Lucas' stunt was hilarious it definitely tipped them off that you were on a date, and if it didn't, then they really are idiots."

"Ugh, I knew that was going to come back and bite me in the ass, but god it was hot. Especially when he told Seth that I was gorgeous. Honestly, I could've listened to him say that all night. But if they know then why haven't they said anything? It's not like them to stay quiet this long."

"Well they probably suspect, but they don't know for sure, and they know if they ask, then there's a good chance that you'll dodge the question."

Alexis had to admit that Jess' logic was sound. While she had planned on telling the guys about Lucas eventually if they had asked her straight out this morning then there was a good chance she would've changed the subject.

"You really should tell them, they'd be happy for you."

Alexis couldn't help the scoff that came from her mouth. "Yeah sure, happy. That's an emotion that most people would feel, but I doubt that they would." Alexis took her phone back from Jess, sent one last message and copied down what had been written on the white board.

11.18 - *Definitely yes to lunch. Where should I meet you?*

Alexis was almost home free after last period finally let out. Lucas and Em were standing by talking about some English assignment they both had while Alexis put her books in her bag. That was when she realised that she'd left one of her human bio books in the science room. "Shit, guys I'll be right back, I left a book in class."

"Do you want us to come with you?"

"No, no it's fine. I'll be like thirty seconds tops."

Leaving her bag behind Alexis made her way back to her sixth period class. Thankfully, Miss Lesch had forgotten to lock the door and Alexis was able to get in and grab her book from where she'd left it propped up against the leg of the desk.

It should've been straight back to her friends and then to the pickup point. Unfortunately, as Alexis rounded the corner she realised that it might not be quite so straight forward. Huddled together yet blocking the entire walkway was April's siblings. Well the ones still young enough to attend Themis College. Joel was a year above them, Carter a year below and April's only sister, Bella, was the youngest at thirteen. Other than their looks, the siblings also shared the same pissed off look. Instinct told Alexis that there was about to be trouble, or maybe that was just pure common sense.

"Sup guys, long time no see ai?"

"Shut up bitch. April had to have stitches because of you." Bella might've been younger than all of them, but she was also wider and had April's mean streak. She bullied others to stop them from bullying her, it was basic eat or be eaten mentality.

"Well actually, Mr McNeil ruled April's injuries as being her own fault. Sorry that I can't be your scape goat today."

"Yeah well here's the thing. April managed to tell us what really happened. Did you know that because of your lies she's been locked in her room? We're not even allowed to see her. We had to talk to her through her window while our parents were out."

"Right, well thankfully your sister's Rapunzel issue isn't my problem. Your parents were shown the overwhelming proof and agreed that April was in the wrong, so if you don't mind, I'm going to go."

Not believing anything Alexis had to say, the siblings had other plans. Carter rushed her and while she tried to dodge it, the fucker was fast. He looped an arm around her waist, dragging her back towards his brother and sister, his other hand was wrapped firmly over her mouth. Not one to go without a fight Alexis struggled against him, but it didn't seem as though her heels making contact with his shins was doing much.

Pushing her against the brick wall, Carter stepped back so that the three of them surrounded Alexis. She had no way of getting past them. It was in that moment that she truly felt fear for the first time in her life. She couldn't joke her way out of this. The Hale siblings were out for blood, she could see it in their eyes. They were like a pack of hyenas and she had a choice, let them beat her to a bloody pulp and then hopefully leave, or fight back and possibly just make them even angrier.

When Bella threw the first punch, Alexis' body made the decision for her. Years of blocking surprise attacks from her cousins had given her some preparation for this moment. Ducking out of the way of

Bella's straight punch, Alexis retaliated by swinging her elbow into Joel's face. When he stumbled back Alexis saw her chance and danced past him, just as she was out of their circle someone grabbed her hair and pulled her back. Reaching up to grab the hand that held her ponytail, she twisted back to face the brat who learned too much from her sister, breaking the hold.

"Bella you always did fight dirty." Not wanting to break the nose of a thirteen-year-old girl, Alexis pushed Bella backwards while also kicking one of her feet out from under her.

The bigger they are the harder they fall.

Carter caught Alexis by surprise and she didn't have time to block his swing before his fist made contact with her face. Everything after that was a blur. Alexis was aware of what was happening, but she couldn't feel it. Her body snapped back upright and charged at Carter. Before she could get within swinging distance though, Joel came up behind her, wrapping both his arms around her waist and lifting her up off the ground. Bella was back on her feet and the brother and sister stood in front of her flailing body held tight by their big brother. As soon as they were close enough Alexis kicked her feet out. She managed to catch Bella in the groin and Carter in the stomach. Not having time to wish it had been the other way around, she flung her head back into Joel's nose. She heard the crack and he involuntarily let her go. Looking up, Alexis saw Lucas and Em at the other end of the breezeway and started towards them.

The last thing she remembered before blacking out was Lucas shouting her name and something solid shoving her to the side.

◆◆◆

Later, when she was told about what they saw, Lucas and Em explained she was only out for a minute, but by the time she regained consciousness it felt like it had been longer.

Miss Lesch realising that she had forgotten to lock the classroom door came back on her way to her car. That was when she'd heard the sounds of fighting and rounded the corner just in time to see Carter shove Alexis into the wall. She'd yelled at the siblings to stay where they were, but they gathered themselves up and stumbled off. Lucas was ready to chase after them, but when he heard Em calling Alexis' name, he stopped short and knelt beside her limp body.

Miss Lesch was already on the phone calling an ambulance. By the time she hung up Alexis was opening her eyes and the three breathed a collective sigh of relief. Lucas gently propped Alexis up in his arms, needing to see her and hold her at the same time.

"Lex, you okay?"

"That depends. Am I dead?"

Emilia let out a snort. "Not quite Rocky."

"Well that explains why I hurt like a bitch."

"The ambulance is on its way, and Mr McNeil is coming to help get you to the office." Miss Lesch surveyed the area, making note of the blood leaking from Alexis' temple and cursing that she didn't have anything clean to press against the wound.

"Don't worry about it, we'll meet him there." Lucas scooped Alexis up into his arms and stood. Not waiting, he set off for the front office. Alexis pressed herself against Lucas's chest and marvelled at how strong he was. She was vaguely aware of Mr McNeil appearing next to them, and someone mentioned a wheelchair. It was at that moment that Lucas' hold on her tightened. Like he never planned on letting her go. Looking up at his face the best she could, Alexis saw a tightness in his jaw.

"Luke?" When he looked down at her she saw how hard his eyes were, she expected them to soften, but if anything, the anger on his face only became less hidden. "Luke, what's wrong?" He didn't reply, but a muscle in his jaw twitched. Alexis suddenly wished that he'd just put her in the wheelchair.

She didn't need to worry for much longer though. Before she knew it they were being rushed through the administration and back to the sick bay where Lucas gently set her down on one of the beds. Em followed them into the room, sitting on the end of the bed, clutching what looked like Alexis' textbook.

She'd forgotten that she'd dropped it during the scuffle. The front cover looked ripped. Alexis looked around the room for Lucas and saw him leaning against a cupboard on the other side of the room. He was staring right back at her. Their eyes met only for a moment before he stormed out of the room. Alexis tried to call after him, but a pounding had started in her head, and all she wanted to do was close her eyes and go to sleep.

"Lex, bub, come on you've gotta stay awake. The paramedics just pulled up okay. They'll be right here. Please just stay awake for a little while longer." Em squeezed her friend's hand, holding a towel to the bleeding gash in her temple with the other. If only they'd just gone with Alexis to get the book, then the last ten minutes would never have happened. Those bullies never would've attacked Alexis while she was with other people. Emilia had seen the siblings as they stumbled away, and they looked in rough shape. Even outnumbered Alexis had dished out a can of whoop-ass. If only she hadn't been handed her own plate of it at the same time.

It wasn't much longer until the paramedics got to the office and loaded Alexis onto their gurney. Em followed them out of the of sick bay and saw that hers and Alexis' bags were sitting next to the reception desk. Looking over at the young receptionist sitting there, Em got the answer to her question before she even had a chance to ask.

"That young man that carried your friend in here, he brought your bags a few minutes ago and then left again."

"Lucas? He came back?" Alexis' voice was weaker than usual, the sound of it had Em holding back tears. She'd never seen her friend in such bad shape. "Yeah hun, he did. He just dropped off our bags."

"Em? Call him, please. Make sure he's okay, he looked really mad before. Tell him I'm sorry."

"I'm coming with you in the ambulance. I'll call him later when I know that you're okay."

There was a soft sound of acknowledgment from Alexis as the paramedics maneuvered the gurney through the doors. Em scooped up their bags and followed them to the ambulance, ignoring the gawking teenagers and whispers. She didn't realise that Miss Lesch and Mr McNeil were following behind until she heard them telling the students to disperse and let the paramedics through. Mr McNeil ended up taking the lead while Miss Lesch came up next to Em. She gently took Alexis' backpack from Em's hand, wanting to lighten the girls load, but knowing that emotionally and mentally, she was carrying more than anyone knew.

Adriane Leschenelle knew more about the goings on in her student's lives than they thought she did. What had occurred the previous week in her human bio class, Adriane had never thought it would come to that. She knew that Alexis had tipped April's chair and she knew why. April was a bully and Alexis was a protector by nature. Emilia, she was a carer. Fierce in her own way, but when it came to looking after herself, she needed someone like Alexis. And Lucas, he cared about Alexis, that much was clear to anyone with eyes. When he left though, Alexis had thought that it was her fault, as though somehow, she'd angered him by being assaulted. Now while there was no question that her assault had made him angry, what the concussed girl couldn't see was that he was angry at himself for not protecting her.

The paramedics loaded Alexis in the back of the ambulance, Emilia insisting that she ride to the hospital with her best friend. Mr McNeil gave assurances that he would be along to the hospital to check on her condition once he'd made contact with all the relevant parents. This prompted Alexis to comment sleepily about how mad her dad was going to be.

The ride to the hospital was short, not as short as it should've been thanks to the after-school traffic but still only ten minutes. Once Emilia got off the phone with Mrs Angelo, the paramedic that rode in the back of the ambulance with the two girls finally asked the question she'd been dying to since the office. "So, this Lucas guy, did he do this to your friend?"

Emilia let out a humourless chuckle. "God no, he

and Alexis just started dating. What she said in the office about being sorry and him being angry, she just thinks that he's mad at her but he's not."

"Well it wouldn't make sense for him to be mad at her, it's not like she asked to be beaten up. Do you know who did do this?"

"Yeah, it's okay though. They won't get away with this." The paramedic gave a satisfied nod.

15.45 - *Lucas, we're almost at the hospital. I'll keep you updated, but you know you're welcome to come see her for yourself.*

Em didn't have to wait long for reply, but just as her phone went off, the ambulance pulled into the hospital. The gurney was unloaded and Emilia was directed towards the waiting room. There she found some seats in the back corner, away from everyone else and sat Alexis' and her own bag on the seats next to her.

15.47 - *Thank you. I don't think that's a good idea right now. Tell her I'm sorry.*

Hours later Emilia still sat in the emergency room waiting area. Tony and Carmen Angelo had shown up five minutes after their daughter had arrived and spent the time since then making phone calls, pacing, and going in and out to see their daughter. In between tests, the worried parents stayed by her side, smiling and holding her, but out in the waiting room Emilia saw their rage. Mr McNeil had come to hospital about an hour after they'd left the school. He assured the parents that there would be serious consequences for the Hale siblings involved in the attack, and that Alexis was excused for as long as she needed to recover from the ordeal, any outstanding tests or assignments could wait.

As helpful as he was trying to be all Mr McNeil did was fuel Tony Angelo's anger. Carmen had to intervene and persuade Tony to take a walk and cool off.

"I'm sorry about my husband. He knows that it's not your fault. He's just angry and can't take it out on the people who deserve it."

"It's fine Carmen, totally understandable. Perhaps it would be best for me to leave. Please let us know how Alexis is doing tomorrow. Our thoughts and prayers are with her and your family."

"We will, thank you so much."

Once he was gone, Carmen had sat down next to Emilia putting her arm around the girl's shoulders. "So what happened today, Em?"

"I don't know. Everything was fine during the day, and then Lex realised she left her human bio book in the classroom so she went back to get it. We asked if she wanted us to go with her, but she said no, and we should've just gone because it must've been when she was coming back that they caught her. It was three against one, but somehow she still had them limping away."

"She's got her mother's fire that's why," Tony said, sitting down on the other side of his wife.

It was a quarter to eleven when the Angelo's pulled into their driveway. Alexis had been released and her parents given instructions to wake her up every few hours to ensure she didn't slip into a coma from her concussion. She was also warned that she'd have a killer headache.

"I'm taking tomorrow off of work, so I'll be here to interrupt your sleep every now and again."

Alexis sighed as she dumped her take out wrappers in the kitchen bin. She'd known that what she was about to tell her parents wasn't going to go over well.

"I'm going to school tomorrow."

Tony and Carmen looked at each other, their faces full of confusion. Their teenage daughter was giving up a legitimate reason to stay home from school.

"Angel, I think that bump to the head really did a number on you. You're talking crazy talk," Tony laughed weakly, wondering if maybe they should take her back to the hospital.

"Dad, I'm serious. I'm going to school tomorrow."

"Do you have a test or something? You know what Mr McNeil said, all your assignments and tests can wait."

Mr McNeil had also assured her parents that there would be severe consequences befalling the Hale siblings involved in the attack, and that all school-work was taking a back seat to her recovery. That was all well and good, but she wasn't about to sit back and let people think that she'd gotten worked over by some hypocritical cowards. She had been, but no one else got to know that. Plus, she needed to talk to Lucas. He hadn't been replying to any of her messages and he'd looked so mad this afternoon. Alexis hated to think that she'd ruined her chances with him when things were just starting to get good between them.

"Alexis, the doctor said that you need rest. You don't have anything to prove to anyone," her mum said, always seeming to know her reasoning before she did. It must've been some kind of mum super-power. Alexis hoped that she would have that super-power one day.

"Yes, I do. Look, I know that I could take the rest of the week off and no one would bat an eye at it. Everyone would understand. They'd feel bad for me, and offer to help me catch up, and tell me how messed up what those assholes did was. It was cowardly, but they weren't totally unjustified. I am the one that messed up their sister's *pretty face* and then got away with it. If I had siblings, then I'd hope that they'd be as protective of me as the Hales are of each other. I'd also hope that my siblings were smarter and a lot more subtle in their revenge, after all we're Angelo's. But that's just the thing, I am an Angelo. I am not giving anyone the satisfaction of thinking that those self-righteous pricks got the best of me. Now, my head hurts so I am going to bed, but I am going to school in the morning, and I will call you if I need picking up."

Carmen got up from the bar stool she'd occupied when they got to the kitchen and hugged her daughter. "I'm proud of you, baby." With a soft kiss to the top of her head, Carmen let go and moved aside so Tony could get his goodnight hug.

"You're a stubborn little shit, you know that?"

"Yeah daddy, I know, and you love me because of it."

"Mm, I might have to rethink that with all the grey hairs you're giving me."

Alexis snorted a laugh and left the kitchen, snagging a water bottle from the fridge on her way out. She made it halfway up the stairs to her room when she turned back around. In the time it took her to come back, her mum had a glass of wine and her dad had poured himself a bourbon. Leaning around the door frame Alexis voiced her final request for the evening.

"When I'm feeling better, I need you to teach me how to fight properly."

CHAPTER 11

The next morning Alexis was regretting her decision to go to school. Her head was throbbing and she was exhausted from being woken up by one of her parents every two hours. All morning they hovered around her waiting for her to give in and admit that she should stay home from school.

Thing was though, she hadn't become known as *testa dura* for nothing. She remembered the first time her dad had muttered it under his breath when she refused to back down about something. When she asked her mum what it meant, Alexis had been so confused as to why her dad was calling her hard-headed. She was six.

That was just it though, she was stubborn and she'd made her choice. Alexis didn't care if she had to put on a happy face all day and pretend that her brain wasn't trying to carve its way out of her skull with a blunt spork.

As soon as she showed up to school, she already had the upper hand against the Hales. Joel, Carter and Bella were going to be expecting her to be hiding from them, just like they should be hiding from any-one who had any loyalty to Alexis or her Family.

There was also the fact that Lucas had yet to text her back after yesterday afternoon. Emilia had told her last night that he'd said he was sorry, but he hadn't actually elaborated on what he was sorry about. Given his lack of response, she could only assume that he was ending their flirtation. That was the part that hurt her the most.

By the time Alexis had dumped her bag on the rack outside her homeroom class, she had resolved that she was going to apologise to Lucas for the drama that he'd been pulled into. Then she was going to let him go.

However, there was a pretty big part of her that didn't want to just let him go. No, she wanted to apologise and then hold onto him. The choice was his though, she couldn't make him stay. They weren't even officially dating.

Alexis tried to find Lucas at his homeroom class, but he was nowhere to be found. She ignored the bell, waiting until there were no more students milling around outside the classrooms. He hadn't come to school today. That must've been it. He was so determined to avoid her that he hadn't even come to school.

Heading back to her own homeroom Alexis tried to get a grip on herself. She barely knew the guy. Up until four days ago he hadn't even been a blip on her radar, and here she was getting all hung up on him. Sure, they got along like a house on fire, but that didn't mean they were destined to be together. She and Seth got along like a house on fire in the beginning as well and look how that turned out.

Two periods.

Two periods were how long Alexis had to bitch to Emilia nonstop about Lucas avoiding her and her own unrelenting desire to convince him that yesterday's drama was just a freak occurrence.

"Dude, it's not though. You're Alexis-freaking-Angelo. Your life comes with a drama included guarantee. I'm sorry to be blunt, but you can't escape it without escaping who you are. That made more sense in my head, but you catch my drift? Oh, and by the way, Lucas is here today. So guess what you two can do with your double study period this afternoon? Sort it the fuck out. And tell him to stop texting me. If he wants to know that you're okay he can text you himself." With a huff Emilia walked away from Alexis and got swallowed up in the mass of students swarming out of their classes for recess.

Emilia had been right to snap, Alexis knew that. And Lucas texting Em? About her? Why would he bother? Did he want to know she was okay so that he could end things officially without having to feel guilty? Or was he really genuinely concerned?

With all kinds of questions swarming through her head, Alexis autopiloted to the their break spot. She barely noticed when Brennan and Seth sat down across from her, she just stared into her yogurt. She didn't realise that she'd finished it until Brennan nudged her knee with his foot. When she looked up at him, his face was full of concern. Before he could actually say anything, the bell rang and she was on her feet and off for her third period class like a shot.

Alexis didn't realise where she was going. Not until she saw it. If anyone had asked she couldn't have told them how she'd even come to notice the spot on the wall. She just saw it and stopped in her tracks. There on the tan coloured brick was a smattering of blood.

Her blood.

Absentmindedly she brought her hand up to touch her temple. Her mum had helped her with her hair this morning, styling it so that it covered up the butterfly bandages keeping her skin together.

"Lex! Come on, class is gonna start."

The voice only just broke through the static in Alexis' head, but not enough to make her stop staring at the dried blood.

Emilia realised that Alexis wasn't just standing in the middle of the walkway to be annoying, she was actually staring at something. Moving to stand next to her best friend, Emilia looked straight ahead, trying to see exactly what it was the Alexis was seeing.

And she did.

"Alexis, don't look at it. You're okay, everything is okay."

When she didn't get an indication that her friend had heard her, Emilia stood in front of her. One moment Alexis stared through her and then she wasn't. Once her eyes seemed to refocus, Emilia moved them towards the nearest girls' bathroom. Once she'd made sure that all the stalls were clear, she locked the main door, guaranteeing them some privacy. Alexis was sitting on the floor, back to the wall. Her eyes were wide and frantic.

"Lex, hun, come on just breathe."

Alexis' breathing was shallow and fast, she was in the midst of a panic attack. Emilia had seen them before. Hell, she'd been through them plenty of times before. She'd just never seen her best friend in this kind of state. Apparently, this week was going to be full of firsts for the pair.

"Lex, breathe with me, come on. In... and out... in... and out." Emilia continued her prompts until Alexis was able to breathe properly on her own.

"Em, what just happened? What was that? I couldn't breathe, and everything was going fuzzy and static-y an-"

Emilia cut her off. "Hun, that was a panic attack." There was a softness to Emilia's voice that wasn't usually there. "Do you remember what happened?"

Alexis closed her eyes and took a deep breath before answering. "I dunno. I was just walking and everything was fine. And then there was this movement to my left, and I looked, and whatever it was, was gone. Then I saw the wall and..."

"Your blood."

Alexis could only nod in response. Maybe her parents had been right about it being too soon for her to come back to school.

But you were right about needing to be here. For yourself.

Her inner voice had a point. Taking a few more deep breathes, Alexis mentally braced herself for the rest of the day. She knew what was coming. All of the teachers would know by now what had happened yesterday. They'd be on the lookout for any trouble, the Hales, her.

As far as she knew, none of the student body, outside of who was there yesterday, knew what happened. It was only a matter of time though. Someone would talk. For all she knew, Lucas could've told all his friends that she'd gotten her ass handed to her by the Hale siblings, and that was why he didn't want to be with her anymore. Too much drama.

That thought alone gave Alexis enough fuel to get

up from her spot on the cold ground.

Gathering up her books and Emilia's, Alexis headed for the door. "We'd better get to class, no need for more trouble."

Without another word Alexis unlocked the door and headed for their human biology class. Emilia had no choice but to catch up to her and take her books back for the rest of the short walk. For the rest of their double period Emilia kept a watchful eye on her best friend. Which wasn't easy considering it involved her constantly turning around to look at her.

There were only so many times a girl could pretend to stretch before people around her thought there was a problem with her.

When class let out for lunch, the two girls took the long way back to Alexis' bag, no need to risk a repeat of earlier events.

"Hey, do you wanna come sit with me and the others for lunch?" Em asked.

"Nah it's okay, you've had to deal with me a lot today. I'm gonna go sit with the guys, haven't really seen them much lately. Thanks though."

Emilia reluctantly let Alexis go off on her own. Ever since her uncle's arrest, and the subsequent friendships lost as a result of everyone finding out Alexis was related to a convicted murderer, she hated anyone seeing her weak. She knew that her weaknesses could be used against her. Emilia hated that her best friend closed herself off, but she couldn't fault her for it, after all, Emilia did the same thing.

◆◆◆

As Alexis approached the guys with her lunch, she was looking forward to some peace and not being watched like a hawk. However, as she sat down, she knew that there would be no peace this lunch period.

The boys had been sitting close, their heads bent together in deep conversation. When Alexis sat down though they had both turned to face her and their faces said it all. They were a mix between concerned and pissed. They knew. How she played the next few minutes would determine their reactions and how bad the fallout would be.

"So, how has the day been going so far?" Apparently, this was the wrong thing to ask as it set off a barrage of questions.

"Why didn't you tell us?"

"Who did it?"

"Was anyone there with you?"

"How could you not tell us?"

"Are you okay?"

Honestly, Alexis was more surprised that they could ask so many questions in three seconds than the fact that they had more concerns about not being told than if she was okay. But she wasn't going to read into that... right now.

"Oh my god, stop! Okay?"

Once the boys had finally finished talking over each other, Alexis gave them the abridged version of what had happened the previous afternoon. "I forgot a book in my human bio class, so I went to get it. On the way back, April's brothers and sister were waiting for me, punches were thrown, groins got kicked, heads got smashed. I went to the hospital, got checked out, all good, now here we are."

Brennan was gripping her hands so tightly she could feel them losing circulation.

Seth was studying her face as though if he looked hard enough he might see what it was that she was hiding.

"So, who found you?"

"Miss Lesch and Emilia."

"How'd you get to the hospital?"

"In an ambulance."

"And how'd you get to the ambulance?"

"On one of those rolling stretcher things." Seth wasn't asking the right questions, and he seemed to have figured that out. Alexis sat there suppressing the smugness she was feeling from showing on her face. While Seth had given up on his awful interrogation tactic, Brennan was just getting started.

"I heard that you got carried to the office."

Apparently, he had a lot more information than Seth had to work with.

"Maybe."

"So who carried you? Miss Lesch and Emilia aren't

that strong."

"Are you calling me fat?"

"No, I'm saying that they wouldn't have risked dropping you, so someone else must've been there to carry you to the office."

From the look that Seth gave Brennan, this was the first that he was hearing of it.

"How do you even know that I was attacked?"

"I overheard some teachers talking about it. Don't avoid the question."

"Well since you know so much about it why don't you tell the story."

"Alexis." He was losing his temper now. Brennan had always had a bit of a short fuse, especially when it came to the people that he cared about. It wasn't fair that she hadn't told them about being attacked, but it wasn't exactly something that she wanted to keep rehashing.

"What, Brennan? Huh? What is it that you want to know?"

"Who was it that carried you to the office?"

"Why do you care so much?"

"Why don't you want to tell us?"

So many reasons.

"Fine, it was Lucas, are you happy now?"

A look of understanding passed over Seth's face. It was like he'd just found the missing piece of a puzzle that he'd been working on for weeks.

"Why didn't you just tell us?"

Before Alexis had a chance to answer Brennan, Seth interjected. "It was Lucas that you were out with on Saturday night wasn't it?"

Alexis didn't take her eyes off the two boys in front of her. She knew that avoiding it would only make things worse but she kept doing it. Why? Because for some odd reason, she'd thought that maybe she would be able to have some of her private life stay private from these guys. But no, they wanted to be involved with absolutely everything.

"Lex?"

When Alexis looked at Brennan, she saw the hope in his eyes that what Seth said was wrong. All it took was a few more seconds of silence from her to confirm Seth's theory.

Brennan's eyes hardened and when he spoke, his voice had a sharper quality to it. "Why didn't you just tell us? Weren't you the one who was all for telling the truth? We're meant to be best friends remember?"

His words cut deep. He was right. Weeks ago, when she'd found out that Brennan had lied about why he couldn't hang out with her, she'd told him that he should've just been honest with her. Wasn't that the point of friendships, being able to be honest with each other?

But what if they force you to lie? What if you know that they're going to blow things out of proportion and act irrationally?

A sudden thought occurred to Alexis in that moment, and her own eyes narrowed at the pair.

"I didn't actually lie to either of you. I told you that I had plans on Saturday. You were all pissy because I didn't tell you who they were with, and then you proceeded to blow up my phone all night trying to get my attention, and then you went to Jessica and tried to get her to tell you where I was. What you did Brennan, that was actually lying." Pausing for a breath she held her glare at the two boys.

When Seth opened his mouth to say something undoubtedly stupid, Alexis cut him off, "You wanna know why I didn't tell you who my plans were with? Because I didn't know if it was worth telling, I didn't know if Lucas and I were actually going to become a thing. And hey guess what, if it hadn't been for you overhearing a conversation Bren, no one would have ever had to know." A stinging started behind Alexis' eyes, and she ducked her head as she shot up from her spot on the grass.

Alexis' escape couldn't quite be described as 'running away', but it was close. She was certainly out of the boy's sight fast enough. Alexis didn't pay much attention to where she was going, she just wanted to get away. Somewhere where no one would see her crying.

God, I'm so weak today.

One of the unfortunate yet foreseeable side effects of not paying attention to where one is going is that eventually, you will run into something. Or in Alexis' case, someone. This time however, the other party was paying more attention than he had been the first time they ran into each other.

Before Alexis could save herself from falling on her ass again, Lucas wrapped his hands around her upper arms, steadying her. He caught a glimpse of her startled, tear stained face before she was looking down at the brick walkway again.

"We've got to stop running into each other like this, one of us is going to get hurt."

When he didn't even get a tearful chuckle Lucas knew that something was seriously wrong. He let his hands drop from her arms, only to grasp her hand in his and pull her towards a section of limestone that was relatively hidden by bushes, without actually stepping into the garden itself.

"Lex, what's wrong? Did those assholes come back?"

Alexis still refused to show her face, she just sniffled and wiped furiously at her cheeks as she tried to control her breathing.

"Alexis, please. I'm sorry that I wasn't there yesterday. I should've been there to protect you and I wasn't, and I'm so sorry. But please tell me what's wrong."

It took a few seconds for his words to register in her mind, but when they did, Alexis' head snapped up and she looked Lucas dead in the eye. Her disbelief was clear in hers.

"You're sorry?"

Lucas wasn't sure what to make of her question. Was she being sarcastic? Did she not expect him to be sorry for not being there when she needed him most, and it was only third day into their relationship?

"Of course, I'm sorry. I figured you must be pissed at me. Thought that if I gave you some space then you'd forgive me when I came over to apologise after school. I wasn't expecting you to actually be here today."

She couldn't believe what she was hearing. For the last fourteen hours she had been stressing out that he was mad at her for involving him in her drama, and here he was freaking out that she was mad at him. It probably didn't ease his concerns at all when she started laughing. It was soft laughter at first, but the more she thought about the absurdity of the situation, the stronger the laughter got.

"Okay, you're going to have to fill me in on the joke here."

Calming herself down, Alexis held one of his hands in both of hers. Mostly because his hands were huge and made hers look baby-sized.

"Lucas, I am not mad at you about yesterday. If anything, I thought you were mad at me. God how could you ever blame yourself for what happened?"

"Why in the world would I be mad at you?" Everything from his tone to the look on his face implied that she was crazy for even thinking such a thing.

"I thought that you were mad because you'd been pulled into the Alexis Angelo drama."

"The Alexis Angelo drama?"

"Yeah. Look, I don't know what you've heard about me around school yet, but I'm not exactly a fan favourite. And sometimes there's just... drama. Look, it's kind of just part and parcel of being an Angelo, you'll have to trust me on this."

Lucas squeezed her hands comfortingly with his. Looking down at the beautiful girl in front of him he thought about the stuff he'd heard. Criminal. Murderers. Mob.

Lucas wasn't sure if what he said next was going to be the right thing to say, but he certainly hoped that she didn't break his nose like she did Joel's. Leaning in close so no one else could overhear, "Well, if what they say is true then you are the prettiest mobster I've ever seen."

If anyone else had said that, Alexis might've been mad. There was something about the way that Lucas' mouth quirked up at the one corner. An almost smirk. She couldn't resist it. She could roll her eyes at his cheesiness all she wanted, but her smile gave away her true feelings.

"Seriously though Lex, I'm not going to believe anything about you unless it comes from you... and probably Em because if anyone could help me get myself out of trouble with you in the future it's her."

Alexis couldn't help herself. Slipping one of her hands free she reached up and cupped his face, at the same time closing the distance between their faces and their mouths. It was a soft kiss, tender and heart-felt. Different to their frenzied, hormone fuelled kisses of Saturday night, but with no less feeling behind it. Alexis broke the kiss when she realised that she'd more or less attacked him again. Jess would not approve.

"So just to clarify, neither of us are mad about yesterday. At each other I mean," his last-minute clarification stopped Alexis from being able to make a smartass remark, so instead she just nodded as she chewed nervously on her bottom lip. "Okay good because I was enjoying that kiss." And to prove just that, Lucas closed the distance between them once again.

From the moment Alexis got to her feet and left them, Brennan had been feeling shitty. He had wanted to talk to Alexis about the fight yesterday, to make sure that she was actually okay but Seth's question about Lucas had thrown him for a loop. He knew that he had let his jealousy cloud his judge-ment, and it had been a terrible thing for him to do. Especially to his best friend. Brennan left Seth to his own sulking. He needed to find Alexis and apologise before she decided that she didn't want to be his friend anymore. He started thinking about all the places that Alexis might go to when she was this angry. His first thought was that she would go to be with Jess, if not there then maybe Em. Once he stepped off the stretch of grass and rounded the corner, Brennan saw her. She was with *him.*

Brennan tried to wrap his head around everything. What he was seeing versus what Alexis had said. She'd implied that her and Lucas weren't a thing anymore, yet here she was running straight into his arms. Literally.

He stood there and watched as Lucas took her hand, leading her towards the limestone wall. He watched as their faces got closer, as she laughed at whatever he said. He watched as she kissed him and then pulled back. He watched as he kissed her back, and this time no one pulled away, not until the siren rang to signal that lunch was over. Even then they didn't separate straight away. He watched as, when they did manage to detach their faces from each other, he pulled her into his side with an arm around her waist.

Brennan didn't notice the other people around him, all at varying speeds as they made their way towards their next class. Even after Alexis and Lucas had left his sight, he couldn't stop seeing them on that limestone wall, kissing. It wasn't until a heavy hand slapped his back that Brennan stopped staring at that single spot in the distance.

"Dude, what are you doing just standing there? You're going to be late." Seth kept walking as he spoke but quickly realised that his best friend wasn't following him. "Dude, what the hell's wrong with you?"

There was a moment when Brennan had to decide if he should keep what he saw to himself and respect Alexis' privacy or if he should just tell Seth what he saw. He could wait and ask if what he'd seen had been what he thought it was, or he could just assume that what he thought, was what he saw.

"Bren?"

He couldn't stop seeing the girl he loved kissing someone else. Someone she barely knew.

"She lied. Alexis lied."

And just like that, he made his choice.

CHAPTER 12

Tony hung up the phone, his expression grim and his heart heavy. Carmen sat on the edge of his desk, one hand mindlessly massaging the back of her husband's head. She always did that when she felt that he needed comfort. Now was one of those times.

"He's really dead?" Carmen couldn't believe it. Ricky was the third death they'd had this month alone. Even for their line of work the death toll was getting too high. Tony didn't answer straight away and Carmen wondered if maybe he hadn't heard her. When she moved her hand away from the back of his neck he reached up with lightning fast reflexes and caught her hand in his.

"There's more sweetheart." With a heavy sigh Tony got up from behind his desk, not letting go of his wife's hand he led her over to the wall to the left.

There on the wall was a large cork board, on it was a giant map of Australia. It was on this map that Tony kept track of all the major Family related activities. Plucking a red pin from the bottom right corner of the board Tony found the tiny town to the south were Ricky had lived and successfully executed his role in the Family.

Carmen looked over the map, drinking in all of the information that was revealed with something as simple as the placement of different coloured pins. Starting from the pin Tony had just pushed through the map, there were red pins spread out evenly along the coastline, trailing all the way down to Albany and then along the bottom coast of the state before passing over the border. Realisation washed over Carmen as though she'd just stood under a freezing cold waterfall. She didn't even realise that she'd let out a gasp, but when she did, Tony knew that she'd seen it.

"They're coming here. They're coming for us."

CHAPTER 13

After Alexis' attack, Lucas couldn't help but feel overly protective of her. Once they got over their misunderstanding he walked her to and from every class he could which sometimes meant running from one side of the school to the other. He was constantly watching the crowds of students moving around them, watching for any sign that one of them wanted to cause the girl tucked against his side, harm. He never saw a threat, but it didn't stop him from doing it day after day. He just couldn't stop seeing her lying on the bricks out cold, her blood on the wall.

By the end of the second day, he could tell that she was just humouring him. Emilia on the other hand wasn't quite so accommodating. Alexis was late coming out of a class due to the teacher wanting to discuss something with her when Emilia sidled up next to him.

"Look Luc, I get it you've got a thing for Lex, but constantly being around is starting to look a little stalkerish." Out of all the things he'd thought she would say, that hadn't been one of them. He was so shocked that he didn't know how to respond at all.

"I'm kidding, sort of," she added with a small smirk playing on her lips. "I do get it. Seeing her like that, you can't unsee it. You know the next day I was so angry that she'd come to school all to prove a point to people who didn't matter that I snapped at her. She thought you were mad at her, and she was all ready to let you go so you wouldn't have to deal with her 'drama', and I couldn't help thinking that she should've been more concerned with herself. It didn't help that you hadn't stopped texting me asking how she was."

Lucas remembered that day well. He hadn't slept at all the night before, and when Emilia had finally texted him back telling him that Alexis was having lunch at the front of the school, he'd left his friends with barely a 'seeya later'. When Alexis had run into him and he'd noticed the tears in her eyes, it tugged at his heart.

"If you hadn't sent that text when you did, I might not have caught her in time, and things might've ended up differently."

Emilia had considered this as well, but after seeing the two of them together, she had come to only one conclusion.

"I don't think so. The two of you just work too well together. It might've taken you a little longer to get together, but you would've ended up together no matter what."

"I didn't take you as someone who believed in fate," Lucas smiled down at her.

"Well if you're going to be in Alexis' life then it's about time we got to know each other properly," Emilia pointed out. That's when it dawned on him, he hadn't asked Alexis to be his girlfriend yet, not officially anyway.

"Shit," he muttered under his breath, but not low enough for Emilia to not hear.

"Finally clicked did it?"

All he could do was stare at her in disbelief.

"It's only the most discussed topic behind closed doors for the past week," was all she gave as an explanation before Alexis exited the classroom.

Lucas smiled at her as he took her tiny hand in his and as the three of them headed to his car, he couldn't help but wonder at how Emilia had *known*.

CHAPTER 14

"Okay now that we've covered the basics, let's work on bursting." Carmen and Alexis had been in the training room for almost two hours now. Carmen had started them off with some basic Krav Maga, knowing her daughter didn't have the patience and discipline for Karate.

"Throw a punch and I'm going to show you how to block and burst in and attack at the same time. What this does is it closes the distance between you and your opponent limiting the ways in which they can keep attacking you. It always gives you simultaneous blocking and attacking opportunity. Now go."

Alexis swung out at her mother, not worrying anymore that she'd actually make contact. Before she knew what had happened, her right arm was locked up in her mum's left, and her mum's knee was pressing against her thigh. Releasing her daughter, Carmen took a step back and allowed her to get her bearings back. When Alexis nodded at her, she went again, but slower this time, explaining what she was doing as she did it.

"Block the attack. As you're doing that, you reach out with your other hand and grasp their shoulder, wrap your arm around theirs and hold your hand against your chest, step into their personal space and bring your knee up as you pull them towards you. For a guy this would be a lot more painful but it's still going to hurt if you're attacked by a woman. Next time I'll show you how to move your opponent from this position to one where you dislocate their shoulder and make them regret ever coming at you. Now I'm going to do the move one more time, and then it's your turn."

Another half an hour later and the two women were calling it quits for the day. Alexis was sweaty and exhausted but exhilarated at the same time. Her mum had barely broken a sweat through the whole session. Alexis felt a new sense of power that she'd never felt before. The lesson had just been basic, but she was more excited about their next training session then she ever had been about self-defence training before. She knew that tomorrow her body would hate her for using all the muscles she didn't even know existed, but it was worth it to feel like she could protect herself properly. Before she made her way upstairs for a much-needed shower, Alexis turned back to her mum and wrapped her in a hug.

"Thank you. Seriously, I love you so much."

She squeezed her arms tighter around her mum in an effort to convey just how much it all meant to her.

Words would never be enough.

"So how did the first lesson go?" Tony asked as he dished out dinner. While he was not averse to making dinner, or even helping his wife while she made dinner it felt somewhat comical that the main women in his life were being violent while he was being a domestic god.

"Really good. Mum taught me how to lock someone's arm in mine so they can't take it back, and tomorrow she's going to show me how to move from invading someone space to putting them in a head-lock."

Alexis' excitement over something as simple as a headlock brought a smile to Tony's face. The events of Monday afternoon had scared him beyond belief. His baby girl hadn't been admitted to a hospital since the day she was born. And while she had owned up to having a bit of a headache when she got home from school on Tuesday, he could tell that there was something she wasn't telling. She hated to admit that she was wrong, hated admitting she needed help even more.

"Sounds like you made good progress. You were down there for a while."

"Well she's a natural born fighter our kid," Carmen smiled proudly at their daughter.

The praise made Alexis sit up a little straighter in her seat. As loving and compassionate as Carmen was towards her family, she didn't heap praise on her child like Alexis had seen so many other mothers do. So when Alexis did something that elicited such compliments, she couldn't help but want to burst.

"Alexis, there is something we need to tell you." Putting his fork down next to his plate, Tony knew that it was now or never. They'd put off telling Alexis about her cousin's death for two days now. She was obviously feeling better. If they waited any longer, it would look as though they were hiding it from her.

"Your cousin Ricky, he died a few days ago. His funeral is on Saturday."

It took a few moments for her to absorb the words that had just been said. It was almost surreal. Ricky wasn't just part of the Family, he was family.

Blood.

Alexis had never lost someone related to her before. Sure her grandparents had died, but that was before she had been born. Ricky had been one of those cousins that she saw a few times a year for big birthdays and Christmas, but he'd always been around and he was always coming back soon. His next visit would've been for her sixteenth birthday in a few months.

"How did he die?" She already knew how though. It was this life they lived. Everyone in the Family died eventually, and ninety-eight percent of them died because of something related to the Family.

"That's not important hun. We're holding the wake here though, so there's going to be a lot of set up happening on Saturday. His parents shouldn't have to worry about entertaining at a time like this," Carmen explained. She dreaded having all the women of the family here that day, in her kitchen, fighting amongst themselves while preparing the food. However, Carmen also knew that there was no way she could pull all of this together on her own without hiring an army of people. And that just wasn't the way that they did things.

"You don't need to be here on Saturday morning before the funeral. Everyone is going to be here, and I know it can be a bit much for you."

Alexis appreciated her mum's offer, but she also knew how insane the family drove her mum. Dad wouldn't be allowed in the kitchen; these women were old fashioned.

"It's okay, I'll be here. After all you need a buffer, and I loved Ricky. I should be here to help."

This time it was Tony's turn to smile proudly at his little girl. She always stepped up to the plate when it counted.

◆◆◆

By the next morning Lucas had thought up an elaborate plan to ask Alexis to be his girlfriend. He was going to take her on a night hike of the national forest park and they were going to sit under the stars. He'd get some chocolate truffles from the chocolate factory she'd told him about near their school, bring a few blankets, it'd be perfect.

At least that's what he thought until he saw her face Friday morning. He'd come to her homeroom before the morning bell so he could ask her out for Saturday night, but seeing her standing there not even noticing the countless number of people brushing past her to deposit their own bags or grabbing books, the thought flew from his mind. She looked like the ground had fallen out from under her.

"Lex? What's wrong?" She didn't seem to hear him at all. When he reached out and touched her arm she jerked back to reality.

"Woah Lex, it's just me. What's wrong?" There was conflict going on in her mind. He could see it in her eyes. Finally she spoke but her voice was shaky.

"My cousin, Ricky, he um, he died."

Lucas pulled her into his arms in a heartbeat. Hers wrapped around his waist like she was drowning and he was her only lifeline. They stayed like that for a few minutes until she pulled away. He didn't need to look down to know that there would be wet patches on his shirt, not from the way she was trying to subtly wipe her eyes.

"I'm sorry, I didn't mean to fall all over you like that." She laughed at herself but there wasn't any real humour.

"Well feel free to fall all over me any time you like," Lucas smiled down at her. When she looked up at him, she let out a genuine chuckle, though it only lasted for a second before her eyes filled with tears again. Wrapping an arm around her shoulders Lucas guided her somewhere more secluded, away from all the prying eyes of their classmates.

Lucas found them a quiet spot between the back of the science block and the old library that was now being converted into an industrial kitchen for the culinary students.

"Do you wanna talk about it?" Lucas leaned against the wall with her standing between his legs. He let her play with his hands in hers as she got her bearings. He figured that she must be close to her cousin Ricky but couldn't personally relate. His dad was an only child and all of his mum's family was in England, which is where she preferred that they stay.

Alexis wanted to tell him everything right then and there. They were secluded enough that she doubted anyone would overhear them, and she trusted him to not tell anyone. He'd stuck around despite all the drama she came with, and he'd been so protective of her since the Hale sibling ambush, but she knew that those reasons weren't enough. He hadn't even officially asked her to be his girlfriend. What was to stop him from just walking away from what they had whenever he got tired of dealing with her?

Then again, she supposed that even being in an actual relationship wouldn't necessarily stop him from leaving if that's what he wanted to do. Provided she trusted him with her secret that is.

Looking up at him, Alexis couldn't help but lose herself in his hazelnut brown eyes. There was so much concern and caring, all of it for her. So she decided to tell him as much of the truth as she could.

"My parents told me last night that my cousin Ricky died on Tuesday. He works down south most of the year so I only see him for special occasions, but he was just one of those really fun and laidback cousins, you know?"

She remembered the time he'd caught her sneaking more cake after she was meant to be asleep while their parents were outside having a nightcap. Rather than telling her off or ratting her out, he'd cut them a slice each, then they'd gone back to her room and watched a movie until she fell asleep. She was almost twelve and he had just turned eighteen. She knew that he'd earnt his button by then and was more than welcome to have a drink with the other adults, but he'd chosen to spend time with her instead.

"He was like a big brother and now he's just... gone. The next time I would've seen him was my birthday. I've known people who have died before but never someone who was blood family."

Lucas didn't say anything, just stood there as she absentmindedly played with his fingers.

Giving his hands one last squeeze Alexis hopped up onto her tiptoes and planted a kiss on Lucas' cheek.

"Thank you for being here for me, you didn't have to."

"Actually yes, I did. I'll always be there for you when you need me," he said, a sweet smile spreading across his lips.

Maybe she could tell him everything someday soon after all.

CHAPTER 15

The Angelo household spent the whole of Friday night preparing for the onslaught of the weekend. Come 8 a.m. the next morning, their house and kitchen would be filled with aunts and uncles to help set up for the wake.

Not all of them were involved with the Family business, so anything that could be perceived as sensitive information needed to be locked away. Not that anything of a sensitive nature was left lying about anyway, but they were a snoopy and assuming bunch.

Tony's office had a new lock installed. He had caught some of the younger cousins practicing their lock picking skills at the last family get together. You can't pick an electronic pin pad.

Carmen bubble wrapped all the expensive and

very breakable ornaments and put them in the attic. Alexis mostly texted with Lucas and Emilia and brought her parents more of this or that. Her parents had a system, and they didn't like anyone messing with the system.

When Saturday morning came, Alexis wanted nothing more than to stay in bed and sleep for another three hours. Four tops. It had been a long ass week, very draining.

Especially when Seth and Brennan started being weird and passive aggressive again for no reason.

Before she had even had a chance to tell them on Wednesday morning that she and Lucas had ended up working things out, they had started ignoring her and wouldn't respond to her with anything more than a grunt. She'd gotten fed up with them halfway through recess, told them to pull their heads out of their asses and grow up.

Lucas was however a godsend. After they had cleared up the confusion on Tuesday, he'd barely left her side other than to go to his own classes. Emilia had commented that he was acting more like a body-guard than a boyfriend, but Alexis decided to leave him be for a little while longer. She knew how guilty he felt about her getting jumped on Monday. She wanted to tell him that he didn't have to protect her but until she was further along in her training with her mum, she didn't want to say anything she couldn't back up. It was also a bit of a comfort having him around all the time.

As for the Hale siblings, they hadn't appeared back at school since they ran off on Monday. Their parents were claiming that they had run away from home, but there was no police report made or a missing child's notice so it was more likely that they were locked up at home until things blew over.

They wouldn't blow over though. As far as Mr McNeil was concerned they were all expelled with the exception of April, who had been in the office serving out her in-school suspension. Alexis wasn't looking forward to April's return to classes next week, but maybe the little bitch had learnt her lesson.

Texting Lucas good morning, Alexis dragged herself out of bed and started getting dressed. It was going to be a long day, and she wasn't going to make it longer for her mum by drawing things out. In fact when she stepped into the kitchen to get breakfast five minutes later her mum had to do a double take.

"Holy shit! Tony I owe you five dollars!" Carmen shouted out to wherever her husband was hiding.

"Ha, told you so!" Walking into the kitchen, Tony was dressed in shorts and one of his 'outside work' shirts.

"What did you tell mum?"

Dropping a kiss on his daughter's head as he passed, Tony grabbed an apple from the fruit bowl on the counter.

"Your mum didn't think you'd get out of bed

unless one of us forced you to. I bet her that she was wrong."

Alexis feigned offence, but honestly, she couldn't have been mad about their bet. She was notoriously lazy on the weekend. If it weren't important to her parents that she actually be present and accounted for today, she would've been back up in bed as soon as she'd had breakfast.

"So what time are they descending upon us?"

It was already seven forty-five and her mum had said that most of the family would be arriving around eight. Knowing them like she did, Alexis guessed that most wouldn't turn up until closer to nine, but only because they were pre-cooking food to bring over. They'd say it was to save time and clean up and Carmen wasn't going to argue. As it was, having so many cooks in the kitchen was chaos. If bringing over their pre-prepared food made things a little less hectic, she wouldn't be offended that they, not so secretly, hated her kitchen.

"Your Zia Marie called and said they'd be about half an hour late. So, you've got time to enjoy your breakfast, and we can all enjoy the peace and quiet for a little longer."

◆◆◆

Carmen had been to her fair share of funerals. As a matter of fact, she'd been to more than her fair share of funerals. It came with the territory of being the wife of a mafioso. It didn't get easier though. Every time they went to a funeral, she couldn't help but wonder how long it would be until it was her husband in the coffin being carried towards a six-foot hole in the ground. She dreaded the day that she would have to put on a brave face in front of everyone while her whole world fell apart.

Carmen wrapped an arm around Ricky's mother, Veronica, and held Alexis' hand tightly on the other side. She refused to think about her daughter being the one in the coffin. Carmen had lost one child already in her life, she refused to lose another. She never wanted to feel the pain Veronica was feeling again.

When the group made it to the area marked for Ricky's burial they all took their seats. The group was much smaller than what it had been at the church. The service itself had been open to anyone who knew Ricky, this however, was just for the closest friends and family.

Carmen herself didn't pay much attention to the priests' words. She kept thinking about Ricky and how young he'd been. His younger brother Liam was one of the pallbearers, along with Tony and Ricky's father Richard.

Liam was only eighteen, and up till today he'd been so eager to follow in his big brother's footsteps. If he still chose to go through with it then he'd be getting his button in a few months. Tony would give him time to grieve, time to rethink his path in life.

Veronica got up out of her seat and moved to the podium where the priest had stood. Richard moved to her side and wrapped an arm around her waist, supporting her. She looked like she needed all the physical support she could get. Taking a deep breath, she calmed herself and moved away from her husband. There was a look of determination in her eyes and hatred. Carmen had seen that look before, and nothing that followed it was ever good.

"My son was such a sweet boy. He was always looking out for his family. The day my boy was killed, his family failed him, but they won't fail him in death." Veronica's eyes cut through the crowd to where Tony sat and she glared at him. "You can rest easy baby boy, your death will not go unpunished. I'll make sure of it."

There was a collective silence that followed Veronica's speech. Carmen stared wide-eyed at Tony while her daughter gripped her hand tightly. Grief or not, Veronica was out of line. She had not so subtly called out the Family, and Tony as its head, for not looking after her son. She was the wife of a made man, she knew how dangerous it was to show such disrespect.

Richard stared at his wife in disbelief, thankfully it only took him all of five seconds to regain his wits and escort her away from the podium. Her only saving grace would be that she hadn't actually used the 'M' word or called Tony out as being the reason her son was dead. Carmen would argue that it wasn't even close to being Tony's fault, but she knew that the mother's grief wouldn't allow for reason or logic.

Once the funeral was over, Carmen and Alexis rushed back to the car in the most subtle and respectful way possible. Tony was catching the next limo back to house, but right now Carmen needed to head back to make sure everything was ready for when guests arrive for the wake. Once they were on the move Carmen pulled her phone from her purse to text Tony but she got distracted by an envelope.

"Lex, text your dad that we're on our way home would you?"

Alexis did as she was asked but made a mental note to ask about the envelope later.

The envelope was plain and unsealed. Peeking inside, Carmen could see the back of photo paper. Pulling out the photos, she kept them turned away from her daughter. When she looked down at the subject of the first photograph, she felt sick to her stomach. Turning it over didn't lesson the feeling. On the back of the top photograph someone had written, *'We're coming for you.'*

When Carmen went upstairs to change she hid the envelope and pictures in the hidden panel of the walk-in closet where she kept her surveillance equipment. No one except Tony and his consigliere Emilio, knew that she monitored their meetings.

Carmen knew more about psychological warfare and body language than anyone else in the Family. While she didn't always participate in the meetings, she watched over them and told Tony which of the capos were hiding something or unhappy with the outcome. She also had the skill set to act as a bodyguard if the time came.

Tony had fought her on everything to do with her being involved in the Family. He didn't want her anywhere near the danger. She was constantly reminding him that when they met, she was already in danger. Carmen was used to this life and the risks that went along with it. She was the daughter of a made man, and he had thought that it was safer for her to stay in the dark, unaware and unprepared. He thought that maybe that way she wouldn't become a part of the life. That naivety had almost cost her, her life and her honour, until she met Tony. Tony and his guys had trained her up to be able to protect herself from her ex-boyfriend. She didn't tell Tony that her ex had been a part of a Family of his own, not until she was sure that he was out of her life forever.

The thing was though, just like her daughter, Carmen was a natural born fighter. Tony had been fond of her and provided her with the best training, even before they were officially together. Within a year she was proficient in three kinds of martial arts and knew how to use a knife in more ways than to just slice vegetables.

A few years after they got married and had Alexis, Tony suddenly became the head of the family. His father had been killed and no one knew who had done it. In an effort to avenge his father's death, Tony spent weeks poring over camera footage and audio clips of conversations captured during important meetings and negotiations. He came up with nothing.

One night after he'd fallen asleep on the couch again, Carmen was on her way back to bed from the bathroom and got curious. By morning she had narrowed down the list of suspects to two based purely on the changes of pitch in their voice and their body language. When Tony woke up, he couldn't believe how much his wife had accomplished in so little time. She'd gleefully reminded him that one of her degrees was in psychology.

After interrogating the two suspects they quickly figured out who it was that had organised the hit, and who it was that was just disgruntled at having been overlooked for promotion again. That afternoon there was an execution. By the next day Emilio was sworn in as the new consigliere.

It was a new world order, a new generation of mafia warfare. All through America, women were taking over their husband's criminal activities when they were sent to prison. In Mexican cartels, women were assassins and executioners. Australia would be no different. They might be behind the times with many political issues, but not when it came to realising that a woman could run things just as well as a man could.

◆◆◆

It was almost ten at night before the last of the mourners took their leave. Carmen poured the three of them a glass of wine, Alexis' containing half the liquid that theirs did. When she passed the glasses around Tony gave her an odd look.

"What? She earnt it this today."

"Oh no not that. Was there no whiskey?"

"No. Your brothers drank it all." Carmen added an eye roll at her brothers in law's antics. Richard she could understand, he'd lost his son, but Lee knew better than to drink so much. He was a loud drunk, and more often than not, would get verbally abusive and a bit racist.

"Bastards. Honey remind me to call Richard tomorrow."

Carmen just nodded and took another sip of her wine before grabbing one of the left-over cheese platters from the fridge.

"Daddy, what's going to happen to Ronnie?" Alexis knew enough about how respect worked in the Family to have realised that Veronica screwed up. She'd obviously had a few drinks before the funeral but that was no excuse for what she said.

Sighing, Tony tried to figure out the best way to make Alexis' understand the gravity of the situation.

"Sweetheart, what is one of the most important things in the Cosa Nostra."

Alexis thought about it for a few moments. Finally she settled on her answer. "Loyalty and respect."

"Yes, but in this case we're talking about respect. I can understand that Veronica is grieving for her son, and the laws of the Cosa Nostra dictate that wives are to be respected."

"But you should be respected too, you're the mafioso."

Tony smiled at his daughter. She knew more about their life than he wanted her to, but between movies and the internet, she had known the ten commandments of the Cosa Nostra before she was nine.

"Yes, you're right. So you see those two rules are in conflict. Veronica is my sister-in-law; my brother is a made man like me. If it were one of his guys then I would tell him to bring that guy in and I'd have a firm word with him and that would be the end of it. But it's not, so I can't and it isn't."

"So what happens now?"

This time it was Carmen who answered, "Now it's

time for me to step in. Veronica needs to know that grief or not she can't behave the way that she did. Ricky senior won't lay a hand on her, we promise. That's just not how we do things. He will be made to leave her at home for any future events until your dad deems her punishment to be over."

"But she's not going to be hurt?"

Tony snorted, "Oh I'm sure that being left out of every social event from here to the rapture will hurt her, but no, she won't be physically harmed. We have rules for a reason baby girl. It would've been one thing for her to disrespect me behind closed doors but not in a public display like that. If I ignore it then it will cause more problems later on."

Alexis saw the logic in her father's punishment. Zia Veronica married into the Family, but she came from one of those semi-important political families. Alexis' Nonno had organised the marriage between his son and Veronica to secure a political alliance with her father. Life was so different in the 80's.

CHAPTER 16

By the time Alexis made it to school the Monday following the funeral, she was mentally and emotionally drained. Her parents had deemed the day before a family day, just the three of them. They'd spent the day watching movies and reminiscing about Ricky. Alexis had told them the story about the cake, and they'd told her about the first time he saw her after she was born. Apparently he was none too pleased with having a little brother and had tried to swap Liam out for Alexis. Her parents had been quite surprised when they went to check on her and found a then four-year-old Liam curled up in her crib with duct tape over his mouth.

The swap had only occurred half an hour before they discovered the switch, but it had been long enough for Liam to get tired and fall asleep. Ricky was found in Tony's office under the desk entertaining his baby cousin. Alexis had no idea what was going on and was more than happy to watch Ricky make shadow puppets on the wall.

They'd all sat in silence for a while after that, lost in their own thoughts. Every time Alexis looked at her dad she would catch him staring back at her. It was a look that said, *'this is why I don't want you to be a part of this'*. That made her think for the first time in a long time, *is it worth it?*

Ever since Alexis found out what her family was really involved in, she'd wanted to be a part of it too. She knew of the dangers of being involved, she knew of the risks and the losses she could face. It wasn't until these past few days that she truly understood though. There had been times when her dad had hung up the phone and told them of someone who had died, a soldier that she might've seen in passing but never properly interacted with. This was the first time that she had lost someone close to her, someone she really cared about.

What made it all worse, was that no one could tell them why. Alexis thought back to Zia Ronnie's outburst at the funeral. She wanted revenge for what had happened to Ricky. They all did. The difference between her and the rest of them, was she blamed Tony. Alexis had no delusions about what happened. Ricky had been in the firing line because he was a made man in her father's crime family. Plain and simple.

What wasn't so plain and simple, was *why?* Why were their men being targeted? Yes, Alexis knew about the deaths leading all the way back across to the East Coast. Her parents hadn't told her, probably so she wouldn't worry, but she needed to know. Ricky wasn't just an isolated event, he was just one in a series of murders leading to them.

Where would it end?

Lucas practically jumped out of his skin when a pair of slender arms wrapped around his waist from behind. Covering the small hands with his own he breathed a sigh of relief.

"Aaron, I told you, we can't do this at school. The teachers would never approve." Knowing what was coming if he let those hands go Lucas held onto them tighter. No rib jabs for him. However he didn't count on Alexis finding another way of getting back at him. He felt her teeth munch down gently on the soft flesh of his arm and let her go.

"Argh you cannibal! Speaking of things frowned upon here."

Turning around Lucas was met with possibly the most beautiful smile he'd ever seen. Without a second thought he leant down and captured her mouth with his. The kiss only lasted for a few seconds before they pulled away, but he could've lasted on that high for the rest of the day.

"How are you feeling?" he asked, remembering what she'd had to deal with this past weekend.

"Yeah, I've been better, but I stayed home with my parents yesterday and we spent the day watching movies and sharing stories about Ricky. Apparently he tried to kidnap me when I was a baby," she smiled fondly.

"And here I thought I was the only one who'd thought to kidnap you."

"Well apparently not, so I guess it's time to step up your game," Alexis gave him a playful wink as they started walking past classrooms headed nowhere in particular.

"Be my girlfriend." He hadn't planned to ask her then and there. He was going to wait until the end of the coming weekend and stick to his original plan. He supposed he could still do that plan and it would just be a regular date.

"You - what?" Alexis had stopped walking and when he turned around to face her, regret brewing in his stomach, she was staring at him shocked.

"Are you serious?"

"Well I did have a whole plan, and there was chocolate involved, but yes, I'm serious. Will you be my official girlfriend?"

She started coming towards him, and for a moment he wondered if maybe she was going to let him down easy. Which didn't make sense since Emilia had put it in his head that this is what Alexis wanted... unless it wasn't and Emilia had been messing with hi-

His thought process was cut off by Alexis taking his face in her hands.

"Yes, Lucas. I will officially be your girlfriend. But you're still doing that thing with the chocolates."

Of course, the chocolates couldn't be forgotten.

CHAPTER 17

In the weeks following the Hale sibling ambush, all except for April were unaccounted for. Their parents were still claiming that the trio had run away after realising what they'd done but no one believed them. Instead there were some rather interesting rumours going around that they had been sent to a strict religious rehabilitation camp for wayward youths.

Whether or not this was fact, was still up for debate, but Alexis had someone looking into it. What her mum had said that day in the cafe, about knowing the people you're dealing with, it had stuck with her. Alexis was determined to know everything she could about the Hale family. There were quite a few things she knew from her years of friendship with April, but the older half siblings were a bit more of a mystery. They'd graduated from Themis College before the girls had started high school and were now off living their supposedly successful adult lives.

At least that's what April would have had everyone believe.

Now, using one's cousins as a way to gather information was not an unheard-of practice amongst Italian families. Especially when some of those cousins were hired explicitly to gather information on people.

Granted, they were hired by her dad, but as the heir to the criminal empire Alexis felt like she was entitled to some of those resources as well. Her dad might not want her involved in the Family business in any way, but what he didn't know wouldn't get her grounded.

It also didn't hurt that after hearing about the attack, FJ had offered to break bones. After reminding him that he could be charged with assaulting a minor, and that he was already helping her learn how to break bones, they settled for him doing some digging instead.

And dig he did.

It was after their second training session together, and they'd offered to return everything to its proper place while Carmen went upstairs to shower before dinner, that FJ went over to his bag, pulled out a manila envelope and handed it to her.

"Here's everything I could find in two days. It's not much, but if you need more than I can look for more."

Looking through the contents of the envelope, Alexis decided that they had vastly different definitions of what 'not much' meant.

"Frankie, this is... wow. It took you only two days to get all this?"

Drew and Sue Hale's entire lives were reduced to a stack of paperwork in her hand. She had copies of their birth certificates, marriage certificate, of which Sue had two, one for each marriage. There was a birth certificate for all of the kids, police report, drivers' licences.

"Police report?" Alexis whispered excitedly. FJ just got a satisfied grin on his face. That had been his favourite piece of discovery as well. Alexis skimmed over the document. She'd known that one of April's older brothers wasn't around, but they all talked about him as though he was studying abroad. It would seem that 'studying abroad' was code for 'in prison for three to five years'.

"Drug dealing. Turns out he was a runner for one of the smaller gangs around Perth. He'd already been picked up a few times before that for petty theft, and a breaking and entering charge, so when they caught him with a backpack full of coke ready to be sold on the street, they didn't hesitate. He got offered a deal to rat out his supplier, but he turned it down and decided to take the jail time."

"Do we know who he was running for?" Alexis asked, flicking through the rest of the documents and photos.

"Not yet little cuz. I've got a few theories, but I want to be sure."

"Well when you find out, let me know?"

"Of course," he stopped and thought for a second, "You know Zio Tony would be pretty pissed with me if he found out that I was helping you with this. He doesn't want you anywhere near this stuff."

Alexis knew what he was getting at. There was truth behind his words, her dad would be pissed. He might even knock FJ around a little. That wasn't what he was hinting at though.

"Frankie, don't you worry about my dad. So long as you don't leave a trail then he'll never find out from me. Whether he likes it or not, one day I will be a part of all of this. For today though, I need to know everything I can about my enemies, and in the event that my dad does find out, I think he'll be able to respect that. You have my back and I have yours."

Francesco Joseph loved his cousin. She was fierce, strong and refused to back down. She was also caring, protective and calculating. He had no doubt that one day he'd be answering to her... if he lived that long. As it stood though, Zio Tony was the head of the family and his word was law. Technically FJ hadn't broken the cardinal rule of *don't involve Alexis in any*

Family related dealings.

After the attack, Zio Tony had been furious. He'd ordered extra bodyguards for Alexis not caring that it had been a schoolyard feud and not a gang related attack. When Alexis had started self-defence training with Zia Carmen, FJ had volunteered to help out as well.

When he'd mentioned Zio Tony's inevitable reaction to finding out about their dealings, FJ hadn't meant that he wanted protection. He was gladly helping out his cousin. It had more to do with what would happen to Alexis when he found out, but also what she planned to do with it.

"Lex, what will you do with all this stuff?"

"Nothing for now, but at least if I have it in my back pocket then I can use it when the need arises."

FJ wasn't sure what he'd been expecting from her. She wasn't one to air dirty laundry to the entire high school, so he doubted that she would tell everyone about April's brother.

"What about the three supposedly run-away siblings?" Alexis asked.

"Ah, well those three, slippery fuckers that they are, are locked up safe and sound in casa de Hale." FJ reached out and pulled a surveillance photo from the bottom of the pile of documents. In it you could see the three siblings sitting around watching TV. It was date stamped for the day before.

"Those lying sons of bitches," a sadistic grin

spread across Alexis' face. FJ had had the same look when he'd seen them just sitting there. It would've been so easy to wait until they all went to bed and then get revenge. But this was his cousin's call. She was the one who had been attacked, so she got to decide how they were punished.

Taking the folder up to her room, Alexis pondered over how she would use its contents. There was a lot in there that she could use against April alone if she ever acted up again. Someone who was as high and mighty as that wouldn't want anyone knowing about her precious brother. She had done the math and Alexis realised that at the time of his conviction, she and April and Emilia had still been thick as thieves.

Guess I'm not the only one with family secrets.

CHAPTER 18

Alexis and her mum slipped into an easy routine when it came to her training. Monday, Wednesday and Friday, before school, they went down to the training room and worked out for an hour. After school they went back down for another two hours before dinner. Alexis was exhausted and covered in bruises by the end of each session. However, after the second week she noticed that she was walking away with fewer sore spots. Her mum didn't ease up though. In fact every time Alexis seemed to get the hang of one manoeuvre, three more counters were thrown at her.

It was the Thursday morning of the third week when Lucas noticed a particularly nasty bruise on Alexis' forearm that hadn't been there the day before.

"Babe, where'd you get that?"

Confused, Alexis looked up at him. "Get what?"

"That bruise on your arm?"

Without thinking Alexis covered the bruise with her opposite hand. That one unconscious move ratted her out. She could've played it dumb and pretended that she had no idea, but now he knew that she knew.

"Um, so truth?" It was better that she told him. After all she'd been hiding her training from him for almost three weeks.

"Yes, truth," he replied.

"So after what happened, I asked mum and dad to help me learn to defend myself. Once I started feeling better mum started my training. Last week she brought in my cousin FJ so she could focus on watching and correcting. FJ is eighteen... and a giant. Like, you giant. Plus he's got an extra forty kilos on me. I know she brought him in to help me get used to fighting men, but goddamn I don't stand a chance against him. He doesn't hold back either, which I like because I need to be prepared for anything. It would just be nice to be able to catch him off guard for once."

Lucas held his girlfriend's hands in his, rubbing soft circles on the back of her hands with his thumbs. On the one hand, it sucked that she had hidden her training from him. On the other hand, he knew that her pride was hurt by the beating she took. With her personality, she wouldn't have wanted to tell anyone about her training until she was able to back it up with some actual skill. He didn't wonder about how long it would've been until she told him if he hadn't asked about the bruise. Instead he came up with a solution to her problem.

"Lex, how about I train with you?" He thought it was a great idea, this way she'd be able to get used to fighting someone so much taller. Then when she went back to fighting her cousin, she'd be a step ahead of where she was the last time. Which from the looks of that bruise, was on the receiving end of a downward strike with some kind of weapon.

Now while Lucas thought his plan was brilliant, Alexis was not quite as convinced. "Do you know how to fight? Cos I don't think I'd be the best teacher. Also when would we do it, and where?"

There wasn't really a way for Lucas to prove his own skillset without fighting Alexis, so instead he pulled her against his body and dropped a kiss to the top of her head. "Baby, don't worry about all that. Just tell me what days you're available and I'll work out the rest."

The funny thing was, when Lucas told her not to worry about something because he'd sort it out, she didn't worry. She knew that he would take care of things.

And that's exactly what he did. That afternoon

Lucas led Alexis through the darkened back hallways of the gymnasium. Alexis pushed back the memories of all the times she'd made out with Seth in these hallways and instead, focused on how strong Lucas' hand felt in hers. She'd messaged her driver, AJ that she was staying back after school to work on a group assignment so he wouldn't be there to pick her up until five-thirty. That gave Alexis two hours alone with Lucas and whatever crazy plan he had.

Finally they reached a locked door at the end of the hall. At least it was locked, until Lucas pulled a key out of his shorts pocket. When the door swung open and they stepped through, Alexis saw they were in the weights room. It was usually only used by teachers and year elevens and twelves doing certificate courses in sports. In the middle of the room were interlocking exercise mats set out in what was probably a sparing square.

"Um, Luc, how did you get a key to this room?"

Students weren't allowed in this room without teacher supervision, something about occupational health and safety.

"I know people," he said with a cheeky smirk. When he didn't elaborate but instead just led her deeper into the room, letting the door swing shut behind them, she decided to let it slide. His connections could stay secret for now.

Dumping their bags next to a rack of weights, the pair started stretching. Considering how spur of the moment their training session was, neither of them had workout clothes. Though if Alexis could fend off three attackers, at least for the most part, in her school dress, then she could spar with Lucas.

So they did. For the first twenty minutes they went through various drills. Lucas figured out what Alexis knew and what she needed to improve. For the rest of their time they worked on the stuff that Alexis was doing with her mum and cousin.

"Come on, you need to think. I'm bigger and stronger than you, how are you going to get out of this?"

"I get it, okay? I don't know how to get out of this." Alexis was getting more and more frustrated. She'd been trying to get out of the bear hug for twenty minutes, and the manoeuvres her mum had taught her to use, weren't working.

Lucas stood behind her, his arms around her torso, pinning hers to her side. Every time she tried to drop her weight forward to loosen his grip it had no effect. With the amount of force she was using, if he ever actually let her go she'd fall flat on her face.

"You're just going to wear yourself out doing that."

A low growl started in Alexis' chest. She knew that he was right, but it didn't make the situation any less frustrating.

"You said that one of the guys grabbed you from behind that day you got attacked, how'd you get out of that?"

"I headbutted him in the face, but I've tried that already with FJ. It doesn't work because I'm not at the right height."

Lucas loosened his grip around Alexis but didn't let her go while he contemplated a way for her to escape. Alexis wasn't complaining though, she liked having his arms around her. If only she weren't so frustrated with her lack of progress to really be able to enjoy it.

"Okay I've got an idea." Lucas relayed his brainstorm to Alexis and had them switch positions so that he could demonstrate on her what he wanted her to try. Five minutes and two resets later, she had him pushed against a wall with an elbow to his throat. Breathing heavily she couldn't help but grin up at her boyfriend.

"I did it."

"Yeah, you did." Lucas was breathing heavily as well. Ever since they started sparring he'd been fighting back his hormones. There was something about how she moved and took control. You didn't expect there to be so much fire just by looking at her.

Alexis noticed that Lucas' gaze had settled on her mouth, and who was she to deny him what he so obviously wanted. Before she had a chance to close the distance though, Lucas pulled her body flush up against his, their mouths crashing together. Alexis was standing on her toes, her hands had made their way into his hair, his were squeezing her waist like it was a lifeline.

They stayed entangled like this until they had to break away for air.

"I wouldn't suggest using that as a defensive manoeuvre when fighting your cousin, but when we're sparring, go for your life." With a kiss on Alexis' forehead Lucas put some space between them even though that was the last thing he wanted to do. "You... are dangerous."

"I have no idea what you're talking about," Alexis smiled innocently. She had wondered if she had the same effect on him as he did on her, and this had just proved that she did.

"Alright, come on you, let's go again."

And they did.

Once Alexis felt confident that she could get out of the bear hug they did some general sparring which ate up the rest of their time together.

The next afternoon Alexis was more than ready for her afternoon training session. While she changed into her workout gear, Carmen let FJ into the house and ran him through her lesson plan for the afternoon. She wanted to give Alexis another chance to get out of the bear hug on her own. Then she was going to show Alexis a way of getting out if that didn't work.

Sparring with someone in a training room was

easy, there was no real sense danger or urgency. You always knew how to counter someone's' attack, but the thing was that out in the real world, sometimes your counters didn't work. Alexis needed to be able to improvise if she ever got into a situation where her tried and tested tactics had no effect on her opponent.

Twenty minutes later, after FJ and Alexis had gone through their warm ups, Carmen had FJ wrap Alexis up in the bear hug attack. They both expected Alexis to drop her weight forwards in an attempt to get FJ to loosen his grip, just like she had when they first practiced this attack the other day. She didn't though. No, Alexis surprised them both.

Bringing her foot down on top of FJ's, scraping his shin as she went caused enough of a distraction for his arms to involuntarily loosen ever so slightly. It wasn't enough for her to escape from them, but it was enough for her to swing her hands backwards and hitting the inside of FJ's thighs.

She used the extra space she then gained to thrust her elbow into his gut. That was the blow that made him bend at middle, and when he did, she jerked her head backwards. Using the back of her skull, she tapped his face hard enough for him to retreat but not hard enough to break his nose.

Finally his grip broke, and that was when Alexis unleashed hell. Swinging around she brushed her elbows past his chin, just enough that he knew to move his head to the side.

Somehow FJ managed to trip over his own feet and fall to the floor. Alexis wasn't far behind. She dropped to one knee, that knee placed rather gently yet firmly on FJ's ribs and pressed her arm against his throat. In seconds he was tapping out.

"Wanna go again?" Alexis smiled down at her cousin, feeling a sense of accomplishment that she hadn't been expecting.

"Alright you two, reset. I want to see that again."

It went a little differently the second time around. That first time she'd caught FJ off guard, but this time he was ready for her. Or so he thought. She waited for his arms to tighten around her and then made her move. Grabbing hold of the thumb of his right hand she pulled it backwards at the same time she elbowed him in the gut with her left arm. Once his grip was broken she repeated her elbow strike. Halfway through the move FJ blocked her arms. Strafing to the side she forced him to follow her. When he struck out at her, she implemented her own attack/defence manoeuvres. Within seconds she had him bent over as she mimicked kneeing him in the face.

"Okay I think we can move onto something else for now," Carmen said from her position on the sidelines, a proud smile playing on her lips.

Training went on like that for a week. Every other day she trained with Lucas. They worked through any manoeuvres she was struggling with in her sessions with FJ, and then did some more general stuff. He even ended up teaching her a few new things. When she asked him how he learnt to fight so well he made a vague comment about his dad teaching him.

The next afternoon when Alexis trained with her mum and FJ, she blew them away with the progress she had made overnight.

By the Friday she was exhausted. Training sessions six days in one week on top of school and homework, she was almost ready to throw in the towel. That was until FJ didn't turn up to their session.

"Mum, where's FJ? Shouldn't he be here by now?"

"He's not coming tonight, his parents needed his help with something."

Alexis couldn't say that she was totally upset that he wasn't coming. She loved her cousin, there was no question. She was just sore and tired of getting pounded on. Alexis knew that he was rougher with her than he normally would be because she needed to get used to taking pain.

It was all part of the conditioning process, it made it easier to bounce back in a real fight when the other person isn't pulling their punches.

It was during their warm-up drills that Carmen finally said what was on her mind. "So, you've been going really well with your training."

Dodging her mother's thigh slaps Alexis wandered what brought on the sudden praise. "Thanks mum."

"If I didn't know any better I'd think that you were training with someone else as well."

"When would I even have time?" There was a fine line when it came to avoiding eye contact. Too much avoidance and you looked guilty, too little and you looked guilty.

"Well you're staying after school a lot the past week."

Dodge. Slap.

"I've been working on a group assignment."

Fake out. Dodge. Slap.

"Really? So where'd that bruise on your neck come from?"

Without even thinking Alexis' hand went up to cover her neck. She'd forgotten all about the mark. Lucas had gotten carried away the day before. She'd noticed it in the mirrors of the training room and retied her hair to cover it, but this afternoon she'd just been so distracted with showing her mum the progress she'd made. Without her mum finding out how she'd made it.

Slap.

"So, who's the guy?"

"What guy?"

Slap. Dodge.

"The one who gave you that hickey. I know it wasn't there when you left for school yesterday morning so it's not from sparring."

Alexis knew that there really was no point denying the truth. She'd have to come clean eventually, and not being able to go to her mum for advice the past few weeks had been gnawing away at her sanity.

Carmen stood up straight and nodded her head towards the water fridge in the corner.

"His name's Lucas. He was the one I went to the movies with a few weeks ago, and he was the one who carried me to the office after the attack."

"So he's the one you've been with in the after-noons?"

"Yes, but we've been training," Alexis insisted. She didn't want her mum getting the wrong idea about Lucas. He'd helped her more in the short time she'd known him than most anyone else she'd known for years.

"Mmhmm, sure you have."

"Seriously, you've seen how much better I've gotten over the past week. The stuff I get stuck on with FJ, I work on with Lucas. He saw the bruises on my arm last week and how frustrated I was, and he just wanted to help."

Carmen studied her daughter for a minute. She wasn't lying, that much Carmen knew. She didn't like that her daughter had been keeping a secret like this for weeks but she also remembered her first love. Besides, if this boy was helping her daughter learn to defend herself, and effectively from what she'd seen, he couldn't be that bad. She would however be the judge of this herself.

"Invite him to dinner next weekend."

By her mum's tone, Alexis knew that there was no room for discussion. If she claimed that Lucas couldn't make it next weekend then her mum would just plan for the weekend after, either until they broke up or the world ended, whichever came first.

CHAPTER 19

In the weeks leading up to Easter break Alexis wasn't spending as much time with Seth and Brennan as she used to. She had tried, but they accused her of having ulterior motives, and Brennan would alternate between clingy and standoffish. It was like they'd turned into PMS-ing girls overnight and she was becoming exhausted by their behaviour. In all honesty it didn't bother her that much that they were acting so crazy. It made it easier for her to spend more time with Lucas and not feel guilty.

Aaron's end of term party was the first time Alexis would actually be seeing Seth and Brennan outside of school in almost two months. Every time she tried to make plans with Brennan he would always give her the same answer, *yeah if the guys don't want to do something.*

She had apologised for getting caught up in her relationship with Lucas and not spending as much time with him as she used to. He said he understood and forgave her. It was clear though that he didn't.

When she had vented to Jess and Aaron about how standoffish Brennan was being, Aaron had reminded her of Brennan's crush on her. She thought that he'd gotten over that, especially after she had made it clear that she thought of him more as a brother.

Whatever feelings were or were not in existence, both Seth and Brennan had told Jess that they were coming to the party. Which meant that Alexis might finally be able to talk to them, call them out for being assholes and then they could all move on.

Maybe.

Hopefully.

For two hours before the party officially started, Jess and Alexis sat around in Aaron's room, a decent sized shed that he'd converted into a bedroom, getting ready for the party. Alexis had offered to help set up and Aaron had welcomed the help. Once Jess was out of earshot, he asked her to keep Jess occupied for a while before the party started. Apparently, he had a surprise for her.

And so here they were. They'd finished setting up

the various tables for food and drinks. Eskies were full of ice and drinks, prepped cold food was in the fridge and packets of chips were sitting in the bowls they would be emptied into once people started arriving. Everything was ready except for the two girls, and whatever it was that Aaron was cooking up.

"So why is it that Lucas isn't here for this? It would be your first party as an official couple."

"He's got some family dinner, but he said he'll come by afterwards so it's not so bad." Alexis didn't bother to hide her disappointment that he wouldn't be there when the party started. But at the same time it might be a good thing, give her a chance to talk to Brennan without him getting all standoffish.

The party had been in full swing for two hours. The heat had everyone going to the eskies for cold drinks. Alexis had managed to find Brennan, but before she'd had a chance to start a conversation, Marty had appeared and pulled Brennan away for a game of beer pong. He'd actually looked relieved to have an excuse to get away from her.

Maybe it was the way that he'd been ignoring her texts for weeks or would only give her short answers whenever she managed to catch him in person. Or maybe it was how he wouldn't commit to plans with her no matter how flexible she tried to be. Whatever the combination, seeing his look of relief, and the smug smile that Marty shot her way, Alexis decided that she was done trying.

Turning away from her ex-boyfriend and friend, Alexis headed for the drinks table wishing that there was something stronger than lemon lime bitters. The eskies had beers buried under the ice for those in the know, but she couldn't stand the taste.

She started thinking about all the times that Brennan had been a shit friend and she'd forgiven him, brushed it off and let him off the hook. There were times when he had done something wrong, but the second she pulled him up on it, he'd try and turn the tables on her, guilt her until she ended up apologising for getting upset that he'd been a jerk.

Whenever a guy had shown interest in her since they became friends, he'd gotten all sullen and withdrawn. It didn't matter that she hadn't said anything about liking them back.

She'd thought for a while that he was just protective of her, the way she was of him. It took her a while to realise that while she thought of him as a brother, he didn't see her the same way.

That realisation had felt like a light being shone into the dark corners a cluttered room. There was unused crap everywhere, but now she could see it all clearly. See it for what it really was. The over protectiveness was really jealousy. She used to believe he stood too close to her because of his anxiety, he'd said that she was a calming presence for him. So she tried not to be bothered by it. But even that, she realised, was just another way for him to lay a claim to her that he didn't actually have.

It had been different when Seth had done it to her. She'd seen it for what it was. But something about her friendship with Brennan had clouded her thinking. She'd been so blinded by the feeling of being needed that she'd ignored all the red flags.

Alexis walked through the house, wanting to find anywhere else to be, somewhere she didn't feel so pitiful, so stupid and naive.

She wandered from room to room, never loitering for more than a few minutes. She was on her way back out to the backyard after doing a lap of the house when Seth suddenly appeared in front of her.

"Lex, can we talk?" He didn't wait for her to reply, instead just grabbed her by the arm and pulled her into one of the bedrooms.

"Seth what the he-" Alexis was cut off by Seth pressing his mouth against hers. One hand held the back of her head, the other wrapped tightly around her upper arm. His tongue was trying to force its way into her mouth. Her brain was screaming for her to do something, but her body wouldn't respond. She just stood there like a limp fish.

His grip got tighter. More painful. Just like that, a switch flipped in her head and her free hand formed a fist and thrust forward into his soft belly. Seth pulled away from her but there wasn't enough distance for her liking. Pushing him away, she side stepped for the door, not taking her eyes off him. She knew that she should be running from him, not looking back. But he was her friend. She had to know why he was doing this.

"Seth what the hell is wrong with you?" she asked, wiping her mouth with the back of her hand. It didn't get rid of the feeling of his mouth on hers.

"I miss you Lex."

"Well this isn't the way you show it, you asshole!" God, how was she going to tell Lucas about this?

Seth took a step towards her. She took a step back.

"Come on, just one more time, for old times' sake," Seth pleaded. She couldn't believe what he was asking her. When she looked in his eyes they were glassy, like he'd been drinking.

"Seth, no! I have a boyfriend."

"Oh come on, that's never going to last and you know it," he made a grab at her, but she smacked his hand away.

"It doesn't matter if you think that we'll last, I really like him and I want to see where this goes."

"But we were so good together."

Alexis scoffed, "Together? We were never really together, we were a *thing*." She emphasised *thing* with bunny ears.

"Whatever we were, I want it back. Please. I miss you."

"You don't miss me. You just miss having someone who put up with your bullshit."

"What's wrong with that?"

Alexis shook her head, not quite believing that this conversation was really happening. "I'm going Seth, I'll see you after break," and she went for the door. She never should've taken her eyes off him though, the moment that she did he made another grab for her.

This time his arms wrapped around her torso and he brought her up against his chest. Her muscle memory and instincts took over. In moments she had him bent over, his shoulder one firm tug away from dislocation. When she'd thrust her head back she heard a crunch of bone and cartilage. Most likely his nose, though from their current position she couldn't see if she had broken it... she could only hope that she had.

"I told you that we were over Seth. I am with Lucas and I have no intentions of screwing that up. So back the fuck off."

With a hard shove she pushed him away from her. Unsteady as he was, he fell to the floor on the opposite side of the small room, narrowly missing the bedside table. She didn't take her eyes off his limp form until she was out of the room, slamming the door behind her.

She tried to keep her shaking to a minimum. The adrenaline raced from her body, her legs shook with every step.

Stumbling through the hallway towards the backdoor she felt like she was drunk. Her vision was blurring. Her breaths were short. There wasn't enough air.

She finally made it outside but still couldn't get enough air into her lungs.

Away. She had to get away.

"Lex?"

Away.

"Aaron, something's wrong."

Have to get away.

She should've left. Shouldn't have come.

"Alexis, it's me, Jess." Gentle hands grasped her own sweaty palms.

"Jess? Jess - I - can't breathe," Alexis gasped out. She was so dizzy.

"Babe, wait here while I make sure my room is cleared out okay."

Aaron. He was here?

Someone - Jess? - put their arms around her. A hand stroking her hair.

She still couldn't breathe.

"Babe!" Hands pulling her away from where they stood.

Where had they stood?

Where was Seth?

Lucas. She needed Lucas.

"I'll lock the door as I go. I'll be back in a few

minutes, I'm going to get her some food and water."

I'm not drunk. She wanted to speak but the words wouldn't come out.

Alexis heard the solid thunk of a dead bolt sliding into place, felt the soft hands of her friend running over her back. Slowly her senses came back to her. At some point her breathing calmed. It hitched again when a key slid into the lock and the door opened. But the second Aaron stepped over the threshold, closing and locking the door behind him, Alexis calmed again.

He carried a bottle of water under his arm and a plate piled high with party food. Alexis gratefully took the water from him, not missing the worry clear as day on his face. She knew that if she looked at her friend sitting behind her, still rubbing soothing circles on her back, Alexis would see the same look.

"I'm not drunk, I haven't drunk anything."

"I know Lex," Aaron said gently. "I figured that if anyone asked what happened then you could just say you drunk too much." *That's if you didn't want to explain the panic attack.*

It was things like that that made Alexis adore Aaron as Jess' boyfriend. He thought about things like that. She knew that he'd keep her panic attack quiet without needing to be asked.

"I'll let you two talk. I've got my phone if you need anything. Feel better Lex." Once more he left the room, locking the door from the outside. Alexis wondered for a moment what would happen if they needed to get out, but realised that she preferred other people not being able to get in.

◆◆◆

Jessica had never seen Alexis have a panic attack. She'd only ever seen her cry twice in their eight years of friendship. Even once Alexis had calmed down and was breathing normally again, there was an alertness in her eyes that didn't die down. Shifting on the bed to get a better look at her friend Jess looked for any visible injuries. She saw a red mark resembling a hand on Alexis' left upper arm. A mark that hadn't been there when Alexis had been getting ready a few hours ago.

"Lex, what happened?" Jess asked softly. When Alexis wouldn't meet her eyes, she tried again. "You can trust me hun, no one's going to hurt you. Please, tell me what happened, who grabbed you?"

Alexis looked down at her arm in surprise, as though only just realising her skin had been marked.

"Seth," Alexis confessed, her eyes still fixed on the red handprint. She poked it. It was going to bruise.

"What? Seth did that to you? Why?" Jess' head spun. Everyone knew that Seth was handsy with his female friends, but she'd never thought him to be violent.

"He wanted to continue what we had..." And so

Alexis told Jess what happened in the darkened spare bedroom. She confessed to their ten-month secret affair that ended after New Year's and why. She told Jess about the first day of school, how mad Seth had been when she didn't show, and then how she'd found out the truth from Brennan. How she'd realised that she was just a distraction until Jess became available. When she'd finally finished telling her story, Jess had now seen her friend cry three times in eight years.

Holding Alexis close, Jess worked up the courage to confess a secret of her own. It was one that she hadn't yet confessed to Aaron though she knew that she should've by now.

"Seth kissed me last Christmas. That night that Aaron and I had the huge fight. After you left, Seth came back, and I didn't feel like being alone. We were watching a movie, I was starting to fall asleep, I should've stopped drinking when you told me to. He kissed me, and I think it was because I'd been thinking about Aaron, and I was half asleep, I kissed back. But then when I realised what was actually happening I tried to stop it. He was kind of on top of me, I had to 'fall' off the couch for him to stop. He begged me not to tell anyone, especially you. Now I know why."

Alexis' mouth formed into a sneer. For a moment Jess thought it was aimed at her until Alexis spoke.

"Are you okay? That son of a bitch, I told him to leave you alone. I warned him. He took advantage of you. God I hope I broke his nose."

"But what he just tried to do to you, that's so much worse than just a kiss." Jess hadn't told Alexis what had happened to gain her sympathy or take away from what had just happened. She wanted her friend to know she wasn't alone when it came to Seth. Wanted Alexis to know that she believed, and maybe know that she was believed in return.

Lucas arrived at the party an hour later. The two girls hadn't left Aaron's room since they'd been locked in. It was only when Lucas confirmed that he was alone that Jess retrieved her keys and unlocked the door, allowing Lucas into the converted shed. He took in their puffy eyes and red noses and was immediately on high alert.

"What happened? Are you two okay?"

Alexis nodded from her place on the bed. She was well and truly exhausted, and all she wanted to do was go home and curl up. Jess' confession had filled in a lot of gaps that Alexis hadn't even realised were there. The picture that those missing puzzle pieces revealed wasn't a good one. It was certainly not one that Alexis wanted to reveal to Lucas here. Even if Seth had gone home.

"We're okay, I just want to go home. Will you take me?"

The concern etched deeper into Lucas' face but he didn't argue. Alexis and Jess said their goodbyes, Jess promising to pass on Alexis' thanks to Aaron. Jess was going to fix herself up before she re-joined the party. Aaron had texted them half an hour ago mentioning that people had seen Seth leaving the party with blood down the front of his shirt. Brennan and Marty had gone with him. That was the only reason that Alexis felt comfortable leaving Jess, knowing that Seth was gone.

It only took a few minutes to walk back to Lucas' car but they felt eternally longer for Alexis. She knew that she had no reason to fear Lucas' reaction to what she was going to tell him. She knew in her heart that he wouldn't blame her in any way. But her head wasn't as cooperative. It kept throwing hypothetical scenarios at her about how Lucas might perceive the... incident. She didn't even know how to classify it in her head. She'd stopped him from taking things too far, so was it an attack? He still tried though.

Rather than taking her straight home Lucas drove up into the hills to the ZigZag. The lookout was named for how the road zigzagged down the hill and had look out points at the end of each hair pin turn. Very clever.

His left hand rested on her thigh for a majority of the drive, only leaving once he reached the ZigZag and returned both hands to wheel. It was unusually quiet for a Saturday night, but Alexis wasn't about to look a gift horse in the mouth as Lucas parked on the red dirt, a large boulder illuminated by his headlights. Once the car was turned off, Lucas turned in his seat to face Alexis.

"So, are you going to tell me what happened?"

When Alexis told him what happened at the party, he'd wanted to drive back just to beat the living shit out of Seth himself. The only thing that had stopped him was when Alexis told him that Seth had left not long after she broke his nose. It also didn't help when she wouldn't tell him where Seth lived.

Twice.

Twice now his girlfriend had been in danger.

Twice now she had been attacked, and he hadn't been there to stop it. To protect her.

It didn't ease his guilt knowing that she was more than capable of protecting herself.

After she'd finished telling him what happened, Lucas had gotten out of the car and gone to her side. Within a few seconds he was sitting in the passenger seat of his own car, Alexis in his lap, her head against his chest as he held her close. They'd stayed like that for almost an hour, ignoring the sounds of passing cars and headlights flashing as they went by.

It was as they sat like that, Alexis told him about what Seth had done to Jess. She kept telling him that she should've stayed that night. She'd told Seth to leave Jess alone, practically begged him. But she should've stayed. He hated how responsible she felt for what that asshole had tried to do.

"Lex what he did, taking advantage of Jess like that, it isn't your fault," Lucas said.

"But if I had stayed. If I had just told my parents that I needed to stay that night, that Jess needed me, he wouldn't have had the chance," she stared at the boulder in front of the car.

"Look, from what you've told me he would've tried something sooner or later. Whether it had been that night or another," Lucas said, rubbing circles on Alexis' back. The car was filled with silence for a few minutes, the only sound coming from his hand against the material of her shirt. After a little while Alexis turned in his lap to look at him, her eyes brimming with tears.

"Why did he even try? He didn't want to be open about our relationship for almost a year, too afraid of what our friends would say. And then he chooses now, when I've moved on and I'm happy with you, to try and literally force his way back in. We promised that no matter what happened, we were friends first. He was supposed to be my friend. Why did he do it?"

Lucas was at a loss for words. Nothing he could say would make it better.

As strong as Alexis was, she was still human. She could beat someone twice her size to a bloody pulp if she set her mind to it, but her heart was just as vulnerable as any others.

"I don't know baby... I really don't know."

CHAPTER 20

Alexis dragged herself from her bed the next morning. Keeping the shorts but opting for a long-sleeved shirt, she dressed in her workout clothes and sent a few 'good morning' texts. Going down to the basement to train was the last thing she wanted to do on a Sunday morning. After last night all she wanted to do was curl up in bed and wallow. But there was a part of her that didn't want to do that. A part of her that was pissed. Seth had broken her trust and he'd hurt Jess.

Jess.

Alexis needed to make sure that Jess was okay. The night before had been a whirlwind of emotions and confessions. Now that she'd had some sleep and a chance to process everything that had and hadn't happened, Alexis knew that Jess needed her. She hadn't missed the relief in her friend's eyes at being able to finally share the events of that night. Jess had probably not spoken a word about it to anyone since it happened.

After working up enough of a sweat so that she didn't feel guilty about only doing half of her workout routine, Alexis showered and put on a fresh pair of shorts, matching them with a long-sleeved top. The weather was doing weird things with the change of the seasons, one minute it was sweltering and the next it felt like stepping into a walk-in fridge, so her covering up wouldn't be suspicious.

"Morning all!" Alexis said as she bounced into the kitchen for breakfast. Her parents turned to her with a scrutinizing eye.

"Who are you and what are you doing up this early?"

Alexis almost objected but then she saw the clock behind her dad's head. It was only eight in the morning... on a Sunday. And she'd been up for two hours already. Alexis felt her expression morph into one of horror and disgust. Doing the math she realised that she'd only gotten three hours of sleep.

When Lucas had dropped her home she'd dodged a conversation with her parents, begging off that she was exhausted and just wanted to get some sleep. That was at eleven. Then she didn't get to sleep until near three in the morning. She'd spent almost four hours tossing and turning, putting together all the pieces, and replaying the events of the evening in her head. Trying to figure out why any of it had happened.

Just like Lucas, she still didn't have an answer.

"I'm going to see Jess," Alexis said, realising that her parents were still waiting for her to answer them.

"Didn't you just spend all of yesterday with her?"

"Yes dad, but sometimes best friends spend more than just one day together."

"Alright you smartass, eat your breakfast." He shook his head at her and slid a plate across the counter towards her. It was the standard Sunday breakfast of bacon, eggs, hash browns and tomato with a glass of pineapple juice.

"So did you have fun last night?"

Alexis knew that she should answer her mum's question truthfully. They wouldn't be angry at her for what happened. She knew that. It wasn't her fault. She was defending herself. She could tell them.

But she didn't.

"Yeah, it was alright. Kinda sucked that Lucas wasn't there for all of it, but once he got there it was better." Maybe that was as close to the truth as she would ever get. For the remainder of breakfast Alexis made small talk with her parents, discussing their plans for the day. Before Alexis left the kitchen her mum called her back.

"Don't forget to ask Lucas over for dinner this week. It's school holidays so you don't have the homework excuse."

"Ugh, yes mum, I will organise with Lucas for him to come to dinner and get back to you, I promise."

It wasn't that Alexis didn't want Lucas to meet her parents, she did. It was more that she was worried about how her dad would behave. He was a very stereotypical protective dad when it came to her dating. He didn't like it, no one was good enough, and he'd try and scare anyone away before they even made it to the dinner table. It was all of that that she wasn't looking forward too.

For now though, Alexis had bigger fish to fry.

Before Alexis had even knocked on Jess' door it was flung open. No matter the time of day, Jess always managed to look amazing. Alexis kind of hated her for it.

"Good morning lovely, would you like some coffee?"

"Good God, yes!" Alexis loved the coffee at Jess' place. They had one of those coffee machines with the pods that always made a perfect cup of coffee.

By the quietness of the house Alexis figured that Jess' parents were out for the morning, which was definitely a good thing considering the conversation the two girls were about to have. Alexis waited until they were both seated on the chaise lounge, hot coffees in hand.

"Jess... what you told me last night, about what happened at Christmas with Seth, are you okay? With everything that happened last night I don't know if I asked you that."

"You did. It was actually the first thing you asked me, so don't worry. Look, it's fine, Seth apologised a few days later, and we haven't talked about it since." From the look in Jess' eyes right then, the whole thing was anything but fine.

"That's not an answer," Alexis prodded softly. Her free hand reaching out to squeeze Jess'.

"I know."

"Why haven't you told Aaron? He's not going to blame you for what happened."

Jess was quiet for a minute, and Alexis wondered if she was going to answer at all.

"At first, I didn't tell him because we'd just fixed things, and I didn't want to bring more drama into it. Then it just never felt like the right time, and the longer I waited, the worse it would be for me to tell him. Now I just want to forget about it."

Alexis could understand that. She didn't agree with it but she could understand.

"You said that Seth apologised?"

"Yeah, only after I ignored him for three days. Then he begged me not to tell anyone, especially you. I just told him to forget about it because I planned to. Then we never talked about it again. He's still really handsy whenever we're together, and it's just so awkward. I push him away and tell him to stop, but he doesn't get it. So I've just been trying to avoid being alone with him."

Alexis scoffed. That was Seth through and through. She wished that she'd known his true colours before ever getting involved with him.

"Why didn't you tell me? I would've run inter-ference, forced him to back off, something, anything. I could've broken his nose earlier."

Jess just smiled at her.

"I know that you would've. I didn't mean to keep it from you. Just every time I went to tell you, I chickened out."

Alexis nodded sympathetically. She knew that feeling all too well. For a year Alexis had been wanting to tell Jess about her thing with Seth, but it took him attacking her for her to suck it up and do it. Even then, she'd been getting over a panic attack.

"Lex, how are you doing?" Jess startled her from her thoughts.

"Me? I'm fine." A lie. Not much better than when Jess had said she was fine.

"What Seth did, nothing excuses that." Alexis remembered the way his breath had washed over her face, the stench of beer. She suspected that he would just say that he was drunk and didn't remember or was messing around. He'd never admit to it being what it was.

The two girls sat there, silently contemplating

their separate encounters with Seth's darker side, wondering how it was that they had missed the signs along the way.

Finally Alexis spoke the question that had been sitting at the back of her mind for longer than she wanted to admit.

"Why do we stay friends with people even when we know that they're toxic?"

CHAPTER 21

Lucas was waiting for Alexis. He'd been pacing the front entry for five minutes, peering through the windows every time he heard a noise outside. When at last he heard the unmistakeable sound of tyres on gravel and the slam of a car door he had the front door open before Alexis was halfway up the path.

It had been three days since he'd picked Alexis up from Aaron's party. Three days since she'd told him about her run in with Seth. She'd done a good job of calming him down before he dropped her off that night, but he'd woken up from a nightmare the next morning and beaten the boxing bag in the garage until his knuckles bled.

He should've been the one comforting her, and yet she was keeping him calm.

Every time he thought of Seth, of him pushing his

tiny - well tiny to him - girlfriend up against a door, trying to convince her to go back to him, the urge to beat Seth's face in had been his constant companion. Now though, Alexis was here.

Too impatient to wait for her to make it the last five metres to the door, Lucas went out to her, grabbing her up in a hug that had her feet leaving the ground. Her arms went around his shoulders, her face buried in his neck. The warmth of her breath against his skin drove him crazy in all the right ways. Just having her in his arms made every bad thing disappear. He knew that in his arms, she was safe.

"I missed you," she murmured the words against his neck, and he had to put her down before he did inappropriate things to her on the porch. Once she was on her own two feet he leant down and kissed her softly on the lips.

"I missed you too." The smile she gave him was like seeing the sun rise. He could've watched it all day.

"Come on, time for you to meet the parents."

When Alexis had been preparing herself to meet Lucas' parents, she at no point thought that she would be avoiding eye contact with her father's new head of security. Her mind was running a million miles a minute. How was this a thing that was happening at that very moment in time?

"Lex, this is my dad Andrew and my mum Louise."

Alexis shook their outstretched hands, looking at Andrew Peters for no more than a second.

"Hi Mr and Mrs Peters."

Louise laughed gently. "Oh, Alexis please, we don't stand on ceremony here, Andrew and Louise are fine."

Alexis had no idea what to do. Her two worlds were colliding in a way she'd never expected.

"Alright well if we're done having a party in the hallway, I'll give Lex a tour."

She had never been so grateful for someone's existence. Smiling awkwardly at Lucas' parents she followed him through to the rest of the house. She'd never had to deal with this kind of situation before.

If the people around you don't know that you know each other, then you don't know each other.

Her dad had told her that once. They'd gone to some party when she was little and a man that she'd seen at their house had walked right by them without even a glance. She'd asked her dad why his friend had ignored him, and he'd explained that sometimes the relationships within the Family were a secret. That was one of those times.

So is this.

Taking a deep breath Alexis adopted a state of calm and took in everything that Lucas was telling her. Eventually they crossed the threshold into a bedroom. As she was taking in the pictures on the bookshelf and the neatly displayed pop vinyls, Lucas shut the bedroom door. She didn't take much notice as he came up behind her, wrapping his arms around her waist. She was too busy studying one photo in particular.

It was a photo of the two of them at school. They were at one of the picnic benches that were scattered around the school for students to eat at. He was straddling the seat and she was between his legs, her back against his chest. Her head was resting against his shoulder, his arms around her. He was looking at her as if she was the most precious thing in the world. She didn't understand how he could feel that way about her. *Her*.

"Aaron took that photo and sent it to me. I liked it, so I got it printed and found a frame," Lucas explained, finally seeing what was holding her attention. She tore her eyes from the photo and turned in his arms, leaning back to look at his face.

"I love it."

Another feeling filled her heart, and she almost spoke the words out loud but choked them back at the last second. Lifting herself up onto her toes Alexis captured his mouth with hers. She poured all of those new feelings into the kiss, hoping that maybe that look in the photo was something Lucas really felt.

Alexis and Lucas spent the next half hour before dinner playfighting and making out. During their initial kiss Alexis had somehow tickled him, which was enough provocation for him to tickle her, not buying that hers had been an accident. When Louise called them for dinner Lucas had needed to take a minute before they left the room. Apparently he liked when they playfought. Alexis was not about to argue.

When they entered the dining room Alexis realised that the universe wasn't done surprising her for the night. Sitting there alone in the dining room across from two empty seats was Miss Peters, her new history teacher. Lucas didn't know that she knew his dad, but he definitely could've warned her about this. Looking up from the empty plate in front of her, Miss Peters beamed at them.

"Alexis, so nice to see you."

"Um, hi Miss Peters." The confusion in her voice made the teacher laugh softly.

"Outside of school it's Clare, I'm guessing that Lucas didn't mention that we're related," her smile was genuine and kind.

Alexis shook her head as she took her seat next to Lucas who had already occupied the seat across from his sister.

"Yeah I did," Lucas defended himself.

"Yeah no. You told me that you had an older sister.

That was it," Alexis glared at him, a hint of a smile on her lips.

"Ouch baby brother, you don't talk to me at school and now you're not telling your girlfriend about me. That's harsh."

The two girls shared a laugh at Lucas' expense. It had him wondering how it was that within seconds of officially meeting they were ganging up on him.

"So, are you going to introduce us properly or what?" Alexis poked him gently in the ribs for good measure. Watching him jerk away like he'd been zapped made it even better.

"Alexis, Clare. Clare, Alexis," Lucas said once he'd regained his composure. It was then that Louise and Andrew chose to enter the dining room, a dish in each hand.

"Well it sounds like you're all having fun," Louise said.

"Just torturing Lucas a little bit," Clare smiled innocently. Alexis sat quietly, suddenly nervous in front of Lucas' parents. It was not a feeling that she was fond of. As if he could sense her unease Lucas squeezed her thigh under the table, a comforting gesture that had her genuinely smiling.

She didn't know what she'd been honestly expecting from dinner with the Peters', but Alexis was glad that all the scenarios she'd thought up in her head had stayed just that, in her head. They'd spent the first few minutes of the meal passing dishes of food between each other, taking as little or as much as they wanted.

Clare told her about how she and Lucas had agreed to not tell people that they were brother and sister. The teachers knew and in the event that Lucas was put into one of Clare's classes then another teacher would mark his work to avoid any allegations of favouritism.

Alexis spent most of the dinner conversation directing all questions back to the Peters' family. She knew though that soon enough she'd have to answer questions about her own. Sure enough by the time dessert was brought out, Louise was determined to find out more about her son's girlfriend.

"So Alexis, what is it that your parents do? Lucas wasn't quite sure." Louise seemed genuinely interested. Alexis wondered if maybe she didn't know anything who her husband worked for.

"Um, my dad owns a construction company." Alexis glanced around, gauging everyone's reactions to see if there were any signs of disbelief. She'd made up a lot of occupations for her dad over the years, owning a construction business was the closest she'd ever actually come to the truth. That and ringleader.

Being the head of a mafia family could be a lot like running a circus sometimes.

"And what about your mum, what does she do?" This time it was Andrew who raised the question. It was almost like a challenge to come up with a more convincing lie.

"What doesn't she do?" Alexis chuckled softly and was joined by Louise.

"I hear that. Being a stay at home mum is definitely a full-time job. Or more like ten full time jobs rolled into one."

If only that was all her mum was.

Before any more questions could be thrown her way Alexis turned the tables.

"So Andrew what is it that you do." She hadn't meant for the accusatory tone to slip into her voice but it was there now.

"I run a private security company."

Alexis made herself appear more interested than she was. "That's must be interesting work. My dad actually just hired a new private security company for his business."

Andrew's tight-lipped smile said it all. She was toeing a fine line here. No one else at the table seemed to find her questions odd but Andrew knew.

Before any more questions could be asked, Lucas stacked his empty dessert bowl inside hers and excused them from the table. His parents let them go and Alexis wasted no time expressing her thanks for dinner before following closely behind Lucas.

AJ was waiting in the car outside. Lucas was in the

kitchen with his mum, and she was wrapping up some dessert for Alexis to take home with her. Clare had gone to bed early as she had plans to go for a dawn hike with some friends, to see the sun come up and all that. This left Alexis and Andrew in the foyer, staring each other down.

"My children don't know who I really am or who it is that I work for, and I'd like for it to stay that way."

There was something about his tone and the way he was looking at her, as though he was assessing a threat, that just rubbed Alexis the wrong way.

"Do you really think that they don't know or even suspect?" Alexis had her reasons to believe that Lucas at least had suspicions.

"I know that they don't. I've managed to keep my business life and my personal life separate, until now. If one day, God forbid, the truth comes out about your family, I don't want my kids knowing that I had anything to do with it."

"In case you weren't aware, people already suspect what my family is."

"Those are rumours, there's no factual proof that your parents have anything to do with the Family."

Alexis was getting fed up with all the beating around the bush. "What is it exactly that you want from me?"

"I don't want my kids anywhere near the Family and I'd appreciate it if you didn't try and get Lucas involved. I'd also appreciate it if you kept my business dealings with the Family to yourself as well."

"Look Mr Peters, you seem to be under the impression that I go around announcing my family status to everyone. I don't. My parents also tried to keep me as far from the Family as they could when I was growing up, but guess what, I've known who my dad was since I was six. So I wouldn't be at all surprised if Lucas knows more about your *business dealings* than you give him credit for."

Before Andrew had a chance to respond Lucas and Louise walked into the foyer, with Lucas carrying a plastic take away container with three pieces of the cheesecake that they'd had for dessert.

"Oh thank you so much. I'm sure mum and dad will love it."

"You're very welcome Alexis, it was an absolute pleasure to meet you."

After saying her goodbyes to his parents, Lucas walked her to the front door where he gave her an all too short kiss goodbye before escorting her out to the waiting car.

"You know you could've just kissed me goodbye here?"

Lucas gave her an incredulous look.

"Yeah... no. I still haven't met your parents and I don't need your driver telling them that I was being inappropriate before I have a chance to make a good impression."

Alexis opened her mouth to tell him that her mum

had already seen the hickey he'd left on her neck but quickly closed it again. No need for him to be freaking out the night before he met them.

CHAPTER 22

Knock knock.

Lucas turned in his desk chair to see his dad standing in the open doorway. The look on his face said that there was something bothering him.

"What's up dad?" His dad took a deep breath before he walked into the room, taking a seat at the end of Lucas' bed.

"So Alexis, how did you two meet exactly?" As normal as the question was, Lucas wasn't sure why it was making his dad so serious.

"At school, I thought you knew that."

"Yes, I did. What I meant was, did she pursue you, did someone introduce the two of you?"

Pursue him?

"We literally bumped into each other after class one day. I'd seen her around and in one of my classes, thought she was nice and cute, so I asked her out. What's this about dad?" Lucas didn't bother to hide his confusion.

"I don't think you should go to dinner over there tomorrow night."

Lucas might've thought it was a joke if it hadn't been for how dead set his dad looked. His own eyes narrowed as it dawned on him what was going through his dad's head.

"And why exactly is that dad?" He just needed him to confirm it. Needed him to say the words out loud.

"I think you can guess why I don't want you seeing her."

"Oh, so it's not just that you don't want me going to dinner, you don't want me seeing Alexis at all. Why don't you spell it out for me dad?" Lucas felt his body heating up, his blood roaring. When his dad didn't answer straight away Lucas decided to goad him into it.

"Could it be that she's Italian? Or maybe that she's not all that into sports? Oh, is it because she's a cat person?" There was a snideness in his voice that he had never dared use with his father until now.

"Don't act stupid Lucas, it's not a good look on you. And you can knock off that attitude while you're at it."

"Well then be straight with me *dad*, why is it that you don't want me seeing Alexis?"

"I think you can do better than her."

"That's crap, she's smart, gorgeous and amazing."

"Try thinking with the head on your shoulders."

With every non-answer from his father Lucas grew more and more frustrated. He knew that it was because of the rumours about the Angelo crime family. He also knew that if those rumours bothered his father that much, then he wouldn't be in business with Tony Angelo.

Taking a deep breath and holding it in his lungs, Lucas forced himself to calm down. If he was going to call his dad out then he needed to be smarter about it.

"Look, if you came in here to convince me to stop seeing Alexis, then the answer is no. You haven't given me any valid reasons for why we shouldn't be together, and I think that when it comes down to it, I'll be the one to decide what it is I deserve."

The muscle in his dad's jaw twitched.

For so long Lucas had gone along with everything his dad said. Done everything he was told and rarely questioned anything. He knew more about his father's secret life than he had ever let on. As far as Andrew Peters was concerned, his family was perfectly in the dark. The day Lucas had discovered the truth, it hadn't made sense. He'd only been ten at the time but then as he got older, more pieces of the puzzle fell into place.

Finally his dad got tired of staring him down and not getting any kind of reaction. He got up from the bed and walked to the door.

"You're grounded Lucas. You'll understand one day that I'm just doing what's best for you."

Before Lucas even had a chance to process the words that had been said – to think about the punishment that had been dished out without justification, his dad closed the door behind him. Lucas almost leapt from his chair, wanting to go after his dad, wanting to continue the argument, get him to reconsider the unjust grounding, but right now, that would only just make things worse.

Fuming, Lucas paced around his room, working out the best way to approach the situation. It was during his endless pacing that his mobile vibrated on the desk.

21.04 - *Home now and just crawling into bed. It was nice meeting your family. I'm going to make you pay for not warning me that our history teacher is your sister though. Night babe xx*

He knew that he should tell Alexis about what his dad said. He knew he needed to more than that he wanted to. Not to hurt her feelings in anyway, which he knew that it would, but because she deserved to know what it was that she was getting into. She should be prepared for the next time that she came over and had to deal with his dad's new attitude.

21.05 - *Night babe, have a good sleep xx*

Not tonight though. Tonight she would be able to sleep easy under the belief that his entire family had liked her. Tomorrow he'd tell her the truth.

CHAPTER 23

"Daddy, I have a favour to ask," Alexis said, leaning against the doorframe to her father's study. All night she'd been replaying her dinner with Lucas' parents and after what Lucas had told her this morning she kept coming to the same conclusion. Andrew Peters was going to try and kill her relationship with his son. She didn't want that to happen but she needed to figure out a way to stop him from interfering.

Then the answer came to her that morning over breakfast.

Tony looked up from his paperwork to see his daughter looking troubled. Straight away he was thinking of ways that he could make that look disappear. Unfortunately, his wife had already banned him from offering to buy Alexis a car whenever she was sad. Apparently, it was bad parenting and didn't actually solve the problem. He still felt like it had merit.

"What's wrong princess?" Tony asked gesturing for her to sit down. She took her usual spot in the armchair on the left, looking down at her hands the entire time. When she did finally speak, it was mumbled and Tony had to ask her to repeat herself.

"Lucas' dad doesn't want us to be together."

A part of Tony Angelo was glad to hear it. He didn't particularly want some hormone driven teenager pawing at his daughter either. There was bigger part though that felt angry for Alexis. Who was this man to decide that his daughter wasn't good enough?

"And why exactly is that?" Tony asked, pushing down the urge he had to do unpleasant things to the man.

"He wouldn't admit to it, but Lucas thinks it's because of the rumours about our family."

Tony was silent for a few moments while he thought about the best thing to say. While the rumours about their family were just that, rumours, there was still the fact that those rumours were true. Confirmed or not. Whatever this man thought he knew about their family, he was trying to protect his child and Tony couldn't fault him that. However he also remembered when he was a teenager and what he'd done when his parents had told him not to do something.

"And what, may I ask, are Lucas' thoughts on these

rumours about our family?"

While it wasn't an unexpected question, it just wasn't where Alexis thought her father was going to go.

"Um, he doesn't care what people say about us. He said that he knows what kind of person I am and if there's any truths to be told about our family then I'd tell him when I'm ready."

"He's a smart boy," Tony said, and he meant it. He wasn't unfamiliar with people's prejudices about the Mafia. They either wanted in, or they wanted to be as far from it and the people involved with it as possible. Even if those people were their closest friends once upon a time. So long as this kid meant what he said and didn't hurt his only child, then he would support their relationship.

"Do you want me to talk to his father?"

"Oh God, no! I was just wondering if you could be really nice to Luc tonight when he comes to dinner. I remember how you got when I was dating Marty, and yes Luc is smarter than Marty, but that's beside the point." Alexis thought about the last time she'd brought a boy home for dinner. Her dad had started showing him photos of his paper target from the last time they went to the archery range. Marty had just laughed and congratulated her dad on his tight grouping, completely missing the thinly veiled threat.

"Mmm, he wasn't my favourite," he mused, remembering when he'd had to hold back from calling him a moronic string bean. "I promise I'll be nice."

"Thank you daddy, I love you," and with that, Alexis instantly perked up. She blew her dad a kiss before practically skipping from the room.

CHAPTER 24

"What's this I hear about you not wanting our kids to date?"

"I meant no disrespect."

"Really? Because the way it looks is that you don't think my Alexis is good enough for your son."

"No! No, that's not it at all."

"Then what exactly is it."

"Clare is past the point of becoming involved, she's got a career. I'd hoped that Lucas would be the same way, stay in the dark about what my job really is and one day forge his own path completely separate to mine. But then he met your daughter and... I don't want him following in my footsteps."

"Are you unhappy with your position within the Family?"

"Tony please don't misunderstand me. We've been

friends for a very long time. This job, what I do, it's who I am. But... this life, the things we see, I don't want that for my boy, for either of my kids."

"What makes you think that Lucas is going to be drawn into this?"

"With all due respect, Alexis is *your* daughter."

"And you think that because she's my daughter, that automatically means that she's going to become involved with the Family." It was a statement of fact more than a question.

"Well isn't she?"

"Not if I can help it Andrew." He let his friend think over his words for a few moments. "Now why don't you just let the kids be happy. They're young, who knows if they'll even last the year."

"But-"

"Let me put it this way, if our kids are anything like us then they're going to do what they want and be together whether we like it or not, and it'll be a lot easier to keep an eye on them, make sure they're safe, if they're not having to hide their relationship. Don't you think?" Tony interrupted before Andrew could make any more arguments.

Andrew just nodded silently.

The message was clear.

He wouldn't interfere.

When Alexis walked Lucas downstairs the last thing either of them were expecting to see was both of their dads walking out of her father's office.

"Dad?"

"Dad?"

Both men turned towards the staircase where their kids stood confused.

"You didn't have to come inside, I was just on my way out," Lucas almost sounded embarrassed.

"Don't be silly, I was going to meet Alexis' dad sooner or later."

"Yeah, we had a great chat just now."

Alexis didn't miss the briefest of nods that her dad sent her way. He had sorted it out. Looking over at Lucas, Alexis saw his eyes narrowing slightly at what was unfolding in front of them. He was suspicious, which was understandable considering the conversation he'd had with his dad the night before.

"Right, well, we'll let you kids say goodnight. Hands where I can see them son."

Now it was her turn to be embarrassed by her father. With her face flaming Alexis grabbed Lucas' hand and led him to the front door.

"I'm so sorry, my dad can be so embarrassing when he wants to be," Alexis buried her face in Lucas' chest, his arms coming up to wrap around her.

"Lex, it's okay. Seriously. Your dad is cool, I like him. I'm also fully aware that he will kill me if I hurt you, but we all know that you'll do more damage to me first."

She could feel his mouth curve into a smile against her hair.

"Did you know?"

"Know what sweetheart?" Tony asked, looking up from the paperwork scattered across his desk.

"Did you know when we talked this afternoon that Andrew Peters was Lucas' dad?"

Tony thought back to their discussion that afternoon. Honestly when he had agreed to fix things, he hadn't known that the man he needed to sort things out with was his head of security.

"Did you know that Lucas is the spitting image of his dad when he was in high school?"

He could see that Alexis was about to tell him off for answering a question with a question, until she realised that his question was an answer. Just not the one she had been expecting.

"You've known him that long?"

"I have. We became friends in high school. He helped me out a few scraps, so I gave him a job. Then when he proved his loyalty to the Family, I gave him another one." He could practically see the clogs turning in his daughter's head.

"So he's a made man."

"No. I made the offer once, but he turned me down."

"Why?"

There was a hint of surprise that he had expected. Being a part of the Family had been his daughter's goal since she found out what he was. She'd never once shied away from it but then he supposed that she'd never really been exposed to the harsher realities of the mafioso. He'd shielded her so well the past few years, ever since she was old enough to truly understand what was going on. Ever since that day she'd snuck into the warehouse.

"He knew what the consequences were of being a part of the Family. The rewards are high, but so are the risks. For Andrew, the risks outweighed whatever reward he might get. By remaining an associate, he isn't bound by an oath to the Family. He helps us of his own free will, and he can leave whenever he wants."

"But he's not under our protection."

Tony fought to control the cringe at the way she said *our*, as though she were already a part of the Family.

"You're right in a way. His refusal of the oath means that he's not a made man which in turn means that he and his family are not protected by our code. However, he is also my oldest living friend. I would never leave such a friend unprotected and in case you've forgotten, he is the head of his own security company."

Alexis was quiet for a moment. He gave her time to

absorb what he'd said. Her knowledge of their codes both terrified him and gave him a rush of pride. He had been exposed to this life his entire childhood. There had been no doubt in his mind that he would one day head the Family. When he and Carmen had found out they were pregnant, Tony had daydreamed about teaching his son this way of life.

Maybe it was that desire alone that qualified him as being a terrible parent. Maybe it was those thoughts that had prompted the universe to take his son away from him before he even had a chance to live.

His wife's face had lit up like New Year's fireworks when he put Alexis in her arms that first time. She'd had to have an emergency c-section and had been unconscious when Tony came into her hospital room with the small bundle of perfection in his arms. It had been the look on her face, that look which had decided Alexis' fate for him. He couldn't allow her to become a part of this circle of violence.

Every time he thought about it, Tony had to remind himself that he loved his life. All those years learning from his father and uncles, working his way through the lower ranks, earning his button, taking the oath. The day he took his father's place was one of the worst days of his life. It was also one of the best. Not wanting to dwell on the memory of his father's death, Tony restarted the conversation with Alexis.

"So, how's your training with mum going?"

"Yeah, really good."

He didn't miss the way she absentmindedly rubbed her right upper arm through her shirt sleeve. Ever since the weekend she'd been wearing tops with long sleeves despite the weather still being quite warm.

"Is everything okay?" He watched her face carefully, waiting for any sign that things were amiss.

"Everything's fine."

There, a slight hitch in her voice. She'd gotten better at schooling her face into an unreadable mask, but her voice still gave her away every time. He looked her over from across the desk. She looked a bit tired, but then again, she was going to bed late the past few nights. He couldn't see any injuries but she had covered almost every inch of skin.

"Sweetheart, you'd tell me if something had happened wouldn't you? If anything was wrong?"

The glint in her eyes was all the answer he needed and it took all the control he had to not explode in rage. She'd gotten better at hiding her emotions, but she wasn't an expert. He had to let her come to him though, if he pushed too hard, she wouldn't tell him anything again.

"Daddy, with all the training that mum has given me, in the event that something did happen, then I can and would take care of it myself."

He opened his mouth to object but she cut him off.

"Besides, what would you do? Put out a hit on

a teenager?" The mocking smirk on her lips made Alexis look just like her mother.

"Fine, but if anyone who isn't a teenager does something to hurt you, then you let me know." An order from father to daughter.

"Yes, dad. Any one of legal age is fair game for you," she rolled her eyes. She didn't believe that he would do anything. She was wrong.

He didn't need to know.

She kept repeating the words to herself with every step she took towards her bedroom. He didn't need to know what Seth had done. What he'd tried to do. Her dad didn't need to know. Besides, she was fine, things could've ended so much worse than they did.

She was fine.

Maybe if she kept telling herself that then it would be true.

CHAPTER 25

Lucas didn't know what to think when he got into the car with his dad. He'd been expecting a lecture for sneaking out of the house, granted it had been with his mum's help since his dad had hidden his car keys. However, his dad just asked him questions about dinner.

"Dad what's with the sudden one-eighty?"

"What are you talking about?"

"Last night you wanted me to never see Alexis again, now you're interested, what gives?"

His mum had told him that she'd tried to reason with his father the night before but nothing had come of their conversation. So Lucas had been sure to be out of the house before his dad got home.

He knew more about the Angelo Family than his dad gave him credit for. Though it was probably for the best that his dad stayed in the dark about the extent of his knowledge about organised crime families. Lucas had known for years just how involved his own dad was. He was content to let his dad think that he'd successfully pulled the wool over the eyes of his entire family.

At least he had been until he met Alexis. From the first moment he saw her, Lucas knew that she had the ability to change his world. It could either be for the better or for worse. So far she had made everything better, though he knew the reality of relationships. Something was going to go wrong eventually but he felt like they were strong enough to survive whatever the universe threw at them.

While Lucas didn't know the position Tony Angelo held within the Angelo Family, he had the same suspicions as everyone else. The difference was he didn't care what Alexis' father did. He only cared about her. When his own dad had sat on his bed and told him he couldn't see his girlfriend anymore, Lucas had wanted to yell at him that he was a hypocrite.

But that would've meant admitting that he knew everything from his father's involvement to Alexis'.

CHAPTER 26

When Brennan finally found Seth the first morning back at school, he was ready for a fight. "Did you have sex with Alexis?"

"What?"

"Did you have sex with Alexis?"

"Bren, it's not what you think."

"Just answer the fucking question Seth!"

"No!"

"Bullshit! You've been hiding shit for months and so has she. You're always jealous when some other guy talks to her, even me. Everyone knows Seth. Everyone fucking knows what you did."

Brennan just glared at Seth as he sputtered to make up some new lie. He'd known that there was something going on. He could never prove it. The way Seth watched Alexis when he thought no one was watching him. The jealousy he saw whenever she was laughing with another guy. He had feelings for her.

Brennan knew what Seth was like. He knew that Seth would hit on anyone without a Y chromosome. Had he really been stupid enough to think that Seth would not hook up with their friend's ex-girlfriend.

Not wanting to waste any more time around Seth and his lies, Brennan left. He walked through the school towards the trade centre, anger slowly building inside him.

With every step he took he thought of another sign he'd missed.

With every step he wondered how he could've been so stupid.

With every step he wondered what was wrong with him.

With every step he hated Alexis and Seth more.

With every step he wished that Alexis had chosen him.

Someone called his name when he walked through the trade centre doors. He ignored them. There was a storm going on inside his head and he couldn't think straight. Every new thought joined the haze of old thoughts, all jumbling together until they were non-sensical.

With every thought he unwittingly brought himself closer to a break down.

He'd never seen Alexis and Seth *together*, but that didn't mean they hadn't been.

Against his better judgement Brennan started wondering about where the two had hooked up. Had it been at school? At parties? His house or hers? Then a memory hit him.

Their year ten camp the year before had been held on Rottnest Island. One night they'd been hanging out in one of their cabins, and Seth and Alexis had a huge argument. She'd stormed off. He'd run after her. Seth had just sat there on the couch looking both angry and full of regret.

He had looked for Alexis for half an hour, but she'd kept herself hidden somehow. Seth had finally come out of the cabin and joined the search for her. Brennan had just gotten back to the house to check if Alexis had returned. He'd seen the whole thing unfold from the darkness of the porch.

Seth had called out her name and just like that she'd appeared from the shadows, walking towards him with only slight hesitance. Once she was close enough Seth had pulled her into his arms and she'd just melted against him. It was there in the way they held each other. Brennan hadn't thought much of it at the time.

He wondered if that had been when it started. It certainly didn't look like that was where it had ended.

How could they do this?

How could she do this?

Seth was a guy, one that didn't have any kind of self-control. If a girl showed interest in him then he was hooked.

Alexis knew better. Alexis should've been better.

It was in that moment that Brennan realised something else. Something that sent him flying into a new rage. Somehow he had walked to the locker room. His fist made contact with the small metal door closest to him.

They knew.

They'd known for months.

Alexis had been annoyingly insistent during that Rottnest trip that the two of them were best friends. She had kept telling him how he was one of her best friends.

Best friends.

He'd almost lost his shit with her one night. Every time she called him her best friend it was another slice at his heart. But now he understood why she'd repeated herself so many times.

Brennan had confessed to Seth one night that he thought he had feelings for Alexis. They'd all been hanging out so much lately and he felt more comfortable around her than he had anyone else before. A few weeks later they'd gone to Rottnest and he'd forgotten all about their conversation.

Seth hadn't forgotten though. Seth had told Alexis about his feelings and must've told her to let him down easy. God he'd wanted her to shut up so badly. And then he'd felt horrible for being angry with her.

He didn't feel horrible now.

Well he did. Just not about being angry at his best friends.

Ex.

Ex-best friends.

Best friends wouldn't have gone behind his back like that, lying for however long they were going at it. They betrayed him. They betrayed Marty. He doubted either of them would care about Marty's feelings though. But right then in that moment, Brennan felt like Marty was his only friend in the world. The only person who had never betrayed him.

So now Brennan would be a good friend to Marty. He'd tell Marty what had happened before he heard it from someone else. Marty and Seth weren't exactly good friends. They only really hung out because they were in the same friend group.

As for Alexis, Marty had been holding a grudge against her ever since she broke up with him. He'd told Brennan once that after they broke up he saw her true colours.

Brennan supposed that now he had too.

CHAPTER 27

Seth was furious. The secret was out and he was certain that Alexis had been the one to spill it. She was always running her mouth about something. Commenting on things that weren't her business to comment on. So what if the girl he liked had a boyfriend? Jess and Aaron weren't going to be together forever and when they did break up, he would be there for her like he had been since he met her.

Alexis was just trying to ruin his chances with Jess. That was it. She was jealous that Jess spent more time with him than with her and she was trying to ruin it. Everything always had to be about her.

Alexis had actually asked him once if he had been thinking about Jess while they were hooking up, if he wished it had been her friend instead. He had refused to answer, knowing that truth would likely end things between them.

It wasn't that he hadn't liked Alexis, he did. She was feisty and hot. The first time he'd hit on her, he hadn't even known who she was. A few months later she'd been dating Marty and all of a sudden he was the bad guy. The terrible friend who had a thing for his oldest friend's girl.

So he'd tried to move on. It was during the three months that Alexis and Marty had been dating that Seth and Brennan started hanging out with Jess more. It was summer break and Aaron was off working one of those fruit picking jobs with his friends. It was character building or some bullshit like that. And that was when it had happened. When he'd fallen for Jess.

Now both the girls he had a thing for, had boy-friends. Until one of them didn't. Marty had been pretty bitter about his relationship with Alexis when she broke up with him. Seth had been a shoulder to cry on and just like that his crush on her was back. Conveniently at the same time that Aaron came back from the orchards and Jess was once again unavailable.

Alexis hung out with him and Brennan more and more. And whenever Brennan had to leave early or couldn't come at all, Seth was still there with Alexis. They had danced around their attraction to each other for weeks. It was like a game of chicken. Eventually he couldn't take it anymore and he'd kissed her. She'd kissed back. They'd agreed to keep it a secret for a little while. Her and Marty had only broken up a few months before then and he was still sensitive about the whole thing.

Then Brennan had confessed that he liked Alexis, and Seth knew that whatever their relationship was, it could never get out. His life would be ruined. They even tried breaking it off at different points but they'd given into their hormones time and time again.

There was one thing that Alexis and Seth had agreed on though, no one could know about them.

Had he been dying to tell someone that he'd hooked up with Alexis Angelo? God yes. Before Brennan had confessed to his own feelings, it had taken all of Seth's will power not to blurt out the truth.

Clearly, Alexis had no such will power.

Seth spotted her as she walked by the dark hallway he was waiting in. Alexis was a creature of habit so it wasn't hard for him to pinpoint where she'd be at a particular time of day.

"Alexis," he called out. She turned towards him, her wariness clear on her face. He had reigned in his anger before waiting for her. He knew that if she felt threatened from the start then she wouldn't agree to talk to him, then he wouldn't be able to get her to admit that she'd told people about them.

When she'd finally stepped into the hallway, he led her further down towards a dead-end of locked doors to rooms that no one used anymore.

He could see her eyes darting back and forth like a cornered animal. He took that as her first admission of guilt. After all, if she hadn't spilled their secrets then she wouldn't have any reason to be nervous around him. The wary look she was giving him made him even more certain that she was guilty.

"What's up Seth?"

"So I heard something today," he paused, watching her face, "about you and me." There it was. The slightest pursing of her lips, the eye roll she couldn't contain even if she tried. He waited for her to say something, anything to defend herself or even give herself away.

"Who did you tell?" he felt the mask slip from his face, his eyes hardening, his mouth turning into a sneer.

A fire sparked in Alexis' blood. He was blaming her for their secret getting out. Jess had been the first to tell her that the secret was out. She'd also been the first to promise that she hadn't spilled the beans.

Things had come so close to ending badly for her after Seth's antics at Aaron's party two weeks ago. When the adrenaline had worn off, she had been a mess, something she was once again feeling while standing in the hallway. A hallway that Alexis couldn't help but notice was far too dark and secluded for her liking.

"For fucks sake Alexis, just admit that you told someone." Seth took a step towards her, forcing her to tilt her head back to look him in the eyes. The bruising from his broken nose was still there, faint, but there.

"I don't have to admit anything to you."

"We both promised that we wouldn't tell anyone."

"We also both promised that we'd end things before hooking up with someone else. Who broke the promise first, huh Seth?" she could see the anger building in his eyes, the way he clenched his jaw.

"Seriously, you told everyone about us because I hooked up with Anna? Grow up."

"Jesus, you're a dumb shit. You actually think I wanted everyone to know about us?" Maybe once upon a time - yes, but things had changed. While there were still too many secrets between Alexis and Lucas for things to be perfect, she was actually happy now.

"You don't want me with Jess. That's why. You're jealous and selfish and don't want us to be happy together, so you had to try and ruin it."

Oh God, he's actually lost his mind.

"Whatever you think you and Jess had, it was all in your head. Her and Aaron aren't breaking up any time soon and even if they did, you're the last person she'd end up with." She knew her words would cut deep. She knew they'd make him angry. The adrenaline was running through her blood so hard that she'd forgotten about being afraid of what he might do. What he'd tried to do.

"She kissed me, but I bet you didn't know that."

"Yeah she told me about what happened after I left that night, all of it. I wonder how interested people would be in knowing that you took advantage of a passed out drunk girl." Blood pounded in her ears and she didn't give him a chance to say anything before she continued.

"Get it through to that rock you have for a brain, I'm not the reason that our secret got out. You seem to have forgotten that shit you pulled at Aaron's party. Most of our year was at that party. Don't you think that maybe someone saw you pull me into that room against my will? Saw me run away. Saw you stumble out with a broken nose. Maybe other people aren't as willing to stay quiet," she ground her final words out through clenched teeth. Just mentioning the events of that night had her heart pounding, setting her blood on fire like it was gasoline.

Seth was quiet for a few moments as they glared at each other. The moment he sucked in air, she knew that what was about to come out of his mouth would be idiotic.

"I swear to God Alexis, if you don't deny everything between us and stop telling people that I *took advantage* of Jess then I'll-" Seth cut himself off, but Alexis sneered as she egged him on.

"You'll what, Seth?"

"I'll tell everyone that those rumours about you being a spoilt mafia princess aren't just rumours."

He didn't disappoint. For once.

Alexis bowed her head. Her shoulders started to shake. He probably thought she was crying. Until she lifted her head and laughed in his face. It was a sadistic laugh that promised nothing good.

It was his turn to look at her like she'd lost her mind. But no, it wasn't her mind she'd lost, it was her patience. Her patience for Seth's bullshit had been limited to begin with and now it was non-existent. Her laughter stopped and her eyes turned to steel.

"You stupid fuck. You actually think for a second that you can blackmail me? You've got nothing on me Seth. The only one who matters is Lucas and he knows everything about us, about me. And let me just put this out there – if I were a *spoilt mafia princess* as you put it, then it would be pretty goddamn brain-dead of you to threaten me. Don't you think?"

Her words seemed to give him pause, made him backtrack and realise that he'd just ruined any and all chances of getting her to agree to help him.

"Fine, but what about Brennan, this hurts him too. He wouldn't believe me when I told him that the rumours are wrong. You know how he feels about you. If you don't convince him that they're lies then he'll hate us both." Seth was grasping at straws now. Anything he thought might convince her to lie for him again.

"You know, you didn't seem all that concerned about Brennan's feelings when you had your tongue down my throat and your hand up my skirt."

Without another thought, Alexis turned and walked away from him. She saw the anger building in him again as he realised he'd lost.

The last straw had broken.

CHAPTER 28

The warehouse was dark and cold. It was actually warmer outside, which wasn't at all surprising since the heating had been turned off months ago. Another torture tactic.

"Mum?"

Silence.

"Mum, are you here?"

Her mum was meant to be here. She'd promised. It was her sixteenth birthday. They were meant to be at the restaurant in an hour.

"Alexis..." That wasn't her mum's voice sing song-ing her name from the darkness.

"Hello?"

Alexis stepped further into the warehouse her mind conjuring an endless stream of horrible things she might find.

"Who's there?" she called out. She waited but the voice didn't speak again. Alexis kept going. Step by step the darkness felt like it was getting denser, more suffocating.

She had to find her mum.

The floor beneath Alexis' feet became wet... and sticky. The suddenness of the change made her start, almost falling. She didn't dare crouch down to feel the floor, to try and figure out what was making it wet. She had a feeling she didn't want to know.

"You came," the Voice spoke again. It echoed through the dark and empty warehouse.

"Who are you?" Her own voice was calm, even. She had no fear to feel. How? She didn't know and she didn't question it.

"Your mother said you would be joining us. I'm glad to see she wasn't wrong. Though it does make all of this a bit awkward," the Voice said.

"She does know me best, you should've listened," she replied. Where was all of this confidence coming from? How was she standing up to something that she couldn't even see?

"Yes, I suppose we should've. However, maybe if you'd gotten here sooner there might've been at least one for you to leave with."

Alexis was suddenly confused. What had the Voice meant by us and what were these ones she was meant to have left with? Before she could voice the questions swirling around in her mind the Voice *spoke again.*

"Everyone tried so hard to protect you and in the end they all paid the price."

"What are you talking about?"

"This!"

With a snap the warehouse lit up with a thousand lights. The sudden brightness blinded Alexis. When her eyes finally adjusted, she wished the lights had never come on.

Panic bubbled up inside of her, a scream rising in her throat.

Blood.

So much blood.

All around her were bodies.

Her friends.

Her cousins.

Lucas.

Her mum.

They were all dead.

Alexis bolted upright in bed a scream bursting from her lips. Slapping a hand over her mouth she felt the wetness on her cheeks. Her heart was beating so hard she thought it might break through her rib cage.

"Lex!"

"Bambina!"

She heard her parents running down the hallway but she couldn't move. Within seconds they were both bursting into her room.

"Alexis," her mum breathed a sigh of relief. She wanted to turn to her, but all she could do was sit there shaking, with tears running down her face.

It had been so real. The blood, the bodies, everything. The faceless man. The man.

Oh god.

She remembered the faceless man. In the seconds before she woke he was the last thing that she'd seen. He was tall and bald, dressed in a suit but that was it. His face had been like a doll's before the features are painted on.

"Sweetheart, it's okay. Everything is okay," her mum soothed her. She could feel her dad's hand stroking her hair, her mum sitting beside her, holding her shaking body.

"What happened?" Alexis tried to speak, to explain. When she opened her mouth though, no words came out. Once she'd taken a few deep breaths to calm down, she started to feel stupid. It had just been a dream but she'd screamed like she was being attacked. She'd scared her parents for nothing.

"Nothing. It was just a bad dream. I'm sorry." She didn't dare meet their eyes. She felt ashamed that she'd let her subconscious shake her so wholly.

"Do you want to talk about it?"

Shaking her head Alexis just leant more into her

mum's embrace. Looking over at her dad they locked eyes and she could see the understanding. She knew in that moment that while his nightmares might be different, they had the same outcome.

Death.

Blood.

Loss.

Being alone.

"I think I'm just going to try and get back to sleep."

"Do you want us to stay with you until you fall asleep?"

In that moment she was four years old again and she almost accepted the offer.

Almost.

"Thanks mum, but I'll be okay. I don't even remember what it was I dreamt about," Alexis lied. She didn't think she'd ever be able to forget the sight of her mother's lifeless body. Or her friends. Later on, when she woke again from a sweet dreamless sleep, she might wonder about why her dad hadn't been a part of the carnage in the warehouse.

With one last tight hug from each of her parents, they said their goodnights and their 'I love you's.

Before the bedroom door shut completely her dad poked his head back through.

"Happy birthday *bambina*."

CHAPTER 29

When Alexis awoke hours later, the nightmare that had her screaming into the night was little more than a fuzzy memory. That is until she went downstairs for breakfast and her parents asked if she was feeling better. It was then that she remembered the horrors her subconscious had conjured.

"Yeah, I'm fine. Just a bad dream I guess," she said looking down at the breakfast in front of her. Raspberry and white chocolate pancakes with whipped cream. Her mum only made them on special occasions claiming they were too unhealthy to have all the time. Alexis didn't mind, it meant whenever they were made she enjoyed them all the more. Her parents were unusually quiet as she dug into her pancakes, probably exchanging looks about her.

"So, guests won't be arriving until four-ish so what

are your plans for the day?" her mum asked.

"Um nothing really, help set up and then get ready."

"You don't need to worry about that, everything is about ready to go, we just need to put the snacks out on the tables before people arrive. Dinner will be ready by six-thirty because God forbid your aunts eat any later than that. There's nothing else for you to do except relax and get yourself ready."

"But-" Alexis tried to argue but was quickly cut off by her dad.

"Lex, it's your birthday. Your sweet sixteen. With everything that's been going on lately you've handled it better than most your age. Your mum and I are really proud of you. Just let today be about you okay."

"Why don't you ask the girls to come over early? You can watch movies in the theatre room. Your dad will make popcorn and I'll make some mocktails and then you can get ready together."

Alexis thought about her mum's suggestion and it didn't sound so bad. When she went to bed last night she'd been more than ready to just help out all day with party set up. She hadn't even thought to ask her parents if she could spend the day doing something else before people arrived.

"Are you sure?"

"Oh my God, if you don't call them, your mother will."

Holding her hands up in defeat Alexis agreed to

message the girls after she finished breakfast.

Half an hour later Alexis had tidied up her bedroom and deposited more blankets and pillows in the theatre room than was strictly necessary. She'd had her outfit for the night picked out for two weeks and practised her make up a dozen times just so she knew that she could get it right when it mattered. Everything was ready for when the girls arrived.

When Alexis sent out the messages to her friends, she hadn't been expecting either of them to actually be free at this late notice. She was happily surprised when they both replied that they were. Jess was already on her way and Em was coming soon with her dad. Apparently their dads had matters to discuss. It took all of her self-control to keep her nose out of it. Her curiosity could wait to be satiated until tomorrow.

Within the hour the three girls were sitting on the floor of the theatre room atop the pillows and blankets Alexis had brought down. There was a chick flick playing in the background that none of them were paying any attention to. They were all more interested in talking about the party and in particular who was coming.

"Is Seth still invited?" Jess asked.

"While I never formally rescinded his invite, he'd

be stupid to actually show up. Besides, we haven't actually spoken since he tried to blackmail me."

"Let's keep in mind that this is Seth and stupid is his default setting," Em piped in, her words dripping in sarcasm.

"Exactly. What are you going to do if he does show up? Wouldn't he be coming with Brennan anyway?" Jess pointed out.

"As it is, I'd be surprised if Brennan showed up. He was barely speaking to me before. Since he found out about Seth and me, he's avoided me like the plague. I don't know if we're actually even friends anymore."

On the one hand, Alexis knew that Brennan was never going to be okay with her relationship with Lucas, but on the other hand she missed him.

She didn't dare to hope that he showed up tonight just in case wishing too hard jinxed it.

"Right... well... anyways... if Seth does show up then I have a plan," Alexis announced, breaking herself from her musings.

"Are you going to let us in on the plan?" Jess asked.

Em just shook her head, mostly to herself. Alexis would only tell them her plan if they were necessary for the execution.

"You'll just have to wait and see. Besides, he might not even show up."

◆◆◆

The party was in full swing. There was still a half hour until dinner but everyone looked like they were enjoying themselves. Lucas had barely left her side since he arrived, looking hot as hell in his semi-formal attire which included a tie. Em and Alexis had shared looks of approval. Alexis' hormonally charged body wanted nothing more than to sneak Lucas into her bedroom and lock the door behind them.

Jess, who knew exactly what Alexis was thinking, sent her own look of approval. That was until she spotted Brennan entering the backyard over Alexis' shoulder.

Alexis, noticing the change in expression, turned around. The gate shut with a click behind Brennan. He came alone. She wasn't sure if she was shocked or not. She wasn't even sure if she was happy about Brennan coming. Just because he showed up didn't mean that they were friends again. She needed to know where they stood.

"Luc, Brennan just got here. I'm going to go say hi."

Lucas was all too aware of his girlfriend's inner turmoil. She couldn't take back what she'd done, and while it hadn't ended well, he didn't think that she

304

wanted to. They'd had a long discussion about past and future choices and the impact they had on forming the person one becomes.

Alexis had been quite adamant that there was no point regretting her choices thus far in her life since they had been what shaped her now. She knew better than she did a year ago and she didn't plan on making the same mistakes. If she'd never made the choice to pursue things with Seth, who was to say that she would've been ready to be in a relationship with Lucas. All of her choices might've been different.

When she'd said that to him, Lucas couldn't help but think about his own choices and wonder the same thing. Would she have chosen him? He had known from the moment he saw her that he wanted to know her. He hoped that his charm and wit would've been enough, but maybe she was right.

As he watched her cross the backyard to greet her maybe-friend, Lucas scanned the faces of the rest of the guests, his gaze always landing back on Alexis. That was until it didn't. Lucas was on the move the second it registered. Brennan was still standing where Alexis had left him, looking towards the house. Lucas fought the urge to look – he needed to find FJ.

❖ ❖ ❖

Alexis' confusion about Brennan's presence was short-lived. From the second she got there, he had been standoffish and distant. It was like he didn't even want to be there. He'd mumbled a happy birthday and just shrugged or gave one-word answers to every question she asked. By the fourth shrug and sixth one syllable answer, Alexis was ready to snap.

"Bren, seriously, is this how things are going to be from now on?"

He finally made eye contact with her, the first time in weeks. She almost wished that he hadn't. She could see the hurt, but she could also see the disgust. He was disgusted by her.

"I think you know the answer to that Lex, after all you are the one who hooked up with my best friend."

"In case you've forgotten, he hooked up with me too. I'm sorry that I hurt you Brennan. I never meant to do that. But I am not the only one at fault here."

"Yeah, I'm pissed at Seth too."

"I'm not talking about that. I'm talking about the fact that ever since I started seeing Lucas, you've been a shit friend. I understand and accept you being mad about Seth and me, but you've been holding a grudge since before you found out about that. I wanna know why."

It was clear by the expression on his face that he hadn't been expecting that particular line of accusation.

"Because – because you ditched us for him. As soon as you got a boyfriend you didn't have time for me anymore."

Alexis scoffed. "That's bullshit and you know it. I tried for weeks to hang out with you outside of school. You would always tell me that we could hang out if you didn't end up doing something with the guys. And when I finally did get you to lock in a time for us you cancelled last minute. Literally last minute. I was waiting outside of the movie theatre for you, tickets in hand as the movie started inside and you messaged me to say you couldn't come."

"Yeah and I'm sure you just called Lucas to come and see it with you."

"No Brennan, I didn't. I went home. I still have the tickets in my room."

Brennan actually looked taken aback. Alexis forced the tears springing to her eyes to stay put. She was determined not to shed a tear in front him. He didn't deserve that kind of satisfaction.

"I am sorry about what happened with Seth. I can't take it back. I will not apologise for my feelings for Lucas or the fact that I just don't feel that way about you. No one can control who they fall for. I loved you like the best friend you were meant to be and that wasn't enough for you I get that-"

"You knew!" Brennan interrupted. He practically spat the words at her.

"Knew what?" Alexis asked, though she had a sinking suspicion what the what was.

"You knew that I liked you, and you hooked up with Seth anyway." And there it was. The first time that Brennan himself had actually admitted out loud to her that he had romantic feelings for her and they were said in anger.

"Yes and no. I didn't know when things first started. I only found out a couple of months in, and you wanna know who told me? Seth. Seth was the one to tell me that you had feelings for me, he was the one to say that we should end things between us, he was also the one to start them back up again."

She waited for him to digest what she'd told him. Later she would think about how she'd just put a nail in the coffin that was Seth and Brennan's friendship. She would also be able to acknowledge that Seth was the one who built the coffin to begin with.

"I don't believe you. Seth would never do that to me." But he did believe her. She could see it. There was a reason that they'd been best friends, she could read him like a book.

"You know wh- What is he doing here?"

Brennan turned to see who Alexis was referring to. Seth.

"Happy birthday, Alexis."

Alexis walked away from Brennan, his smug words ringing in her ears. He'd brought Seth here, helped him sneak in. *It's okay, you had a plan in place for this... remember?* The voice in her head that sounded like her mum was right. She did have a contingency plan for if Seth showed up. She reached into the pocket of her dress feeling for her phone. If anything happened, help was just a phone call away.

He followed her through the crowd up to the house. He was far enough back that she wouldn't be able to tell he was following her. When he got to the side door he saw how she'd left it open. Not by much, but enough, almost like subconsciously she wanted to be followed.

He thought that he'd have to wait for her to get out of the toilet for them to be able to talk, but she wasn't in the powder room and the door that led to the rest of the house was open. She couldn't have gotten too far into the house. He was only a dozen steps behind her.

When he got to the hallway, he listened out for any sounds of movement, any sign of where she might've gone. Moving down the hallway he saw a lamp on in the living room. He could hear voices coming from the kitchen, all of them women, none of them were Alexis. It did occur to him that she might still be in there and just not talking, and if that were the case then he'd just wait for her.

The sound of a door closing came from his left. He headed for it. He could hear heels on the wood floors. He knew her footsteps when he heard them.

As he turned into the hallway, he saw the back of her turning into a room at the end of the hall. The door closed softly behind her, but it didn't matter. He'd found her.

Standing in front of the door, he had to take a moment to ready himself. He wasn't entirely sure what it was that he had been expecting by coming to the party. It had been so long since they'd talked or had a proper conversation.

He was ready to forgive her for the things she'd said. The things she did.

He opened the door.

He wasn't sure what he'd been expecting to see when he walked into the room, but it hadn't been Alexis standing there in the theatre room, her arms crossed as she looked him dead in the eyes.

"Hello Seth."

Truth be told, Alexis hadn't really believed that Seth wouldn't show. He wanted everyone to believe that nothing had gone on between them. If he didn't show up to her party then people would know that something had gone down and no amount of denying it would keep them from believing that they had a history.

While she wasn't at all surprised that he'd followed her into the house, she hadn't necessarily thought he would do it. When she'd gone through the side door, she'd just been going to try and steal some food from the kitchen and maybe sneak a mouthful of her mum's wine. Then she'd seen him making his way through the crowd in her periphery. Maybe he was going to talk to someone else?

Nope.

As she turned to close the sliding door, she saw him heading straight for her. He was too focused on easing past people that he hadn't seen her hesitate at the door. Yes, she had a plan in place for if he showed up, but she hadn't expected to execute it just yet.

That didn't matter anymore. Time to put it in action. Alexis made her way through the house, slipping her phone from her pocket. It took her longer to find the person she wanted to text than it did to actually write the message.

Theatre room. Five minutes.

Seth wasted forty-five seconds of that time in the living room. She had to quietly open the door next to her and then close it loudly just so he knew which direction to go. Not wanting to waste any more time she headed down the hallway to the theatre room, not daring to look back to check if he was following. She didn't have to wait long to know that he had.

The door opened, causing the light to spill out into the hallway.

"Hello Seth."

"Happy birthday Lex," he smiled at her like he used to, back when they had a secret that was just theirs. Last year she might've fallen for it.

"What are you doing here Seth?"

"You invited me, remember?"

"Was me breaking your nose not clear enough. Or how about the last conversation we actually had. You remember, at school, the hallway. Someone smart would realise that all of those things added up to no longer being invited."

"Yeah see, you say all of that, but if you really didn't want me to come tonight then you could've had someone else tell me. I think you want me here because you miss me."

"You're disgusting."

"You're playing hard to get."

"Are you serious right now? Do you honestly believe that after everything, I would actually want to be with you?"

"Well Brennan already knows about us, not like he's going to forgive either of us anytime soon so why not keep going?"

"Maybe because I have a boyfriend, you disgust me, oh and I don't want to."

"Careful Lex, after all, I am in your house, with all of your friends outside. Imagine what I could find and show them as proof that you're part of one of the biggest crime families on the West Coast."

"No Seth, I think you're the one who wants to be careful, because I have a recording of you trying to blackmail me to stay quiet about what you did to Jess."

Seth's eyes widened for a second before narrowing dangerously.

"You're lying."

"Oh really, you think so?" Alexis unlocked her phone and brought up the recording of that conversation and pressed play.

"Who did you tell? For fucks sake Alexis just admit that you told someone."

"I don't have to admit anything to you."

"We both promised that we wouldn't tell-"

She paused the recording, not needing to go through the entire thing to prove her point.

"You stupid bitch, you recorded us?"

"Of course I did, you think that after Aaron's party I wasn't going to protect myself?"

"Look I'm sorry for what happened, I was drunk, and I missed you."

"You tried to force yourself on me."

"I was drunk!"

"That doesn't make it better, Seth. If you kill someone when you're drunk, you still killed someone. You don't get away with it because you were drunk."

"Funny that you of all people would bring up murder, considering your family's history."

"Get out of my house."

"Not till you delete that recording."

"Yeah that's not going to happen." The words had barely left her mouth when he lunged for her. Or tried to at least. With all of their arguing, Seth hadn't heard someone coming down the hallway and he hadn't noticed when that someone stood behind him.

FJ had appeared while she'd been playing the recording. It had taken all her self-control not to look at him and give away that he was there. She hadn't really wanted anyone else to know about what was going on but she knew that FJ would keep her secrets, it's why she messaged him in the first place.

Seth struggled against the arm around his throat. He was tall but whatever extra weight he carried was just baby fat that he had yet to shed. FJ was two years older and had real muscle plus he was a trained fighter. Seth had no idea who or what hit him, literally, and the more he struggled, the tighter FJ's grip got.

"Seth, you made a mistake coming here tonight, and you made an even bigger one following me into my own house. You just couldn't leave well enough alone could you? Did you really think that I would wave the only copy of this recording in your face? I release this and everyone knows what kind of person you really are. You think you accusing me of being a mafia princess is actually going to stop me from releasing it? Everyone already thinks that I am. I could tell them they're wrong until I'm blue in the face but they'll never believe me. Which is exactly what you'll be facing if I release this. No one will believe that you're not a sexual harasser. No one will trust you. Oh and just so you know, I recorded this conversation as well. You're screwed."

"Alexis, please, we're friends," Seth gasped out.

Alexis gave FJ a look and he eased up just enough that Seth could breathe easily again, then she turned her attention back to the dirtbag in front of her.

"No, Seth, we're not. You ruined that friendship months ago. Then you went ahead and burned whatever hopes we had of coming back from it, and then you tried to intimidate me into lying for you. Now you've come into my house, with my family and friends, on my birthday, to convince me to what? Literally kiss and make up?"

He seemed to realise that he was fighting a losing battle and changed tactics. "Fine, what do you want?"

"Leave me alone, leave my friends alone. That includes Jess by the way, and if you ever sexually harass anyone again then both recordings get released. Do I make myself clear?"

His eyes narrowed again, his mouth twisting into a sneer. "You're a bitch." And just like that he found himself not breathing again.

"I'll take that as a yes. Now, since you're clearly an idiot, I'll speak slowly. You. Are. Uninvited."

That was all FJ needed to hear to drag Seth from the room and down the hall. Alexis followed behind. She knew that if it had been her dad he wouldn't have followed. Something about it being a power move. Unfortunately, they needed to take Seth through the front door so they wouldn't cause a scene in the backyard. Which would definitely have alerted her parents to an issue and that was just not something they needed to deal with tonight of all nights.

She opened the front door but stayed inside as FJ pushed Seth down the path towards the road. She couldn't hear what was being said but when Seth started walking to the end of the street she could guess. FJ took out his phone and made a call, never taking his eyes off of Seth's retreating figure.

Once FJ hung up the phone he turned around and made his way back to the house. She started to smile at him in thanks but when she saw his face she knew he wasn't happy with her.

"What the hell was that?"

Glaring at her cousin, Alexis gestured towards the kitchen where both their mums were currently getting dinner ready. Then she cocked her head back towards the theatre room. Just like her dad's office, it was sound proofed. Once the doors were closed she gave him a quick rundown of what had gone down with Seth and why she needed to involve him in the first place.

"Tonight he thought that he could get me on my own and intimidate me. I've already proven that I can fight my own battles, but he needed to know that even when he thinks that I'm alone, I'm not. There will always be someone in the shadows, looking out for me. I didn't mean to use you but I needed to make a point. He can't just threaten my Family and get away with it. I'm sorry I made you mad."

FJ sighed but pulled her into a hug. "I'm not mad at you baby cousin. I pretty much told that dick the same thing anyway. If he thinks that he can make a move against you and not get his ass kicked then he's got another thing coming."

She squeezed him a bit tighter. "Thank you for being on time."

"You're welcome, but don't do anything like that again, not for a long time at least. It was weird how much you reminded me of Zio Tony." His words made her pull back just enough to see his face.

"I reminded you of my dad?"

"Yes, but in a good way."

She couldn't stop the smile that spread across her face. Seth following her into the house hadn't been her plan A, not even her plan B or C. So she'd had thirty seconds to come up with a whole new plan, and she'd had to think 'what would my dad do'. She must've thought right.

"That means a lot FJ."

Alexis and FJ managed to slip out to the backyard minutes before dinner was brought out. While a majority of the party goers wouldn't question why Alexis was late for dinner and subsequently been missing for fifteen minutes. Her parents would. They had a sixth sense about shady business, probably from years of experience. Since her mum was in the kitchen the whole time Alexis doubted that she would've noticed anything. Her dad though, had been outside and might've noticed that she wasn't.

"Is it all sorted?" Lucas slid up next to her, his arm going around her waist.

"Yep, I'd say that if he's smart he got the message but past experience has shown him to be very stupid."

"That's what I don't get, any self-respecting guy would've gotten the hint the first time around."

"Well I guess he's not very self-respecting," she countered with a smirk. "Thank you for trusting me to deal with him my way."

"You're welcome. Besides if I hadn't seen FJ go into the house at the five-minute mark I was going in myself. Almost went anyway. Just thinking about if something had gone wrong-"

"It didn't baby, and even if it had, I could've taken care of myself. Tonight's theatrics weren't about me showing him I can take care of myself, I proved that when I broke his nose. Like I told FJ, tonight was about proving that other people have my back even when I don't."

"But technically you did have your own back because you told FJ when to come after you."

"Technically yes, but Seth didn't know that."

"You're a devious little thing aren't you?"

"Why yes sir, I do believe I am."

Before he could think up a reply she gripped onto his tie and pulled him down, catching his mouth with hers.

◆◆◆

The rest of the party passed by with far fewer dramatics than it started with. Jess told her that Brennan left a few minutes before she and FJ came back outside. Which meant that the phone call Seth made was most likely to him. There was no doubt in her mind now that Brennan had brought Seth with him.

By ten o'clock, a majority of the family had left, most of them having young kids who needed to go to bed. It might be a Saturday night but a tantrum was a tantrum no matter what day it was.

Alexis' friends from school had left not long after. Em and her parents took Jess home and Lucas left not long after with his parents. Now Alexis sat with her mum and dad in the kitchen discussing the party.

"Well I have to say, by all accounts that seemed to be a success," her mum beamed, proud of herself. She was always the perfect hostess.

"Mm, though I don't know why you bothered inviting that Brennan kid. He left before dinner was even served."

Alexis wasn't sure how her dad had even noticed one seemingly insignificant party goer, especially at a big Italian-do like theirs.

"Um, yeah Brennan and I aren't exactly seeing eye to eye at the moment."

"What happened? You two used to be thick as thieves."

Her parents might have trouble keeping all of her friends straight, but when it came to the inner circle, they were pretty on the ball. Which made it harder to hide when there was drama she didn't want to talk about.

"He isn't a fan of me being with Lucas," Alexis confessed looking down at her plate of birthday cake. She was suddenly rethinking having a second piece.

"Pft, shock," her dad scoffed.

"What's that supposed to mean?" she asked.

"That kid has had a thing for you since day one. I knew it the second he trailed after you the first time you brought him over with your other friends."

And just like that the floodgates opened.

"Well there you have it. He doesn't want anything to do with me anymore because he's jealous that I'm with Lucas. Never mind the fact that we were best friends for over a year or that it's not my fault I never felt the same way about him. He's been dodging me ever since Lucas and I became official, all those times I've said I was going to be out for dinner and then suddenly stayed home, that was him cancelling plans. He left me outside the goddamn movie theatre like an idiot."

Her parents were at a loss for words. Then she found herself wrapped in her mother's arms as her dad stroked her back.

"Why didn't you tell us?"

Alexis scoffed at the question but answered the best she could with her face pushed into her mum's shoulder.

"Because despite everything I thought that we were still friends and I missed him, but I knew that the second I told you two how he's been treating me then he'd never be allowed in the house again," a dry laugh escaped her lips.

"Well you're not wrong. It's a good thing I didn't know before because I would've kicked that punk out the second he got here." Tony Angelo never failed to disappoint.

"And that's why I didn't tell you. Tonight proved that we'll probably never be able to go back to the way things were."

"He'll get over you choosing Lucas." It didn't sound like her mum believed her own words.

"He can get over it or he can't. I don't care anymore. Him and Seth aren't worth it anymore." She didn't like the tone of defeat that accompanied her words but there was no denying the truth anymore. Brennan didn't want anything to do with her and Seth was never going to stop trying to either get in her pants or manipulate her into doing what he wanted. She deserved better than them and she had it.

"Right well enough of that then. It's time for your presents." Her mum gave her a final tight squeeze before letting her go.

"Finally! That pile has been staring me down since we came in here." Alexis looked at the offending presents. They had been piled neatly onto the kitchen counter once the food was cleared away. Her mum had a notebook and pen ready nearby to write down who gave what so thank you cards could be sent. *We might be criminals but we're polite criminals.* Alexis remembered her dad joking the first time she'd questioned the thank you cards.

◆◆◆

Half an hour later Alexis had opened all of the presents on the counter and there was a detailed list ready for Alexis to write out the thank you cards. Something that wasn't going to be done until Monday night. They were all recuperating the next day. Alexis put the dishes in the sink and was ready to say good-night when her mum pulled out one last gift, seemingly from thin air.

"Before you go to bed sweetheart there's one last present for you," her mum said, setting the small box on the stone counter in front of her.

"We saw it and thought of you straight away," her dad chimed in. Intrigued and excited, Alexis carefully undid the bow and opened the box. Inside sat a silver leaf pendant on a silver chain. Inside the leaf were swirls and curls. It was beautiful.

"I love it," and she meant it. Alexis wasn't one to wear a lot of jewellery. She had a jewellery box full of gifts that while beautiful, and some quite expensive, she would rarely, if ever, wear. Jewellery was an easy out gift, something people buy as a present when they're not sure what the person really wants. And the thing Alexis always wanted was something that wasn't jewellery.

But this, this was different. Alexis rubbed the silver leaf between her thumb and index finger following the lines. She didn't ask what it was that made her parents think of her when they saw it, she couldn't explain it herself but she knew that this necklace was a perfect fit for her.

After final goodnights, Alexis went upstairs, a silver leaf hanging from around her neck and a smile that could've been seen from the moon.

CHAPTER 30

Carmen pushed the trolley full of groceries through the car park. The shops had been insane for some unknown reason and she had a hell of a time getting through the checkout. She'd take an armed assassin over a slow check out operator any day of the week.

As she made her way towards her car, the hair on Carmen's arms suddenly stood on end. Years of experience and naturally good instincts told her that someone was watching her.

Slowing her walk ever so slightly, Carmen looked around for anything suspicious, but then, just because she couldn't see it didn't mean it wasn't there. Anyone who saw her stop would just think that she'd lost her car, as though she was ever that forgetful.

After a few more minutes of 'mindless' wandering, Carmen still hadn't seen anyone that looked out of place so chances where they were waiting in a car somewhere. Slipping her phone from her handbag Carmen unlocked it and called Cole, her personal driver-slash-bodyguard. Normally he would've come with her whenever she went out, but she'd told him to watch the school this morning.

"Cole, something's up. I'm fine, stay where you are. I want you to keep a closer eye on Alexis. The second that anything out of the ordinary happens, you get her out of there." Once Cole confirmed that he understood the instructions Carmen hung up. She had made her way back to her car while on the phone, not wanting to waste any more time, after all, she had ice cream.

With a deepening sense of something about to go wrong, Carmen loaded her groceries and deposited the trolley in the collection bay a few cars down from hers. It wasn't until she got into the driver's seat that she saw the envelope on her windshield. Getting back out, she looked through the windshields of all the surrounding cars, trying to see anyone watching her. Immediately she could tell that there was more than just a note inside. It was thicker and heavier. Not unlike the envelope she'd found in her purse the day of Ricky Jr's funeral. Sure enough, there were photos inside. The last set of photos had put her on edge. This set though, it sent a chill down her spine and made her blood boil at the same time. These weren't photos of herself running errands. No. These were photos of Alexis.

At school.

Eating lunch. In class. Arguing with Seth and Brennan. Smiling with Lucas. Walking with Jess. Talking with Emilia.

Carmen didn't waste any more time. As soon as she was back in the driver's seat, she had the car started and was peeling out of the car park. Pressing the voice command button on her steering wheel, Carmen put a call through to her husband.

"Tony. We have a problem."

CHAPTER 31

Tony had spent a lot of time out of the house since his nephew's funeral. His sister in law's outburst might've been out of line, but she wasn't totally wrong. He kept telling himself that everyone who took the Oath knew what it was they were getting into. He made it very clear that once they were in, there was no getting out. And one by one they all spilt the blood, burnt the card, and spoke the oath.

Veronica knew that. She reaped the benefits of his brother's success. She lived in the house he bought with dirty money and wore the expensive jewellery he claimed to buy 'on sale'. Yet she had the audacity to lay the blame for her son's death on his shoulders.

Tony knew that he wasn't responsible for Richard Jr.'s death, yet here he was, driving six hours to the bottom of the goddamned state on the off chance he might find a clue that would lead him to his nephew's killer. That's why he was doing it. Not because of guilt but because whoever was responsible for Ricky's death hadn't just killed a *capo*, he'd killed family.

◆◆◆

Albany. Roughly four-hundred kilometres from Perth and the home of Ricky's operation.

Tony was losing what little patience he had when he first walked into the warehouse. It was always a warehouse. Every once in a while he'd like to shoot out someone's kneecaps somewhere with a nice view. Unfortunately, the logistics of that were not on Tony's side. Realising this did nothing to curb his ire.

"You know what Lou," Tony bent over to get eye level with the guy currently tied to a chair. "I'm getting really tired of hearing you say you don't know anything." They'd driven six hours to get down here and now this *faccia di merda* was lying to him.

"I'm telling you the truth boss," Lou audibly swallowed. "I swear to God."

"You swear to God, ai? Right, well here's the truth as I know it to be. Ricky dies mysteriously, then you don't check in for a month and no one has seen you, then you all of a sudden crawl up out of the wood-work like a *madonn'* cockroach! Now give me one good reason why I shouldn't put a bullet through your

328

skull right now for abandoning your capo and your post?"

Tony was so close that he could smell the seafood Lou had for dinner the night before. He stood up straight, his mouth curling in disgust as he raised his gun. Lou's eyes went so wide, Tony thought they might actually pop right out of his head.

"Because! Because I can tell you where they were headed next." Tony lowered the gun just a fraction. "They were headed up to Busselton. The guy has a thing for staying near the coastline. He doesn't like being too far inland."

Well that was new information.

Tony took a step back, lowering the gun fully but never actually taking his finger off the trigger.

"That's a very interesting tidbit you've got Lou. However it does raise another question, how do you know that?"

It seemed to dawn on Lou in that moment that in his panic to stay his execution, he'd only signed his death warrant twice over.

"I don't- He- Ricky-" the stench of urine filled the immediate area causing Tony to roll his eyes.

"Ty! Get over here."

Ty left his spot against the nearby doorframe, where he seemed to have been happily enjoying the show.

"Make this *testa di cazzo* talk, but don't kill him until we've verified everything he has to say."

"You know your Italian always comes out more when you're riled up."

"*Non essere una merda.*"

"*Come ti pare*, boss," Ty replied with a cheeky grin. That was all Tony needed to hear before he holstered his gun and left the warehouse.

Part of Ricky's job had been running the freight company and maintaining the warehouse, as well as fudging a few records so no one was any the wiser about what the trucks were really hauling half the time. He'd been damn good at it too. Maybe that was why this mystery person had taken him out, because he was good at his job.

Tony had been trying to figure out the connections between all the men that had been killed across the country since the reports started pouring in. At first the deaths over East had happened so quickly that no one realised that the deaths in South Australia were being reported at the same time as the ones in New South Wales and Victoria. Once they crossed the border into Western Australia, the reports had slowed down significantly.

It was almost like this guy was playing with them.

But why?

By the time the first true screams of pain started, Tony had already considered a half dozen options for who could be coming after his Family and then dismissed them methodically. He'd even briefly considered it being an inside job, especially if a lifer like Lou could betray his capo so easily. What Tony couldn't figure out was who it would be if it were an inside job. His brothers didn't want the responsibility of being the mafioso. His sisters were the same. They'd always wanted the benefits of the life but never to actually be actively involved. Veronica was the only one he could think of who had it out for him, but that was only since her son died.

Wasn't it?

"Boss, you're gonna wanna hear this," Ty called from the doorway.

Tony had been pacing behind the warehouse, lost in his thoughts. His tracks were visible in the dirt, the laps growing in length.

When Tony reached the doorway, Ty didn't look pleased. If anything he looked ready to put a bullet in someone right then and there, if he hadn't already.

"What'd he say?"

"You're going to want to hear for yourself," Ty said through gritted teeth. Tony could've demanded that Ty tell him right then and there but rolled with it. If Ty said he'd want to hear for himself, he probably wanted to hear for himself.

"Alright, out with it asshole, what have you got to say for yourself."

When Lou didn't immediately start spilling his guts, Ty came up next to him and started pressing down on one of his already broken fingers.

"*Non ti sento*, Lou," Tony taunted when nothing

but silence came from Lou's mouth. Ty let go of the broken finger and moved to one of the three unbroken ones, pulled a hammer from a loop on his belt and started lining up the blow.

"Agh! Ricky was a rat! Okay! A traitor!"

"*Stronzata*!" Rage course through Tony so quickly he didn't even realise he'd backhanded the asshole until his head was snapping to the side. Taking a deep breath Tony calmed himself, waving off Ty who had stepped forward to hold Lou in place.

"You're trying to tell me that my nephew flipped?" Tony walked around Lou, reaching inside his jacket for his gun.

"No. He had a side business with some Serbian and wasn't kicking up like he should've but he was my *capo* wasn't he? You put a goddamn kid in charge and look where he ended up!"

Bang!

"Alright let's get this mess cleaned up and get back to the city."

Ty just nodded and cut the duct tape keeping Lou upright in the chair.

"How'd it go, *ciccino*?"

It had been late when Tony got in the night before and he hadn't been in the mood to talk business when Carmen woke up to greet him. But now in the harsh light of day, it was time.

The two of them were in his office, Carmen perched on the edge of his oak desk, the photos that had been left on her car the day before beside her, as Tony studied the map on the wall with all the pins.

"Not good. He said that Ricky-" Tony cut himself off, not wanting to disgrace the memory of his nephew by saying the words out loud. Carmen waited for him to finish but when he didn't she started putting the pieces together herself. The shame on his face at just thinking about what Lou said, only meant one thing.

"Ricky would never betray the Family. Whatever Lou said, he's a goddamn liar." Carmen had known Ricky almost his entire life. He was one of the first of the cousins to see Alexis when she was born. Carmen was there when he took the Oath. There was no way that he was a traitor.

No way.

"How did you-"

"Know? Because of the look on your face. You were ashamed to even be thinking it and I know you, you're not ashamed of much."

Carmen was right and they both knew it. Tony had long ago accepted all aspects of this thing of theirs. He took the Oath seriously and he expected the same of everyone else who took it.

"So we agree, Ricky wasn't a traitor." Carmen nodded in agreeance. "Then that means Lou was,"

Tony concluded.

"Or someone convinced Lou that Ricky was," Carmen suggested.

"Honestly, I'm not sure which one is worse right now."

"We need to call a meeting," Carmen realised.

"I'll call Emilio and the others."

"And I'll run to the store." Tony just looked at his wife like she'd grown a second head.

"You're thinking about dinner right now?"

"No *ciccino*, I'm thinking that this meeting is going to be going for hours and eventually you're all going to be hungry and I need to get more food."

CHAPTER 32

Suffice it to say that the meeting did not go well. As soon as her dad's crew left, Alexis had been called down to his office and told that she wasn't to leave the house until this mess was sorted.

From the look in his eyes she knew better than to object. He concocted some lie to tell the school that she'd gotten sick and would be out until further notice. Even had the Family doctor sign a certificate for the front office records. No one was allowed in or out of the compound without a heavily armed escort. She wasn't allowed out – at all.

Alexis could've survived with a little time off school, except for the fact that none of her friends were allowed to visit her, Emilia being the only exception. She wasn't even meant to tell the Lucas the truth in case he let it slip that she wasn't actually sick.

Seven days of being locked up in the house with only her parents. Even the housekeeper had been given paid time off.

Five days of having nothing to do because she'd finished all of her schoolwork. She'd even worked ahead by the second day.

None of her favourite shows could distract her from the loneliness that she could feel creeping in.

It was one thing to isolate herself, but when isolation was forced on her it was just suffocating.

Sunday night Alexis came to a decision. She was going to school the next day. She was going to see her friends and be bored by her teachers and sit through the ridiculous school assembly that was the literal definition of *this could've been an email.*

She found her dad sitting in his study, pouring over files and a map.

"Daddy, can we talk?"

He didn't even look up from his desk, just waved her forward.

"What's up princess?"

Maybe it would be easier if he wasn't looking at her.

"I want to go to school tomorrow."

"Well we both know that's not going to happen."

"I'm sick of being locked up in this house."

That made him look up. She hadn't meant for her tone to become so clipped.

"In case you've forgotten Alexis, you are locked in

this house for your own safety."

Safety.

The thought was almost comical to her. In what universe did he actually think that she was going to be safe? She was the daughter of the Mafioso. She may not have experienced a threat quite like the one they were facing now, but she remembered times as a child when her mum would keep her home from school, distract her with games and movies. She remembered her dad coming home limping, or favouring some part of his body, blood drying on his clothes. She remembered her uncle going to prison and the cruel taunts of people she once thought were her friends.

She remembered it all.

She would never be safe from the risks that came with being a member of the Family. It didn't matter that she hadn't made the oath. She was a target purely by association. Not everyone had a code like her dad did. Not all rival families were against hurting kids or women.

"Someone threatened me, didn't they? That's why you and mum were freaking out after the meeting last week. That's why you haven't let me leave the house. Isn't it?"

He didn't say anything, he just stared at her. The silence in the room was deafening and it was only broken when he finally got up from his chair and made his way across the room to her. Alexis wasn't sure what she was expecting until he pulled her into his arms. Instinctively she wrapped her own around his waist, her face against his shoulder.

"Daddy, I refuse to live my life in fear."

"But at least you'd be living."

"No, I wouldn't. Because living in fear isn't really living, dad. You and mum taught me that."

With a kiss on the top of her head he pulled away, a sad smile on his face.

"Yeah, well I regret it. At least if you thought living in fear was okay you wouldn't fight me about keeping you safe."

"You can keep me safe and still let me go to school. Besides if you keep me home any longer someone is going to call child protective services, and then where will we be?"

"I think once I explain the situation to them they'll understand."

"Yeah, somehow I don't think that informing them of the threat of some unknown assailant will sway them to see things your way," she said, quirking her left eyebrow.

"You are aware that if I let you go to school tomorrow you're not going to know a moment of peace. I'll have guys trailing you from class to class. You might actually wish that you'd just stayed home."

Alexis gave it some genuine thought. She knew that he would make good on his promise. Her miniscule amount of freedom would come with consequences.

"Fine, but they need to blend in, at least look like they could pass as year 12's, or teachers even. No one else should be able to pick them out of a crowd."

"You drive a hard bargain."

He could've locked her in her room. He could've had a guard at her door and outside under her window. He could've kept her in the house until the end of times. But he'd chosen not to. Or rather his wife had told him not to. She'd known that Alexis would only humour them for so long before she started chomping at the bit. Carmen had told him that when Alexis finally wanted out, he had to let her out. It didn't mean that they wouldn't watch every move she made.

Alexis was aware of the threat on her life, and yet she still wanted to go outside where it wasn't safe. He marvelled at her sometimes. Back when his youngest sister had been Alexis' age there had been some particularly violent threats made against her. No one had known until then that she'd been dating a boy from a rival family. She had broken it off when he tried to get her to betray Family secrets and feed him information.

His sister had hidden in her room for weeks. Even after they dealt with the threat she hadn't left the house for another month. Maybe it was knowing who it was that was threatening her that had scared her the most. Then again he would've thought that the threat of the unknown would be worse. Never knowing who it was that was out to get you, any stranger in a crowd could be the one to pull the trigger.

Alexis was either brave or in denial.

CHAPTER 33

Three weeks.

It had been three weeks since they had gone into DEFCON 3.

Two weeks since Alexis had been on constant high alert, not allowed to go anywhere without a team of bodyguards. Just like the house arrest, this had grown tedious. Every corner Alexis turned at school she spotted one of her dad's undercover bodyguards. They blended in well enough, except for the fact that sooner or later everyone would start wondering why there were so many new 'students' and 'teachers' in the middle of the school term. Also why no one seemed to actually have a class with any of these new people.

Her mum kept reminding her that it was for their own good. Dad just wanted to make sure they were protected.

Alexis had been quick to point out that her mum could protect herself, that she was a weapon all her own. Alexis had watched her train with the guards. She moved with a speed and grace that only came from years of dedicated training. Her skills with a gun were surpassed only by her skills with a blade. She was like some kind of lethal anti-hero. Alexis hoped that one day she'd be half as good as her mum.

It was as they drove home from one of their few approved outings that her mum once again tried to convince her that this was all for the best.

"Sweetheart, I know you hate not having your freedom, but trust me when I say that this could be so much worse. There was a time before you were born when the Family was under threat. All of the women and children were ordered to go into hiding. For months I couldn't come home." The gentleness in her mum's voice didn't detract from the seriousness of the words.

"I love your dad's family, but I never want to be cooped up with them like that for any period of time ever again," she said as they pulled into the garage.

Alexis laughed, imagining her mum and aunts stuck together for that long. It was lucky they had all come back alive. As she got out of the car her mum's phone rang. Looking back Alexis saw the troubled look on her mum's face and felt the tension come back into her shoulders. Her mum just waved her away.

"I'll be in in a moment," she mouthed.

There was a feeling in her stomach, like she should stay and listen, but at the same time she knew her mum wouldn't be happy with her if she did. So she left, the feeling in her gut eating away at her with each step.

CHAPTER 34

"Hello, Carmen."

Her heart stopped in her chest. The air around her turned thick and heavy. Dread settled in her stomach like a rock. Of all the voices she could've heard over the phone line, why was it *his?*

"I know you recognise my voice. Have you dreamt about me since we parted ways? See I've dreamt about you, every night in fact. Do you want to know what I dream about?" There was something in his voice that screamed 'unhinged'.

"What do you want?" Carmen spat, finally finding her voice. He just continued on as though he hadn't heard her.

"I dreamt about your world falling apart, like mine did. I dreamt of all the fun ways I could destroy everything you have ever cared about. I think I'll start with Alexis. After all, wouldn't it be fitting for you to lose her like I lost my father. Though... I didn't really *lose* him, rather I killed him. I think you're going to do the same."

"My parents are already dead Stefan."

"No, no, no. Oh my sweet, beautiful, *stupid* Carmen. Not your parents. Your daughter. Your sweet pretty Alexis. She doesn't look a thing like you by the way. Perhaps that'll make it easier."

"I'm not killing my child you lunatic."

"Think of it as a mercy Carmen, because if you don't kill her, I will. Then I'll kill your husband. Then his family. But I won't kill you, not at first. You'll watch them all die, and I'll make you wish that you had ended their lives yourself."

Carmen could barely contain her shaking. She hadn't felt fear like this since she was nineteen years old. Pushing all of those old feelings back down into the hold they'd tried to crawl out of, Carmen steeled herself.

She was the wife of the mafioso. She was a weapon of her own design. She had lost one baby and raised another and that baby grew up into a beautiful and strong young woman. She'd be damned if she let this ghost from her past destroy everything good in her life.

"What will it take for you to leave my family alone?"

"Oh, bargaining now are we? But you see my

sweet, I already told you what I want. Your daughter's head on a platter."

"Pick something else. You're not getting Alexis."

There was silence on the line for a few moments, Carmen wondered if he'd hung up.

"You."

"What?"

"You. I want you to give yourself up to me. Tell your husband that you're leaving him and come to me. Do that and I won't touch your precious little family."

"Swear it."

"I swear."

If there was one thing Carmen had learnt from her relationship with Stefan Marković, other than the fact that he was an abusive sociopath, it was that his word meant nothing. He couldn't be trusted.

When she agreed to leave her family for him, she knew that all she'd be doing was prolonging the inevitable.

Once she was in his grips again, he would kill everyone she loved. There was no doubt in her mind. So no, she wasn't going to go gently into the night.

CHAPTER 35

Carmen was ready.

She was ready for all of this to end.

That's what she kept telling herself.

She wasn't ready to leave her freshly turned sixteen-year-old daughter, or her husband of twenty years.

She wasn't ready to miss her only child graduating from high school, going to university, or becoming a member of the Family. Or both. Alexis was a high achiever after all. She wasn't ready to miss her daughter walking down the aisle or have children.

Carmen was not ready.

But she had to be.

She had been given a deadline and that deadline was approaching like a speeding train. She had the choice to get off the tracks or stand her ground and pray to whatever God there was that it stopped in time.

Carmen had been waiting for Stefan to arrive for exactly twenty-three minutes. She'd arrived at the warehouse early and it had given her more than enough time to scout out the surrounding area. She'd picked this particular warehouse because it wasn't connected to anything that had her husband's name on it. Nor was it connected to anyone that was a member of her Family. In fact it was a warehouse that had been linked to a Filipino gang. They'd abandoned it until the heat died down. Unfortunately for them, if everything worked out in her favour, they were about to be thrown into a furnace.

The sound of car doors closing alerted her to the arrival of her oldest foe.

It was time.

The silence of the warehouse just made her heartbeat sound that much louder. It almost drowned out the sound of feet crunching on gravel. When she had picked this particular warehouse two nights ago, there hadn't been gravel anywhere near it. She'd poured bags of it herself in the night. It was because of this forethought that she knew about the two thugs going around the back of the warehouse, probably to secure any exits and then ambush her if she tried to run.

Good thing she didn't plan on running today.

The roller door that she'd left unlocked clattered upwards. A square of light illuminated three dark silhouettes.

"My, my, my, if it isn't Carmen Esposito. It's been a long time but you're still as gorgeous as ever."

Carmen's skin crawled the second he started talking. His voice was like a thousand snakes hissing in unison.

She needed to focus on something other than the memories of what he did to her.

"Angelo." Her link to her husband and her daughter. Her link to her Family. In family there is strength.

"Excuse you?"

"My name, asshole, is Carmen Angelo. I got married, and you didn't send a wedding present," she mused as though they were old friends joking around.

"Why would I send a present to the bastard who stole the love of my life?" He was still quick to anger. When he got angry, he got sloppy and he made mistakes.

"Why would you ever think that what we had was love?"

For a moment, she thought that he might completely blow his top. His fists were clenched so hard his knuckles turned white. He looked ready to take a swing at her.

Wouldn't be the first time.

But then as quickly as the wind changes so did his expression. It was no longer one filled with rage, but regret.

She didn't trust it.

"I'm sorry *dusho moja*, I'm sorry that I hurt you so long ago."

My soul.

He used to call her that all the time. She'd thought it was sweet until she realised that he only used it as another way to keep her under his control.

"I was so lost without you, for so long. Everything I did, it was to get you back."

"So you put a target on my daughter's back as a way to get me back?"

"She's an obstacle to us being together. You have some false sense of maternal guilt to protect her. This can all be over if you just call off the guards. My men don't need long," he practically purred. He acted as though he was doing her a favour by killing her only child.

Her hands went to rest on her hips. Her fingers brushing the metal circles in her belt.

"You said if I gave myself up to you then you would leave my family alone."

And then there it was. The sinister smile she knew had been hiding under those sad, remorseful eyes. The true face of Stefan Marković.

She hooked a finger through one of the metal

circles. Thanking God for custom made clothing.

"I lied. I know you better than that. Family is everything to you. You would never truly turn your back on family and they would never abandon you. So I'm going to give you one last chance to do what's best for them. Either you end them yourself or I will end them for you."

"How about I just end you?" Without missing a beat Carmen pulled on the metal circle, unsheathing a throwing knife with her left hand, and letting it fly all in the same breath. Her right hand went to the gun tucked into the back of her pants.

By the time Stefan yelled out, she was putting a bullet through the skull of the goon on his right.

It was time that she ended this.

Carmen stumbled from the warehouse, a hand pressing against a slice in her abdomen. She could feel the poison taking effect. Her legs were starting to go numb and soon she wouldn't be able to walk at all. Her vision was starting to blur.

She'd failed.

Stefan was still alive. The knife had missed its mark, not by much but it had been enough. The bastard was still breathing.

And she was almost out of time.

Propping herself against the alleyway wall Carmen

struggled with the zipped pocket of her top. Her fingers were starting to fail her too.

It took her too long to get her phone unlocked. Tears formed in her eyes as she thought about the last moments she'd had with Alexis.

Seconds felt like minutes as she hit the speed dial. Her breath became more laboured. The world around her started to get darker.

But that didn't make sense.

It was only the middle of the afternoon.

Wasn't it?

Ringing. There was a ringing in her ear.

"Carmen, where are you?"

"Tony?"

Tony was here?

She was going to be okay.

"Carmen!"

"I love you."

"Where are you *ciccina*?" Tony begged.

There was a moment of clarity and she remembered. Alexis. She did this for Alexis.

"Tell Alexis I love her."

"*Dammit drive faster*. Carmen, we're coming, just hold on, okay? I'm coming!"

I love you.

CHAPTER 36

Alexis was ready to go home. All day she'd had a pit in her stomach that she couldn't explain and a nagging in the back of her mind as though she'd forgotten something important. She just couldn't find it in her to focus on anything her teachers were saying and even during recess Jess had called her out for being off with the faeries. Lucas had suggested that if she wasn't feeling well then maybe she should go home, but it wasn't a feeling of being sick that had her distracted. Besides, she had a big project due next week in Media and needed all the time she could get on the computers.

Alexis was sitting next to Lucas at lunch, absent-mindedly nibbling at her sandwich. If someone were to ask her what was in it she wouldn't be able to tell them without opening it up. Her friends must have realised that there was no hope for her attention span that day and just continued their conversations without her. She'd tell them what was wrong once she was feeling better.

It was almost the end of their lunch break when someone called her name. When she looked up to see who had called for her she saw that it was a middle-aged teacher that she'd never had before. Come to think of it she had never seen him at school before that moment.

Bodyguard.

"Alexis, your father is at the front office, you need to go now. I'll bring your things." There was a calm urgency in his voice.

The nagging feeling that had been bothering her all day disappeared but it was replaced with a pressure that threatened to crush her skull.

She didn't waste another second. Lucas was hot on her heels as she made her way to the office. There was something about the way the bodyguard had looked at her, the urgency in his voice, there was something wrong and she needed to know what it was.

All she wanted to do was break out into a run but there were so many people. People walking, people sitting, people in big groups and small groups. Too many people.

Her heart started beating faster the closer she got to the office. She could see it now. One more corner and she could see the doors.

Fifty metres.

Forty.

Thirty.

The doors opened.

Twenty.

Her dad stepped out into the mid-afternoon sun.

Ten.

He turned to her.

Five.

She stopped.

His eyes.

The windows to the soul.

His soul was shattered.

Nononononono.

No.

"No."

"What's wrong?" Lucas grabbed her hand tugging it softly.

He didn't know.

Alexis gasped for air.

I love you so much baby girl.

Her hand went to the silver leaf hanging from her neck.

I am so proud of you.

Her legs couldn't hold her up anymore.

You will do whatever is right for you.

Someone was holding her.

Finish your breakfast and I'll drive you to school.

"Alexis, baby, breathe."

Have a good day, sweetie.

"I need to get her home, Lucas."

"I can help-"

"Lucas."

Alexis couldn't understand why her mum looked sad that morning, but she was running late to meet Em so she didn't stop and ask. She just hugged her mum goodbye and bolted from the car. Not even looking back.

"I'm so sorry Tony."

Alexis felt herself being moved but she couldn't do anything. She felt strong arms under her knees and back. Someone was carrying her.

I love you.

I love you.

I love you.

When Alexis woke up she couldn't remember going to sleep. In fact, she didn't remember coming home. Her head felt fuzzy. How did she get to her room? Looking around she saw that her dad was sitting in the armchair next to her window.

"Dad?" The last thing she remembered was... school. "What happ-"

The bodyguard.

The office.

Her dad.

His face.

"Lex, I-"

"Where's mum?"

It wasn't true. It couldn't be true. Her dad had to be upset because of someone else. Someone else died but it wasn't her mum. It couldn't be her mum.

"Lex, I'm so sorry."

He got up from the chair and made his way to the bed. Sitting on the edge he turned to face her and she could see how bloodshot his eyes were. His hair was the most dishevelled she'd ever seen it. He'd discarded his tie completely.

"What happened?" Did they sneak up on her? How did they find her? How did they get past the guards? Questions swirled through her mind and she found it hard to breathe again.

"She knew... someone... long time ago... she went ... wanted to... went to protect you... us... they cut her ... poison... she called me..."

Alexis' eyes focused on her dad again, properly. She'd only registered half of what he'd been saying but those last words stuck with her.

"She called you?"

He just nodded.

"What did she say?" It felt like some invisible hand had reached through her chest and was holding her heart.

"She said that she loves us."

Everything from that morning came rushing back.

The way her mum had held her a little bit longer than normal when she came down for breakfast. Driving her to school. The multiple 'I love you's. They were an affectionate family but none of them said 'I love you' that much in one morning. She should've known.

That was what drove it home like a hammer. Her mum had known that it was the last time they'd see each other. And she had just jumped out of the car because she was late to meet her friend. Not even late to school. Just late to talk to Em. She should've realised there was something wrong with the way her mum was looking at her all morning.

"Lex? Come here baby."

When she didn't respond her dad moved further onto the bed and pulled her into his arms.

Her body wracked with sobs. If she were to look up she would've seen her dad's face mirroring her own. Tears like rivers on his cheeks. His body shaking with grief. His own heart in splinters on the floor. The only thing keeping him from screaming into the darkness of night was the girl in his arms.

She was just as fragile now as the first time he held her. He'd known how to protect her and take care of her back then. Even buried in his own agony, he wanted to protect her, but he couldn't. With all of his influence and all of his men, he couldn't put her broken heart back together. He was powerless.

As the two of them sat there for what must have been hours, holding each other and crying, until

finally Alexis seemed to pass out from exhaustion. All
Tony could think about was how Carmen would know
how to fix this. She would know how to put the pieces
back together.

CHAPTER 37

Alexis didn't remember much of the last few days since her dad had picked her up from school. Every night she cried herself to sleep rereading the letter her mum had left on her desk. Alexis always remembered the nightmare she had every time she fell asleep.

At first it was a whole lot of nothing. It wasn't light and it wasn't dark. It was just nothing. Then her mum's body appeared. It was in the centre of the nothing, lit up by a spotlight. Alexis was running to it as fast as she could, but she was getting nowhere.

Then suddenly she was standing over the body. When she knelt down, it looked as though her mum was just sleeping, so Alexis reached out to squeeze her arm, just enough to get her to wake up. But she didn't. Her mum's body felt wet and sticky, and she pulled her hand away to see what it was, but her hand was clean. When she looked back at her mother's body it was covered in blood, but there were no wounds that she could've been bleeding from.

Alexis scrambled to check her mum's body, maybe if the blood wasn't hers, then that meant she wasn't hurt and if she wasn't hurt then she was alive.

That was when she woke up. There was no finding out one way or the other if her mum was truly alive or dead. And when she woke up gasping for air it was always to the same realisation.

Her mother was dead.

Alexis was overtaken with anger. It was a new feeling. Since the night her dad told her what happened, all she'd been able to feel was grief.

Her blood started feeling like it was boiling in her veins. Someone had killed her mum. Killed her for trying to protect her family.

Alexis threw the blankets off and charged downstairs to the training room, unleashing her anger on the fighting man dummy in the middle of the room.

It isn't normally in the middle of the room.

By the time Alexis calmed down enough to be able to think straight, she was covered in sweat. It was an effort and a half to untie her knotted hair and twist it back into a plait.

She looked around the room and remembered all the times she'd been down here with her mum, all the things she'd learnt. She looked to the right wall of the room and saw all the fighting weapons in their spot. Her mum always made her put things back where they belonged after each session.

Alexis remembered the first time they sparred with rattans. She'd had bruises on her forearms and legs for weeks. But they were nothing compared to the cuts she got from the throwing knives.

Going over to the wall Alexis took down the sheath of throwing knives before strapping it to her wrist. Then she positioned herself across the room from the precision target.

Her mum had found one shaped like a human torso.

Her mum. Who died in an alleyway. Alone.

The first knife was flying across the room before Alexis realised she'd thrown it. It missed the target by a good thirty centimetres.

Relax your body.

It's what her mum always told her.

Stand up straight.

She pointed both arms towards the target before pulling her right one back, bending at the elbow just so. She shifted her weight, bringing her right arm forward. The knife left her hand and flew towards the target.

Hit. Right shoulder.

She did it again.

Chest. Dead centre.

Again.

Again.

Again.

Alexis spent an hour throwing the knives and retrieving them. Over and over.

Shoulder.

Heart.

Head.

She was always just slightly off centre when she aimed for the head.

Taking a moment to rest, Alexis thought about all the times her mum had shown her to throw knives.

The way she'd stood.

The stiffness in her wrist when she let the knife go.

Never taking her eyes off the target.

She had one knife left in the sheath. Taking it out, Alexis closed her eyes and took a deep, steadying breath.

Then she opened her eyes and looked at the target. It wasn't a wooden cut out anymore. It was the faceless man from her nightmares. The one who she saw in the darkness while she crouched over her mother's lifeless body.

She let the knife fly.

MAFIA HIERARCHY

Boss - Don/capo famiglia. Head of the family, makes all the important decisions. All members of the family pay tribute.

Underboss - Second in command. Ready to stand in for the boss and is usually groomed for the eventual take over. Some families have two underbosses.

Consigliere - Chief advisor to the boss. Doesn't need to be a direct relative of the boss. Offers unbiased information based on what he sees as best for the crime family. Third in charge.

Caporegimes/Capo - Captain of a crew of soldiers, anywhere from 20 - 1000+ soldiers. Report directly to boss/underboss.

Soldiers/Made men - Lowest rank within the mafia. They run errands, do whatever they can to hope to make a name for themselves. Can be as young as 16.

Associates - Anyone who does business with the mafia but isn't a member. Can be any ethnicity.

To earn one's button - In order for an associate of Italian descent to become a made man they have to earn their button. This includes committing a contract killing and taking the oath of omertà.

ITALIAN - ENGLISH

Bambina - baby girl

Ciccino/ciccina - sweetheart/honey

Come ti pare - whatever you say

Costa Nostra - our thing, Mafia

Faccia di merda - shit head

Madonn' - goddamn

Mamaluke - idiot

Non essere una merda - don't be a shit

Non ti sento - I can't hear you

Stronzata - bullshit

Testa di cazzo - dickhead

Testa dura - stubborn/hard-headed

ACKNOWLEDGEMENTS

I might have come up with Alexis and her story but I never would've been able to get this far without the love and support of so many people.

Matt, you've been my biggest cheerleader. The pompoms are okay but I think you need to reconsider the short skirt. Ever since I told you about my dreams of being a writer you haven't stopped supporting that dream.

Mum, you've read and re-read this book more times than I care to count. Thank you for wanting everything to be perfect for me. We've probably missed something but it's okay. You taught me that rejection didn't mean that my book wasn't good enough, it just meant I had to believe in it more than everyone else.

Dad, you've been helping me run through scenarios since I was twelve. Thank you for letting me beat you up, bounce ideas and theories off you and letting me grill you with very minimal questions as to why. Where mum was reason and logic you were railroad spikes and jumper cables.

Lauren, you have listened to me rant and rave and vent about everything under the sun and not only that, but you've created the masterpiece that is this book's cover art.

The four of you have inspired me in so many ways and none of this would've been possible without you.

Special thanks to Dani for reading through and editing the early incarnations. Renae for giving me your honest opinions and believing in me even when I forgot to. Kel, you definitely kept what small amount of sanity I have left from crumbling away this past year.

To all my friends and family who have believed in me and waited somewhat impatiently for this release since you found out about it a month ago, thank you.

To everyone who has read this and hasn't immediately thrown the book across the room, thank you. If you did throw this across the room or have the urge to, I get it. I really hope you stick around for the next one. I write because I love it but it wouldn't be the same without you, the reader.

A very special thanks to all the caffeinated drinks I consumed during the writing of this novel. Writing until 3 or 4 a.m. wouldn't have gone nearly as well without you. Then again maybe if I'd been a little more coherent there wouldn't have been so many grammatical errors to fix (sorry mum!). I will however maintain that some of my best lines came from a 3 a.m. caffeine haze so Dare, V, here's to you.

ABOUT THE AUTHOR

S. J. Smith lives with her fiancé and two ragdolls in Perth, Western Australia. She found her love of writing stories when she was six years old. This is also the same age she discovered a love of video games. Since then she has spent her time finding a tentative balance between the two.